HUMAN TO HUMAN, DUST TO DUST

As smoke rose from the burning gun, the Sharwani rushed us. Granite stunned two of them, then I knocked the third down, his throat in my hands. And then suddenly I was wringing his neck, screaming in English, "Pig, son of a bitch, used your own son, tricked us."

And he died and went limp. More aliens rushed us. I sat up and screamed. Then I realized their shoulders were round and they were our own Jereks, from the Institute of Control. I put my hands over my face and cried. They pulled my hands down and put plastic cuffs on me, as though I were a wild animal myself.

The Barcons bent over the strangled Sharwani, thrusting trocars up his neck veins and arteries, but one of the Jereks clicked a stopwatch and said, "Brain death, stop."

One of the Jereks came up to me and checked my skull computer, then asked, "Is it easy for you to kill?"

The conclusion to *Becoming Alien* and *Being Alien*
by Rebecca Ore
"One of our finest new SF voices!" —Michael Bishop

BEN BOVA'S DISCOVERIES

BECOMING ALIEN by Rebecca Ore
NAPOLEON DISENTIMED by Hayford Peirce
ETHER ORE by H. C. Turk
CORTEZ ON JUPITER by Ernest Hogan

BEN BOVA PRESENTS

BEING ALIEN by Rebecca Ore
THE THIRTEENTH MAJESTRAL by Hayford Peirce
PHYLUM MONSTERS by Hayford Peirce
FATHER TO THE MAN by John Gribbin
HIGH AZTECH by Ernest Hogan *(forthcoming)*

HUMAN TO HUMAN

REBECCA ORE

A TOM DOHERTY ASSOCIATES BOOK
NEW YORK

HUMAN TO HUMAN

A Tor Book
Published by Tom Doherty Associates, Inc.
49 West 24th Street
New York, NY 10010

Cover art by Wayne Barlowe

ISBN: 0-812-50045-8

First edition: November 1990

Printed in the United States of America

0 9 8 7 6 5 4 3 2 1

= 1 =

In the eighth year of the Sharwani Problem, my wife, Marianne, my son, Karl, and I lived on the sixth floor of a building in Lucid Moment District in Karst City, on an artificial planet light years from Earth. We were odd, even for humans, her with her radical parents, me a parole breaker. Humans would have blushed to know we represented them in space.

A few days after our son Karl's seventh birthday, he spent the night with his nursery group. It was our first day together alone in weeks. Marianne woke up first and dressed slowly, wrapping her long black hair in a headscarf. She said, "The Sharwani remind me of my parents. They're busy bombing and occupying planets, but we're too morally massive to just crush them."

"You think we're being repressively tolerant?" Marianne had got me to read Marcuse the year after Karl was born and I thought the idea was slightly hilarious. The Sharwani, like terrorist bombers, killed people in small bunches. The Institute of Control simply kidnapped Sharwani families to study. The Sharwani thought they were fighting a war. The Federation was studying a fractious new mammal.

"Tom, so the working conditions are better, the people whose languages I study don't have lice. The Sharwani . . . I want to do more. Just being a linguist is so ordinary, even here."

She'd come from Berkeley where all sorts of oddnesses coexisted, but even so. "Isn't the ordinariness something our minds make from the data?" Berkeley, when I first saw it, reminded me of Roanoke.

She didn't answer, just walked out of her bedroom to the front room. I followed her and watched her fingers touch our imported Terran furniture as if seeing if the feel matched what her eyes saw. We had two huge rooms front and back, six bedrooms, three to a side, off the central atrium. She went to the window and looked down. "Okay, it's different here. The streets are plastic."

"Do you sympathize with the Sharwani?"

"I gave up planning to kill people for causes when I saw what that did to my parents."

"You're bored," I said as if our whole conversation had been a puzzle that I'd just solved.

Marianne said, "They ought to change the tires on that bus." Plastic electric buses rolled on tires muffled by our street's soft pavement. Now that the bus companies switched to what Marianne called jelly rubber, the bus support crews put on fresh tires when the old ones picked up too much dirt to be translucent. Then she said, "Karriaagzh would like to house a Sharwani couple here, make over one of the rooms into a secure space. I'm going to talk to Karriaagzh today if you wouldn't mind."

"Marianne, don't you think having kidnapped Sharwani move in would be upsetting to Karl?" Karriaagzh was the Academy Rector, a huge grey bird with yellow eyes, mangled feathers under his uniform, legs that bent backward at the knee, totally without any sense of species. Since his own people decided not to join the Federation, he was an isolate, so lonely he fed toilets as if they were his babies. Without Marianne, I could have become a human Karriaagzh. I didn't really want dangerous duties, but didn't want my wife to think I was a coward.

"Karl thinks all sapients play together perfectly. He ought to learn there can be friction."

I said, "Okay. If you want to get more involved."

The day after Marianne talked to Karriaagzh, my computer terminal dumped three small books on the Sharwani into my printer. I could almost feel my skull computer—the one that normally translates from Karst Two to sequential languages—being tapped, biopressures noted.

We were the perfect household for a captured pair of Sharwani. Earth didn't know there was a Federation. If a Sharwan ate one of us, no home government would complain.

Marianne and Karl came in. Karl opened the first book to a picture and said, "Pretty."

They had angular facial bones, hollowed-out cheeks, thin-lipped mouths, more angular between nose and upper lip than humans. Blond to brown hair, facial hair extending onto the cheekbones in both sexes, blocking an utterly human look. I remembered the one I'd seen live—smaller than human average, but like most species, they could have as great as a two to one size range.

Marianne said, "Males and females aren't noticeably dimorphic in either size or secondary sexual characteristics." She sounded pleased and annoyed at the same time. Human trouble between the sexes, she claimed, stemmed from us being neither dimorphic enough to have complex sexual group mating systems, nor nondimorphic enough to have stable pair bonds.

I wondered if Marianne wanted to be a big female

Gwyng, all swollen armpit webs, birth hairs from pouch to vagina, nostrils clapping, up to her shoulders in males, competing with other females for marsupial pouch beasts—things like Holstein-colored rhinos—to parasitize. Bossy lady Gwyngs like my sponsor, Black Amber, tended to both attract and repel my wife.

"Don't go into these people's room, Karl," Marianne said. "Tom, you're not sorry I told Karriaagzh I was bored? He said we'd have help with them."

I said, "Karriaagzh thinks danger cures boredom."

First, we needed a security room. Two olive-feathered bipedals with backward-bending knees and arms, not wings, and a human male descended from the Tibetans stranded here over four hundred years ago came in with a tool cart and polycarbonate sheets and bars and began dismantling the hall wall of the room next to mine. The carbon plastic and metal studs didn't surprise me as much as the real plaster on expanded metal lath.

The Tibetan and I rigged a hoist down the atrium so that the scraps could be taken only a few steps, put through the atrium windows, and lowered to the courtyard. Dropping plaster and lath down into the courtyard was better than messing up Marianne's sister's handwoven carpet in the front room, worth a year's minimum wage on Karst.

I watched the two bird-types slot the first polycarb sheet in a three-sided metal frame. We all then wrestled it into position on the floor where the wall had been and bolted the frame to the building joists. Then we installed the second sheet, the one with doors in it. Where the polycarb sheets butted together, the birds smeared glue and reinforced the joints with polycarbonate bars.

The door system was odd—a smaller door about two feet high by a foot and a half wide with an electric eye, Class Five locks for that, set within an equally well-secured regular-size bigger door.

"That's a little too large for a food door," I told the work crew, well remembering the food slots in the Floyd County jail when I was busted for helping my brother make drugs.

"The child needs free access," the Tibetan said.

"He's of the age where they leave the mother's side to play with other children," one of the birds said as he cleaned his hands with paper towels and solvent, prying a bit of hardened adhesive off one of his black forearm scales.

I asked, "When are they coming?"

"Soon. Karriaagzh broke role and went for them himself."

Karriaagzh didn't just recommend danger as a defense against boredom to others.

I asked, "What did the History Committee say?"

"Nothing," the first bird said as the Tibetan and the other bird hooked up the security systems. "Karriaagzh's foolhardiness appeals to those mammals. They think one hundred twenty-five years is too long a term for a Rector. Are our lifespans too long for you mammals?"

"He enjoys showing up in dangerous situations," I said.

"But he shouldn't. He represents a very vital drive in the Federation—expansion," the bird said, handing the other bird a circuit testing box from the tool trolley.

The Tibetan asked, "Do you think Earth will support expansion if Earth is contacted?"

"I have friends in both camps," I said. "And I don't know what Earth would do. Join the Sharwani, probably."

Marianne came in then and caught the last couple of exchanges. She laughed, knowing I didn't want Earth to be contacted.

The Tibetan said, "What Service does affects Support and Free Traders. And we don't get to affect those decisions." He looked down at Marianne's hips and thighs. The Tibetans had been breeding out of the same stock for five hundred years. New human women might be genetically inspiring, but the look he gave Marianne's crotch annoyed me.

Marianne smiled and looked from the Tibetan to me. She then went up to the polycarbonate wall and felt it with her fingers. She asked, "Will we get our Sharwani soon?"

I said, "Karriaagzh caught them."

"Poor baby."

"The Sharwani baby?"

"Karriaagzh," she said. "Tom, have you checked your messages lately? Black Amber left a message on my screen asking why you hadn't replied."

The Support crew went dead quiet, working their job without speaking.

I went to my room and laid my palm against the handplate, pressing harder than usual against it. The screen lit up and I began reading: NEED TO TALK TO YOU NEXT THREE DAY BREAK. BLACK AMBER, SUB RECTOR, ACADEMY AND INSTITUTES.

Meaning *visit*. I typed in: ARE KARL AND MARIANNE INVITED, TOO?

PREPROGRAMMED ANSWER, KARL INVITED, TOO.

My wife's placental pregnancy and labor grossed out Black Amber. Also, placental females, especially the sapients, had odd sex lives by Gwyng standards. Not that some Gwyng males didn't appreciate the human brain's function as a sexual arousal organ, mere thoughts serving as pheromones.

I typed in, I'LL TAKE THE BUS, then shifted into work matrix and left the machine up, ready to check on my cadets. Outside my door, I heard the work crew packing their tools and Karl coming back from his nursery group. He babbled in Karst One about bird doodoo and tinkle getting mixed up.

"Daddy, are the pretty people going to live there?" he said when I came out. He opened the little door within the larger door and knelt down to look around inside.

"Don't go near them unless I tell you it's okay."

"Do I *have* to go visit human people over the break?"

"She's your cousin," Marianne said, although the child in question wasn't a cousin by any kind of blood, but rather the daughter of an ex-lover of mine and Marianne's sister's ex-husband, Sam Turner. Sam, with his then wife, had come from Earth to Karst looking for a place to be merely human. Cousin enough, Marianne often said, so far from Earth. "And they'll be at the beach."

"Black Amber wants us to visit her, Karl and I."

" 'Karl and I,' " Marianne repeated, her fingers clenching slightly. She looked at me a moment, then said, "Maybe I can get someone to smuggle me back to Berkeley for the weekend."

"You don't particularly like her."

"She's nasty to Karriaagzh, and not just because he triggers anti-raptor defenses. If they were both the same species, she'd still hate him. He's in her way."

Karriaagzh's lifespan was in Black Amber's way; he had to die before she could become Rector. "Will you be upset?"

"When I married you . . ." She didn't finish, just went up to the clear plastic wall and pushed on it, fingers flattened against the polycarb. "It's all right. I volunteered us for the Sharwani."

"You said Karriaagzh promised help."

"Black Amber is being a *bitch*." The last word was English.

Karl said, in Karst One, "Don't talk in species language."

We hadn't taught Karl English. Languages shaped the brain, so Marianne and I thought that if he never learned English, he could avoid human problems. He looked so much like Marianne, dark hair, thick lower lip that jutted out, not-so-thin lip on top either, the nose that he raised and lowered in expressions he'd borrowed from aliens—my son, seven years old, biologically human, perhaps, but not semiotically.

The Institute of Control team waited in the transfer truck while Marianne took Karl to his nursery group. She'd wanted to tell him that the truck had our new housemates in it, but I knew he'd fuss to stay. She hadn't thought that lying to Karl was right, but I said it wasn't lying, really.

Rain was coming down outside windows gone clear in the gloom. Just as Marianne got out of the bus, two black shiny guys, skinnier and more pointed-nosed than humans, if the almost mirror skin wasn't clue enough, rolled an awning from the back of the truck to our building entrance.

I watched them from above; that foreshortened perspective made them all seem vulnerable. The van doors opened, but the awning screened my view of the stretchers being unloaded. Marianne stopped, looked up at our floor. I didn't know whether she could see me. Normally, residential windows reflect light, but then the glass today was clear. Below me was all wet glitter—alien skins, the plastic roads, windows reflecting windows into infinity.

I sat in the front room by the elevator, feeling chilled as though I'd been rainsoaked, too. My cock stirred vaguely in my pants, more restlessness than serious arousal, but I wished I could be alone with Marianne before the Sharwani arrived.

The elevator door slid down. "Help us, Tom," Marianne said. The two Shiny Blacks—I'd made up my own designations—and we humans pushed the two gurneys out of the elevator.

The Sharwani adults were drugged unconscious. Their child clung to one and kept speaking to it in a soft voice. We wheeled them into the room with the polycarb wall and lowered the gurneys to the floor.

"They are beautiful," Marianne said.

I didn't remember the Sharwani as lovely, but I'd met them only once before in near combat conditions, an interrupted first contact with another species. Nasty little Sharwani bombed a two million–population city to bluff another new species away from the Federation.

These captives looked like what ferrets crossed with angels would aspire to be: blond hair, cheekbones like pyramids hidden under skin that went from bare to fur as dense as moleskin, fur on the points of the cheekbones and along the jaw. Dense eyelashes matted with gum now gave them a hurt look. I pulled the sheet off the male—he wore a brown Federation-style tunic and pants. To conceal species differences, our tunics covered our middle leg joints and the pants were baggy. The male Sharwan also wore a shock bracelet and a second ID bracelet on his left arm.

Marianne said, "The female's right wrist is broken." She made a move to pull the sheet off the female, but the baby lashed out at her.

One of the Shiny Blacks from the Institute of Control said, "If you'd go out for a few hours, we'll finish the installation."

The other one said, "Your black opaque-skinned conspecific plays music at Wanderers' in the Green Light Building, three parks inland."

It took me a second to realize they meant Sam Turner, the black man who'd been married to Marianne's sister, Molly. I wondered if the Shiny Blacks made up a name for us, too, like the window-skinned ones. Marianne said, "Yangchenla will probably be there."

Funny thing, even though I loved Marianne better, I didn't really like seeing Yangchenla happy with another man. "She can be a real bitch, too," I said in English, "but I miss human music."

Human music was what Sam Turner played. Turner's training came both from Oakland black clubs and equal opportunity laws bearing down on Juilliard. When he was really hot, all of what we humans could be came through on either his harpsichord, his digital piano, or his woman's Tibetan drums. Black man, married to an Asian woman born on Karst, Sam denied all limits other than the purely human.

He was lucky. Humans these past two years were a fad, considered representatives of a culture in the cusp between the primitive and the techno-bore future where all the machines on all the planets evolved into one chain of forms.

Sam said, privately, that humans passed the cusp around the time of Mozart and began teching down toward functional forms ever since. He didn't date the music he played for the cusp-culture lovers, though.

Marianne said, "I miss Sam."

The Shiny Blacks watched us decide to go hear Sam and his group. "Get your rainclothes," the female with her tiny breasts just under her clavicles said. "We'll stay until you get back."

So we left the Shiny Black couple with the unconscious Sharwani and went out in raincoats and clear plastic hats through the wet parks behind the buildings. One park over, odd lights bounced through the raindrops onto plants that looked like red glass or brown dead things, evolved under suns harsher than ours.

By the time we got to the Wanderers' Club building, I felt ambivalent about seeing other humans, especially ex-lovers with ex-brothers-in-law.

The Green Light building front was made of white tile with chrome inlays under a writhing mass of green neon tubes, with enough red lights to intensify the green for those species who saw that low in the light spectrum. I put my hand in front on a dark tube and felt heat—visible as infrared to some species. Marianne said, "I've seen buildings like this before."

"They just opened a few weeks ago," I said.

"In San Francisco," Marianne said.

With infrared tubes, I thought. The green tubes covered the first two stories of the building, twisting, writhing, yet not so brilliant as to be obnoxious to the people living on the street. Green Light Building housed clubs instead of people; the lobby was jammed and full of sweat and gland odors of over fifty species. The graphics for Wanderers' lit up over the elevator, and we filed in with other species evolved from tropical brachiators. A different club light lit over the second elevator and a mob of crepuscular-types got on that one, large eyes reflecting the lights. Then our elevator doors closed and we began going up, a couple standing in the corner muttering about us being the same species as the musician. Turner Musician—they'd translated his name into the closest Karst One equivalent.

Marianne touched me on the side and smiled when I looked at her. She said, "He's still family, really."

The elevator doors opened and I saw Yangchenla in a red, shiny sheath dress talking to an Ahram, who ground inch-long molars and rubbed his skull crest as he looked at her. He was almost completely bald headed, not just along the crest ridge. Yangchenla slid a data card into a handcomputer and began writing on the scribe pad. I figured she was hustling a better deal for the gig. Sam came up behind her and wrapped his arms around her waist, then noticed us and slid his hands up under her breasts and smiled, showing teeth.

Another Ahram said to us, "Chip?"

I shuffled through my cards, handed him the credit chip, and said, "Both on this."

Yangchenla seemed to have cut her deal by the time I looked back. The Ahram's crest was quite red, and even his scalp seemed flushed a little. Yangchenla scribed a bit more on her computer; he smiled a little and the red left his crest skin. Sam unwound his arms from her body and went up to the music stand. Two Tibetans were waiting in the dark there.

Marianne said, "Big crowd." We threaded through

the bodies and sat down, the only humans in the audience. "How expensive was it?"

"All right for them," I said, suspecting Yangchenla got Sam a percentage of the gate. "Half a day's minimum wage for each of us." I couldn't really say what that would be in dollars, maybe twenty-five each, as minimum buys more here than minimum would have bought on Earth.

Marianne said, "It's okay if mood changers are included." The one Karst word she used included all legal chemical mood changers: drinks, drugs, electric apparatuses, vibrators—the works.

I said, "Dinner should be."

Sam sat down at his harpsichord and played Bach. The stage under him began to glow, throwing shadows and lights on his face that made him look almost ghoulish. The Bach piece jerked out of the harpsichord, electrically nervous, each note cut separate, more space between the notes than Bach usually got on Earth.

Marianne breathed in deeply when Sam segued into jazz made from broken bits of the Bach. The Tibetans beat drum beats like little bombs. My mouth went dry.

Complex aggressive music. Human music.

The music cut its closure in the air. I almost clapped Terran style, didn't, then wished I had. Marianne leaned her lips near my ear and said, "I'd like a tape of that to play when I'm nervous about the Sharwani."

The house lights came up and small fuzzy creatures like serious teddy bears began bringing around small vials of liquids. One of them paused at our table and backed off to take a photo of us with Sam in the background, then went about its business.

Marianne said, "Somehow, I don't think we could ever be an ordinary human couple."

I was about to say, *what happens if we're contacted*, but realized if Earth did make contact with the Federation, we'd still be odd, rescued by aliens from a criminal record in my case and post-doctoral boredom in

Marianne's. I said instead, "I just want to be a complete me."

She jerked her head back and looked at me as if I'd surprised her. "Are parts missing?"

I shrugged. Sam began with a tape—Wagner's "Ride of the Valkyries." The audience began to seem almost afraid of us, then Sam and his sidemen took the Wagnerian motifs and twisted them, almost mocking these aliens for the fears that Wagner stirred. I looked over at Marianne and saw her teeth glinting behind her lips.

I realized I was angry and didn't quite know why. I wondered about us humans.

When we got back, the female Sharwan was pacing the room, her head hair flared like a Persian cat's ruff, darker hair showing underneath, looking like undyed roots. She looked around when we came in. The Shiny Black who was awake said, "The male and the child seem calmer."

Marianne asked, "Do they understand our language?"

"Some Wrengu. Karriaagzh's team captured them on Ersh's planet."

I said, "I know Wrengu. Ersh was my first contact person from the Wrengee, a creature halfway between lizard and feathered bipedal sapient, scales the size of saucers along his sides that he could raise, eyes like a kitten's, that dark blue, but shaped wrong. "Maybe it's only fair that I have to deal with these people since the First Contact team I was on couldn't stop them."

Marianne said, "We both have to deal with them."

The Black Shiny male woke up finally and said, "Ersh wants to meet them. We're not sure that's a good idea."

Marianne said, "Where's Karl?"

"In his room. The feathered nursery mother stayed until he fell asleep."

Marianne said in English, "He loves to cuddle up to feathers. I'm just not fluffy enough."

The female Sharwan leaned her hands against the polycarb, the one in a cast looking bruised under the plastic, and pushed. She trembled and then spat at us, a projectile spitting that sounded like a rock, not liquid, against the barrier.

"We've left language tapes," the Shiny Black male said. "Explain to them what the situation is." He and his mate left us then with our captives.

The situation was that the Federation species outnumbered the Sharwani more than five hundred to one. Some Sharwani wanted to set up a Sharwani-dominated planets system. Ersh told me five Sharwani helped him escape the twenty thousand other Sharwani controlling his planet. It wouldn't have been fair to the good guys to run a genocide operation on them, even if the Federation did such things.

And the poor-ass Sharwani thought they were fighting a war.

Marianne said, "I can't sleep yet."

"They can't get out."

She and the female Sharwan locked eyes, like two pit bull bitches.

I woke up with Karl's fingers gripping my chest hair. Marianne was sleeping beside me, her hair spread all over her face. Karl said, "The Sharwani can't get Mom, can they?"

"They're caged behind armored windows."

He looked at me as if used to lying daddies. I couldn't remember being so sophisticated at seven, but did remember eleven-year-olds like little men before puberty scrambled their first maturity. "Karl, we'll leave them behind the polycarbonate barrier—the armored windows—until we get back."

"It's like restraint rooms. One of our daddies was in a Control restraint room once."

Which species, I wanted to ask him. "One of the people in the children's group?"

He looked down at his nails, then up at me with Marianne's dark eyes, his mouth straight, muscles locked against expression. "We're not supposed to know."

"Keep your secret then."

He smiled and said, "Okay, it was the pug-faced male. He got in a fight with another pug-faced male. Nothing serious, only it's gotten Sul worried . . ."

"Bir's son? He's . . ." I remembered him as more like a domestic animal than a sapient baby, walking on four legs, as precocial as a baby pig.

"He's learning fast now that he's walking like us. Dad, he says we treat him funny, but he just this year got smart enough to talk."

"Try to forget that he was more like a pet once."

"Okay, but he's afraid to grow up and not be like our other daddies. Male Domicans fight a lot."

"Tell him he'll be happiest being what he is. . . . No, don't tell him anything, just be his friend."

Karl got out of bed as if he had been surprised to act like such a baby and wanted nobody to mention anything about sleeping with us. "I liked him better as a pet. Now he talks back."

"Live with it," I said, getting my uniform out. Marianne opened her eyes and smiled. I suspected she'd been listening all along. I turned to her and said, "You going to be okay? I could see if Black Amber could talk to me in the city."

"I'll have the nursery group here a couple of days running, so I won't be alone with them," Marianne said. She pulled down her nightgown as she unwound herself from the covers. Yangchenla was never such a restless sleeper. "But does Karl have to go?" Marianne's breasts rolled under her gown as she stood up. She came up close and didn't kiss me, just breathed on me with her arms around my neck, crossed at the forearms. I pulled her right up to my lips and heard Karl groan behind us as we kissed.

I pulled back and said, "*Sappy*, huh?"

He didn't understand the English word, but got the tone. "You said species language limits brain development," he said, then he worried the inside of his lower lip with his teeth. "I don't want to be here alone with them."

"Not even with your mother?"

"The child one can get out of the littlest door. His people bombed Ersh's planet."

"Karl, we're counting on you to tame the little one," Marianne said. "You're not afraid, are you?"

"Why are you asking me that?" Karl said. "You're afraid, too."

"I thought I'd feel okay about leaving them in the security room," Marianne said.

"Do you want me to cancel then?"

"I'll ask Karriaagzh what to do. He gave them to us."

= 2 =

On the day Karl and I were to leave for Black Amber's new house, Marianne woke up early and went to the security room. I found her there, staring through the clear wall at the Sharwani. The female Sharwan asked in Wrengu that sounded tremendously rehearsed, "Why am I here?"

"We're studying you," I said. "Others of you, too."

She asked again as if she hadn't understood my own Wrengu, "Why am I here?"

Marianne said, "Karriaagzh is sending over someone who knows their language."

"Are you sure you'll be all right?" I asked, touching her on the shoulder.

"Fine," she said. "You must go see your sponsor."

Karl and I went downstairs to catch a city bus to the transfer point for the coastal buses. He wasn't sure he liked Black Amber, but he liked some of the other Gwyngs, even if he couldn't understand what they said, his skull bones still growing, not ready yet for the temporal bone to be replaced with a skull computer.

The bus ran on an elevated road over the northside slums. Karl spotted Tibetans below us and said, "I don't want to play with the country humans again."

"Karl, they're relatives, too." I saw the building where my brother Warren killed himself—his ultimate drug deal. We'd tried to save him, but the brain rebuilding, he thought, was an alien invasion. Why had I bothered to get him off Earth? Something in me died with him. I never was sure whether that part of me needed to die or even precisely what I'd lost.

Karl and I transferred to the coastal bus at the North Gate. After we adjusted the seats to fit us, Karl pulled out his reader, put a data card in the slot, and began reading. I looked over and saw pictures. A computerized picture book—he wasn't that different than I was at the same age, even if his best friends weren't human.

Then we were out in the country, a sandy coastal plain that Marianne said looked like south Mississippi. On one side of the road, mechanized plows cut across the field like giant shuttles; on the other side, two people of indeterminate species waded out on the flats with tongs and baskets, so primitive a food-gathering system I knew they had to be high officials escaping their terminals.

I could skip the primitive. "Karl, do you like this?"

Karl looked down at his reader, shrugged, and said, "If Rhyodolite isn't there, I'll be bored. Look, we're close." He pointed at Gwyng herds, the large two-ton marsupials that hosted their young, the smaller blood beasts with ropy neck veins, and the latest Gwyng craze, cloned Jersey cows for milk, one-quarter cream.

About an hour and a half later, the land began to rise, more rocky, more like California or the north coast of Black Amber's Gwyng Home island, which was foggy and had diurnal bats and near-sapient seal-things. But here wasn't really foggy, just cloudier than Karst City.

"I thought we were close," Karl said. He looked back at his reader and changed cards.

"She's moved," I said.

The bus driver said, "Officiator Red Clay, we're approaching your destination." I looked ahead and saw Black Amber's new house. She'd built in stone, not of planks woven together like a giant basket, light coming in at every plank crossing. I'd seen one stone house on Gwyng Home—very superior Gwyngs there.

The bus seemed to zoom in on the house, which got bigger and bigger. My eyes fooled me, or the relative clarity of the air where I'd expected fog. The huge house rose almost as raw as the bedrock under it, no true right angles—as if right angles belonged to the poor Gwyngs' plank and plastic building traditions.

Finally, as the bus began to climb up to the entrance, I saw Black Amber standing under a stone arch entrance, long arms spread, furred knuckles pressing either side of the arch. The stone around her looked both ponderous and unsteady. Black Amber wore a green Gwyng shift, armholes cut out to the waist.

The bus stopped and Karl and I got off, a flight of steps below her. Lichen everywhere. How, I wondered, did she get the lichen established so quickly? Her face was impassive, wrinkles sagging slightly, folded along her mouth, along her nostril slits, which moved in and out slightly like furred gills.

"Red-Clay and child," she said in Karst Two that my computer transformed out of sonar-pattern language into sequential tones I could hang meaning on. For a second, I regressed to the stage where her speaking was meaningless noise until the computer whispered in my brain. Karl moved closer to me, then, as if he'd caught himself being afraid, stepped toward Black Amber.

"Black Amber," I said, coming up to her, stopping a step below. Her shift had gold threads woven in it, almost duplicating the gold in Karriaagzh's Rector's Uniform. I put my bag down. She folded her arms around her, hooking her thumbs behind her neck, looking much like a giant bat with her elbows at waist level, the webs collapsed at her sides. I brushed her with my left arm, then she unfolded her arms and took me up against her left side, the web slightly clammy against my. Karl's jaw muscles clinched as he watched us.

"You seem/are anxious (about what: several guesses)," she said, my computer layering the meanings with little pauses.

"Marianne, my Linguist Mate, is with the people from those who fight us. Why didn't you want her to come?" Black Amber probably could understand the noise I made for *Marianne*, but I doubted she could attach a meaning to *Sharwani*.

"You didn't ask the Rector bird for them. She did. She deserves to be alone with them." Black Amber looked at my bag as if wondering what to do with it, then her small Karst One–speaking fuzzy servant came out and took the bag. She twitched her nostril slits in her muzzle and rubbed her sharp chin, then said, "Do you like my new house better?"

"It's impressive," I said. Did she simply invite me here to make Marianne uncomfortable?

Her brow hairs flared slightly as if what she heard carried the implication of "trying to impress," or she'd sensed my irritation, then she simply said, "Yes," and led us inside.

The floor was basket-woven, very awkward underfoot for a flat-footed ape, like walking on a lumber pile. Through the weave, I saw steel joists. Along the stone walls were brushed-steel platforms at knee level. On the platforms were Gwyng tube sofas like open cocoons and feather-filled mats covered with something like coarse linen, handwoven no doubt, and so terribly expensive unless Marianne's sister Molly cut a deal with her Gwyng lover's adoptive mother.

But where were the other Gwyngs? Karl looked up at me and said, "Where are Rhyodolite and Amber-son?"

I wished I'd brought one of his friends along. "Have you been ill?" I asked Black Amber. Gwyngs were group creatures, constantly in physical contact with each other. Instinctively, they isolated the sick.

"No, I have not been ill." She went over to a table covered with translucent plastic globs—all colors—and picked up a blue glob like dribbled wax about five inches tall. Staring into it, she turned it in her hands and didn't speak for a while.

Karl whispered, "Can I play with those, too?" I knew that Gwyngs saw polarized light patterns and wondered if the plastic globs were patterned in a Gwyng-meaningful way. The room had a brutal elegance except for all that tacky plastic, not like Black Amber's first beach house at all.

I asked Black Amber, "If you haven't been ill, why are you alone then?"

"The Weaver and Rhyodolite are here. Cadmium is no longer." For a horrible moment, I thought she meant dead, but she continued, "Gone from my social life, but he breathes." She continued to stare into the plastic.

"Rhyodolite and Molly are here," I told Karl, then I asked Black Amber, "Can you read the plastic?"

"Art objects for not-limited brains," she replied. "The Rector Bird . . ." She didn't finish her statement, but I saw blood engorge her web veins slightly. "Your food is here, eat first alone/talk first with me, you decide."

Karl and I had to eat our disgusting vegetables out of her presence. Karl said, "I'm hungry. Where's the food?"

She said, "Follow," her rolling stride and short bowed legs working well on the plank-basket floor. The rooms flowed into each other, no set purpose to any other than the food room. When we got there, I saw that she'd gotten a table and chairs for us. Gwyngs just ate, when they were hungry, from a vein or udder in the field, from a bottle in the house, microwaved warm or not.

I opened the chest coolers until I found the non-freezing one with some cheese and raw fruit in it. ''Do you have baked yeasted wheat paste?'' I asked, meaning bread. There was a Karst One term for bread, but for some reason the computers in Gwyng skulls conflated it with the concept for beer, the same ''yeasted'' root, I guess.

She opened a cabinet and pulled down a warm loaf. I took it and it cut like fresh bread, mashed slightly by the knife. Black Amber oo'ed when I swallowed my saliva hard, her lips pursed as if to kiss. ''Yes, new baked. I knew the bus schedule,'' she said. ''I leave you to your un-beer and seed pulp. Enjoy and come back to the first room.''

After she'd left, I found a glass and poured Karl some milk, hoping it was Jersey, not mixed with marsupial. The cream line looked authentically Terran.

Karl drank some and said, ''At least, I can play with Rhyodolite.'' I nodded, thinking that I could speak English to Molly if I wanted to. Was Sam's ex-Berkeley wife still Rhyodolite's lover, I wondered, or was he less erotic now that she could understand him better? I felt odd about feeling so hard toward Molly. Coming to Karst was Marianne's idea; Molly and Sam struggled to make places for themselves as craft weaver and musician.

I finished my cheese and bread quickly. This house of Amber's gave me the creeps. Maybe she'd been very angry lately and smeared the juice from her thumb glands over the entranceway stones, warding off the other Gwyngs? Her last son wasn't here—hers out of her own womb and pouch. Maybe she had been sick and was lying? Wy'um of the History Committee, her favorite mate, where was he?

When Karl and I got back to the main room, Rhyodolite and Molly were huddled by Black Amber on one of the steel platforms. Funny, Molly took more space than they did, a social distance. And, as usual, I'd forgotten how small Rhyodolite was, not having seen him in several months. He was only about five feet tall on his true legs, a bit shorter than when I'd seen him first, disguised as a human with extended thigh bones.

Karl ran up to him and embraced him sideways, rocking his body against the Gwyng. Rhyodolite could understand Karl, and Karl knew some hand signs.

"Red-Clay, help us defrost Black Amber," he said.

She'd been in a cool-down torpor then, a Gwyng social stress escape. "Should I heat some oil?"

Molly said, in English, "Gwyng Home thought this house was pretentious for one who won't outlive a certain bird."

I wondered how Black Amber paid for the house, but only said, "Oh."

Molly asked, in Karst One, "Is Marianne all right alone with them?"

"They're behind reinforced polycarbonate and she's got someone who speaks their language with her."

Rhyodolite looked at me and, in a slow ripple, squeezed one nostril shut, on the off-side from Black Amber.

Black Amber said, "We will expand my social group soon."

Rhyodolite looked at her, his eyes rolling to white beneath the skull eyeshield. I noticed then that Black Amber looked age-wrinkled. The wrinkle folds, under the fine velvet fur, were thinner, not as plump and regular as Rhyodolite's.

She seemed annoyed by our silence and said, "We will (insistent/predictive) have more company."

Molly went "*Sheesh*," and lay down on the cushions, shifting her legs to plant her feet on the floor. She put her forearm over her eyebrows. Black Amber got up and walked away. Rhyodolite said, "Yes, Sub-Rector Black Amber."

Molly asked, in English, "Seen Yangchenla lately?"

"At a music club in the city just this week," I said, also in the same language.

"I saw her at the beach wearing a bathing suit copied out of *Vogue*. All the Tibetans want to wear modern human clothes. They look like jerks. Act like them, too."

"They're bored with each other," I said. We still spoke English. "One of the Support guys was coming on to Marianne."

"Stop talking English," Karl said. "Rhyodolite, they're telling secrets."

Molly fished around in a bag she had slung over her shoulder, a cloth bag that blended in with her handspun clothes, and took out a cigarette. Rhyodolite lit it for here—odd to see him trained in male human manners that compensated for our general male dominance. Human male manners reduced him to pet status. I said, this time in Karst One, "Sam was looking good."

She sat up and blew smoke at me.

Rhyodolite signed to Karl and they both got up and walked toward the door Black Amber had gone through earlier. I said, before they passed through the doorway, "Ask Black Amber what she wanted me to come here for?"

"Company for the Weaverfish," Rhyodolite said before disappearing around a corner.

I looked at Molly. She sat up, hunched over, arms and knees covering her body. "I still love Rhyodolite," she said, "but I need humans, too."

"We didn't run you out."

"You loathed seeing me with Sam, to begin with."

"Don't accuse me of being a racist, Molly. There were black and white marriages in the mountains early on." I was thinking in my mountain dialect again, translating "early on" into Karst as best I could. "And he has a human relationship now." What was she after?

I looked at her again and her knees moved apart, thighs loosened. "Molly?"

She closed her knees. "I don't want a human sex partner. I just need more human contact. I want to see my nephew."

"He's here now."

"But you don't like me." She lay back down on the mat, feet sliding to the floor, and smoked her cigarette.

"So it's been tense here?"

Molly's body wiggled, but she didn't say anything until she'd smoked the cigarette down to the filter. She stubbed the filter out and said, "We weren't sure she'd come out of her latest coma. When she came out, she wanted you here. She's been studying Karriaagzh's language, the one her brain will process. I can't imagine why. No, I'm afraid I can imagine why." Molly pulled herself back into a sitting position and I saw tears spill out of her eyes. "I'm different now, as if being around Gwyngs pulled things out of me, but . . ."

I knew what she was talking about; each different species of sapient drew out from each other emotional and mental things we couldn't get to through our conspecifics. "I tried to live without my own kind, too."

"The Tibetans think I'm horrid. They accept you, even after you dumped Yangchenla; they love Sam; I'm . . . what do the Tibetans call me?" She giggled. Neither of us knew what Tibetans called her, really, but surely they had some fierce little expletive.

I said, "Yangchenla called me a pouch hole licker when she thought I was having an affair with Black Amber."

"I thought maybe that's why Black Amber asked for you. Wy'um's senile and the Gwyngs abandoned him. One of his sisters stole Amber-son."

"No, I never slept with her. Wy'um? Amber-son? Oh."

"Why didn't you? Too stinky for Gwyng sex?"

"I'm not going to answer that. Come visit. Bring

Rhyodolite.'' I told myself that Molly was, after all, my wife's sister, and more family than Sam and Yangchenla and their daughter. ''Why did Black Amber build such a large house if she has so few other Gwyngs around her?''

Molly said, ''Display. It's mostly outer shell.''

Black Amber, Karl, and Rhyodolite came in with four other Gwyng males, all whinging in Gwyng language too complex for Federation computers. The new Gwyngs looked slightly rumpled, as if they'd raised their fur recently and hadn't smoothed it after the fuss was over.

I hung in through a half hour of their social mobbing. Rather than party until I dropped among them, I found Black Amber's servant and had him show Karl and me to our room. We walked through two huge empty halls—shells, just as Molly had said, steel beams showing in the walls, a synthetic floor.

''All hollow,'' Karl said just before the little bear opened a door into a medium-size bedroom.

The room was set with two sleeping mats. Karl looked at me as if being in the same room with Daddy but not Mommy was a bit intense. He pulled out his reader and his radio-controlled puppet—four-legged and of no determinate species—set them on a stool by his bed, and asked, ''Can we go home tomorrow?''

Karl and I ate breakfast in the food storage room, trying to ignore the Gwyngs who came in and sipped various liquids, talking away in Gwyng and watching us closely. Black Amber picked up more company this morning, two females in Gwyng shifts that consisted only of a neck band, a strap over the pouch hole, and a short skirt over the hips. The males we'd seen the night before came in, still looking rumpled, and rummaged through all the coolers and cabinets before heading outside.

Then Rhyodolite came in with a modified tossing disc, alien cousin to a Frisbee, and held it out to Karl.

Karl said, "I don't really want to."

Rhyodolite said to me, "Tell him I have to take care of him while you talk with Black Amber."

"Karl, maybe we can go home as soon as I talk with Black Amber."

Rhyodolite bobbed his head—annoyed—but said nothing more. Karl looked from Rhyodolite to me and then said, "Marianne the Linguist wants us to come home. We've left her with dangerous people. I didn't want to."

Rhyodolite said, "Tell him that wasn't my doing."

"Karl, Rhyodolite says he didn't do it."

My son slowly finished his milk and took the glass to the sink. When I saw that he was about to wash it, even more slowly, I said, "Go on with Rhyodolite. I'll wash up." He grinned and took Rhyodolite's long-fingered hand. Rhyodolite looked back over his shoulder at me and pursed his lips into a Gwyng smile.

I washed our glasses and plates and put them with the other glasses in what looked just like a dish drainer on Earth, except for the broad oval Gwyng straws, wider than a human thumb.

They grew odd muscles in their throat at the base of their tongues. Looking at the straws now, one in silver, the others in glass or plastic, I remembered what the muscles had looked like when my brother cut into a dead Gwyng.

Black Amber came in and picked up the silver straw. Before she said anything to me, she poured out a glass of pure cream and drained it, the lump between her jawbones bouncing. Then she said, "Your linguist/mate called. Karriaagzh has turned her into a prison keeper (displeases/pleases)."

"Displeases and pleases who?"

She didn't answer, but said, "We could turn inward

and strengthen the relationships we have. Perhaps bring in those who rejected us the first time, but no more.''

"We need to get to people before the Sharwani do.'' I realized I wasn't being diplomatic, but she had called me away from Marianne.

Her hands dropped, elbows bent, and her thumbs curled back, pushed back by the anger glands at their bases. I froze and watched her hands as she stepped toward me. Her left hand seemed to float up, the gland hole glistening.

"Black Amber, I'm sorry.''

"You're afraid of me?''

"Black Amber, I'm sorry I was rude.''

She nibbled her right gland, swallowing the secretion, but her left hand stayed up, swollen just above the wrist. Just as I thought she was going to drop that hand, it darted toward me and smeared the peppery juice down both sides of my cheeks. Then she ran the gland hole down my nose. Now I was angry.

"So you support Karriaagzh? He wants to contact your people, give them gate technology. Perhaps the Universe is destroyed and recreated with each gate leap (history failing to be a sensible continuum of gradual advances).''

"Are you serious?''

"Would contact with your species be bad for you?''

"I don't know. Marianne would approve.''

"So she should be left with the dangerous ones— good training for expanded human contact (sapient killers, babies dangerous to mothers being a bad start).''

Black Amber seemed to believe that evolution was intentional. I thought she was smart enough to know better. I said, "Birth must be rough on children, too.''

She sucked her left hand noisily, then said, "Better to have nymphs.''

I almost said something about the number of Gwyng nymphs that died, but realized that Black Amber's nymphs all died now that she'd used up her birth permits. "You asked me here to talk?"

"For company for the Weaver." She oo'ed and rubbed her belly up to the pouch hole. My own belly muscles tightened and my shoulders went up, arms half bent. Why did Black Amber want me to sleep with Molly, cheat on Marianne?

"I'm married to her sister."

"Marianne is with Karriaagzh now," Black Amber said. "He draws no species lines. His sex objects don't even have to be alive."

One of the other Gwyngs stuck his head in the door and sniffed once before backing off. She said to me, "Disruptor spray in the top doorside cabinet. Break my molecules."

Gwyngs were incredibly sensitive to the anger juice odor, but the Federation medics invented a molecular disruptor to break the odor up. Gwyngs didn't kill, or so Gwyngs claimed. They just bruised and bloodied. I sprayed as I wondered about the evolutionary reasons for angry Gwyngs to warn off other Gwyngs.

"Couldn't you come visit us? We've got another spare bedroom."

"Don't you approve of my house here?"

"Very nice, Black Amber."

"I invested in hydrogen crews from Gwyng Home. Tap gas giants for volatiles." She looked pleased with herself. I wondered if she'd used her Sub-Rectorship or her friends on the History Committee to wrangle possession of a non-habitable gas-giant system.

Cynical of me to wonder. I said, "Congratulations."

"The Federation is useful, as a trade body."

I was wondering how we could get away from this conversation when Rhyodolite, Molly, and Karl came in, sweating, flushing blood through webs, radiating exercise heat. Karl threw open cooler doors until he found juice, then sat down on top of a counter to drain most of the bottle. Molly found a beer while Rhyodolite held ice chunks against his webs. Molly and Rhyo chattered about how good a catcher Karl was getting to be.

Karl looked over the bottle and said, ''Thanks, I know.''

Rhyodolite koo'ed over that and said, ''Tell him, Weaver, we remember when a thrown disc toppled him off his feet.''

Karl finished the bottle and said, ''Now we go home.''

Black Amber spread her long fingers over his face and neck and wiggled them as if trying to massage out the negative language. Karl opened his mouth as if he planned to bite. As I shook my head, Black Amber jerked her hands away and said, ''Red-Clay's son, you should bite captive bad-sapients for us.''

He said, ''You don't scare me, you old—''

''Karl,'' Molly said.

Black Amber seemed defeated by that one temporal morpheme, left dangling. ''Go home.''

I said, ''Karl, you're going to have to bear with us.''

Black Amber said, ''No, take him home. We can talk in Karst City (fear Bird spies, though).''

''If you need to talk to me about something, Karl can wait a few minutes.''

''I need you/your support.''

''No, I can't wait a few minutes,'' Karl said.

''Just relax, Karl.''

Karl turned pale. I thought he might cry, but he looked away from us, then got up and went out.

Rhyodolite said, ''Go with him.''

I followed him to our room and saw him playing with the puppet, getting it to jump up on him with its forelegs as if it were a dog. Without looking at me, he said, ''Black Amber is mean. She hates my mother. Are we bad?''

''No, just different.'' I wasn't really sure, though.

Karl said, ''Why are we called refuse-people?'' The

slang Karst One word *refugee* had its roots in something equivalent to the English for *refuse*.

"It's nasty to call you that. You were born here, and the kids who use that word are just being stupid. Only a few people of any species are smart enough to discover gate technology and the math. Most people aren't any brighter or better than you."

"Are humans too stupid to make gates?"

"No, not basically." I couldn't tell him about Yangchenla's uncle, who'd figured out the system secretly, but reinvention didn't count, anyway, and Karl was smart enough to understand that.

He knew I was concealing things from him and sent the robot running toward me so fast that I flinched. Victory over Daddy. He set his jaw muscles and began packing. I packed my own bags and then cuddled him against me. "You're a good kid to be so patient with us."

"Yeah," he said, "and you're stupid to leave Mom alone with the Sharwani, even if they can't get her, really. And even if Karriaagzh helps her."

But she seems so tough, I was about to say, but I got the bus schedule in Karst One instead. We had about a half hour to wait.

= 3 =

Karl ran out of the elevator to greet his mother but stopped so abruptly his shoes squeaked. When I got out, I saw Karriaagzh sitting on the floor against Marianne's knees, pupils of his yellow eyes contracted. His Rector's uniform lay folded on the coffee table.

I smelled the glue before I saw the feather splints and the falconry book opened beside Marianne. She'd sloppily mended his grey feathers where his usual clothes had broken them. Karriaagzh slid his nictitating membranes slightly out of his eye corners. "Good afternoon, Rector," I said, looking at Marianne, like *why?* Had Black Amber been telling me Marianne was having an affair with Karriaagzh? The glue smell would cover up any other smells.

She said, "Karriaagzh knows Sharwanisa, but they didn't want to talk, so he sent out for the falconry books and feather repair tools."

"Did they try to tear down the polycarb?" Karl asked.

"No," Karriaagzh said, sounding even more hoarse than usual. "You must play with the young one." He stood up, unfolding his bent back knees and rising to his eight feet of height. Karl frowned slightly. Karriaagzh bent his knees slightly and looked around the front room as if he'd misplaced something.

One membrane didn't retract into the inside eye corner. It looked scratched and bloodshot. He saw me looking at it and said, "I went inside to talk to the Sharwani. The female attacked, again. Psychologically, perhaps the Sharwani need to be able to hurt us, at least individuals of us."

"How are they?" I asked.

Karriaagzh's crest flicked. "I refrained from breaking her other wrist."

I went back to the room where the Sharwani were. The female came up to the door and said, in mediocre Wrengu, much less grammatical than her earlier question, "Keep giant feathered sex-scale-ripper away." *Sex-scale-ripper* was an odd curse for her to use, but Wrengu came from non-furbearers, without an attitude toward *assholes*.

"We all wanted to bring sample Sharwani here for a talk," I told her in the same language.

"You non-understand how complex situation is," she said. Veins swelled up around her eyes. I didn't know if that meant anger or frustration, or what.

"My mate is learning your language."

"How do you know which language among many is ours?"

"The sex-scale-ripper told us which language."

The veins shrank back. The Sharwani child came up and said something in their own language. She picked him up and cuddled him against her, turning away from me. The male looked up at me and either bared his teeth or smiled.

I went back to the front room. Karriaagzh said, in Karst Two, so Karl couldn't follow, "We (you and Marianne personally) might/could leak information to the human governments. I know a bird-kind who speaks English.'' Karriaagzh's brain could grasp both the sequential call-derived Karst One and the sonar-based Karst Two. I wondered if he could learn Gwyng languages as Black Amber was learning one of his.

''Do you know how ridiculous it would be to smuggle in a bird to Earth, find a scientist who'd listen, and get my people involved in this?''

''You still don't trust yourself?'' Karriaagzh asked.

''It's most other humans I don't trust. Karriaagzh, isn't premature contact against Federation policy?'' I said, wondering if Marianne, with her old Red saving-the-Universe fervor, had already gotten involved.

Karriaagzh's bill flew open, but before it snapped together, he stuck his fingers in at the mandible hinges. ''Black Amber corrupts (you/everything),'' he said.

''Marianne, aren't you sick of being played between the two of them,'' I said. Karl wiggled back against an armchair and then went rigid, trying to be invisible, wanting to hear what grownups fought about.

''I want to see more humans,'' she said. ''And you're being played between Black Amber and Karriaagzh, not I.''

''Molly was at Black Amber's.''

Marianne handed Karriaagzh his clothes as she said, ''I'd like to see Anne Baseman again, my other Berkeley professors.''

I said, ''We met a mathematician in Berkeley who was working on something like gate theory.''

Karriaagzh pulled on his tunic, then his pants, one hand down inside them smoothing his feathers. He said, ''Carstairs stopped working/thinks aliens will feed him the information.''

I said, ''The aliens he met don't know anything.''

Karriaagzh said, ''We have physically disguised contacts other places than Berkeley . . .''

''So, let them leak—''

". . . but they are more obedient to the Institute of Analytics and Tactics than Alex in Berkeley."

I remembered Alex the Ahram, scarred head where his skull crest bone and overlying muscles had been removed. Now looking like a human blond with an unusual baldness pattern and a rather massive jaw, he snuck around Berkeley smoking high-potency marijuana and telling everyone he was an alien. Marijuana had an inhuman effect on him.

I said, "I don't want to go back."

Marianne said, "Karriaagzh, let's wait a little. I don't want to be from an unequal species if our guys can figure it out themselves. What are the chances?"

"Ten years to fifteen years," Karriaagzh said. "What if the Sharwani find your people? The History Committee is forcing us to guard the Federation's planets first."

"I'm not in a hurry to meet officials from Earth," I said, remembering jail, congealed Lysol in the cell corners thick as jam.

Karriaagzh said, "Your people would be happy to work with you. You've been law-abiding ever since moving here."

As if I'd been a bad guy before the aliens reformed me. "Humans abandoned me."

"Come on, Tom," Marianne said in English.

Karriaagzh settled down on his hocks again, his face feathers twitching. He picked up Marianne's tone, or knew that much English. He said, "You abandoned yourself, perhaps."

My head rocked back on my neck. "Let us try to get the Sharwani tamed. That's enough for me and Marianne to do."

Marianne and Karriaagzh looked at each other. He rose, then she handed him the box of feather-mending equipment and the falconry book stolen from a Terran library by a shape-shifted creature who probably got drunk in human bars and wept from loneliness.

Marianne said, "I don't like being a jailor, Tom."

"You volunteered us for this," I said. "You want to let the Sharwani run around the house?"

Karriaagzh said, "I'll go now," and stalked to the elevator, lifting his hocks high behind him.

As soon as the elevator doors closed around him, Karl spilled out the contents of his suitcase, found the robot and adjusted the controls so that it walked with knees bent backward. "Poor bird," he said. "He needs a few people like him."

Marianne said, "Maybe we could go to Earth for just a visit, not run Karriaagzh's operation."

"You wanted us to take in the Sharwani family, now you want to go to Earth. First, we've got to deal with the Sharwani," I said, slipping out of my shoes and then heading for the back room. I needed at least one beer.

Beer, in the Federation, came in squatty little cans that took up less space than any shape other than a sphere. Spheres rolled; squatty little cans stacked. I put twelve in the flash chiller.

Marianne came in and rubbed my neck and shoulders. "Did that bitch feed you guys?" she asked in English, breasts pushing against my back.

"I could stand to eat," I said.

Karl came in, his robot, still in Karriaagzh mode, following him. He said, "I'm hungry, too."

Marianne said, "Let's feed our prisoners first, so I don't feel guilty." She looked through our foodcooler, a chest model with hand-revolved bins—energy efficient—and brought out Sharwani analogs to beans and carrots. The cut-up roots were almost beet red.

The flash chiller beeped and I took out a beer still tingling from the sonics that kept it from freezing around the edge of the can. While Marianne heated the Sharwani's food, I popped the beer open and sipped. Warren said once that when you really want a beer, you're generally so thirsty that cold piss would taste good. Warren wasn't much on alcohol, I thought, hoping I wasn't going to get depressed for thinking about him again.

My mind flashed letters: I OBLITERATE ALL YOU FUCKERS. Warren's suicide note, big as a billboard on the wall over his body. I shuddered as I swallowed the beer. Neither my son nor my wife noticed. For half a second I was pissed that they hadn't seen, then thought, just as well.

"Do you really want to go back?" I said to Marianne.

Karl said, "I want to meet more humans, too."

Marianne said, "Karl, you couldn't go."

I said, "It wouldn't be dangerous for him. He's a minor."

Karl said, "Mother, you and Dad feed the people out there. I can fix our food."

Marianne said, "Great, Karl, you're getting to be quite the adult," as she put the Sharwani food on three plates. They used soft plastic wafers the size of tea saucers to eat with; I found a speck of dried food on one and scraped it off before folding them and sticking them into the food.

When we got to the Sharwani room, the male was in the toilet and the female was pacing the floor, her fingers going through her head hair, picking at the fur over her cheekbones. The child began wailing when he saw us. I unlocked the small door and slid the plates in.

The male came out of the toilet, both eyes bruised.

The female shouted over her child's wails, in Wrengu, "Divide us."

"Tonight, we can sedate you," I shouted back. "Barrier tomorrow."

The two Sharwani looked at each other and made odd whistling sounds almost like warning cries—maybe their laughter, maybe not. Their child stopped wailing and began mouthing his wristbone, knobbier than the equivalent human bone. All three of them froze, looking like geometric sculptures, the male's facial and head hair down, the female's flaring, then the female kicked her plate across the floor. It clattered on the back wall.

"We're as much stuck with you as you are with us," I said, wondering how much Wrengu she knew.

The Sharwani woman sank to the floor, fingers over her eyes. Blood began to seep down below her palms. I sealed the food door and started to pull a lever to gas them unconscious, but she looked up at me and said, "Veins break when upset."

The male pointed to his left eye and said, "Natural." He said something to his mate, and she threw her head back, blood leaking from the tissue around her eyes, and said something harsh back to him.

He didn't turn his back on her as he got the plates for his son and himself. She finally got up and, not looking us in the eyes, asked, "Can be more food if I . . . ?" Lacking the Wrengu word for *clean up*, she began picking up the plate and food that had fallen off it.

Marianne sighed and went back to the kitchen. I heard Karl talking to her, neither voice audible enough to carry signal.

The female said, "If I do you order, what?"

"See other Sharwani we hold."

"Surrendered Sharwani?"

"Some surrendered, some captured," I said, wondering if I'd promised something I couldn't deliver.

"For that, I'll . . . work with," she said. She went into the toilet box and came out with her eyes looking as bruised as her mate's. Marianne brought in a new plate and some paper towels. The female Sharwan shoved the plate with the dirty food out, and took the towels and the new food. She squatted down by the door and scooped up the food with the plastic wafer. "You know, have . . . people telling about me?"

"I don't know why you were brought here," I said.

Marianne reached toward her as if she wanted to pat her through the polycarb.

Karl came in quietly and said, "Night meal is ready."

Marianne said, "Thank you, Karl," and we followed him back to the kitchen.

He'd fixed strips of Yauntry villag—something like a translucent bean curd, only chewy—and a salad with strips of cheese cut up over it.

"You ate this when they captured you?" Karl asked, smiling so hard I wondered if he'd heard about me saying, "Piss on their cheese," when the Yauntries first televised my capture.

"Yes, Karl, they had cheese, too," Marianne said.

Karl looked at me and giggled. We ate the salad while he sliced off a few pieces of Jersey tongue for himself. I thought he had weird eating tastes for a seven-year-old.

"Dad," he asked me, tucking a strip of tongue in with his hand that held the knife. When we both scowled at his manners, he chewed, swallowed, and then said, "Can you always end up liking people after you get to know them?"

Marianne said, "You can't like whole species, really. You like individuals, or not."

"Dad, do you like the Yauntries now?"

"Some of them, yes, very much."

"After they killed people?"

"They were scared," I said.

"But the Sharwani aren't scared. Are they going to be bad people?"

"Some of them just make mistakes."

He put down his carving knife and looked down at the beef tongue strips he'd cut for himself. "I bet Jersey lactators think we're bad people."

I was about to tell him that Jerseys weren't people when I remembered we had Buddhist relatives, more or less. Nearest next of kin. "They don't suffer as much as sapients when we kill them. And they wouldn't have been born except for us."

Marianne said, "If you don't want to eat meat, Karl,

we can fix you vegetarian meals. Then you can be a good guy to the Jersey people.''

''If they can't use language, we can own or kill them?'' Karl asked.

''If they never use language in their life cycles, we can own them if they tame to us,'' I said.

Karl looked at me and said, ''That's tricky.''

Marianne pushed her napkin against her lips and rolled her eyes at me. Then she stiffened and asked, ''Are you afraid of the Sharwani in our house?''

''If you are brave, I can be, too,'' he said.

''Well, let's both try to tame them and teach them our language,'' she said. ''You can help us by working with the little one.''

Karl prodded his strips of tongue with a finger and said, ''I bet he bites poison.''

That night, Marianne lay down beside me in my room, flat on her back, not touching me for a while. Then she said, ''Did you sleep with Molly?''

''No.''

''I hope you turned her down without hurting her feelings.''

''I hope you . . . Black Amber said Karriaagzh was here.'' I didn't know if I wanted to ask her if she slept with Karriaagzh or not.

''Karriaagzh is just a friend.'' She rolled over and put her cheek against my shoulder, began running her fingernail around my nipple. It almost stung.

I, too, hated being a jailor. The next morning, when I brought in the cart with their first-meal bowls, the Sharwani female was standing with her shoulders at a forty-five-degree angle to the barrier. She slowly moved the first two fingers of her left hand, nails skating the polycarb surface. Her eyes were half-shut. She only wore the pants bottoms and had an almost flat furry chest with naked skin around the armpits and on the belly. The fur tapered into a V going between her flat nipples.

She looked up at me, finally, and then almost unhinged her jaw to scrape her lower teeth across the plastic.

"Marianne," I said. I took one bowl off the cart.

Marianne and Karl came in and stared. The male finally came up to the female and pulled her away from the glass. He shrugged. Marianne took a bowl off the cart and slid it in to him. He took it and backed away, using his fingers and the flexible plastic disc to shovel the food in.

The female sat down in front of the food slot and called in her language. Her son came out of the toilet cubicle with wet hair and spoke to her in Sharwanisa, their language. Karl said, *"Ouvootriyala."*

I looked at him and he said, "It means 'I'm sorry' in their language, Dad."

The child took a tentative step toward Karl, but his mother grabbed him and rocked him up against her belly. I slid two other bowls. Marianne said, "I think she's going crazy. We need help."

I went to my terminal and typed in a message about what was going on. The computer flashed back at me: A SHARWAN WHO IS COLLABORATING CAN HELP. SCHEDULED YOU FOR GENERAL MEETING THIS AFTERNOON, 4TH TIME BLOCK, 2ND TOWER, 19TH FLOOR.

When I told Marianne about the meeting, she said, "I don't want to be prejudiced, but maybe we need martial arts lessons?"

"Or handguns?"

"Too redneck," she said.

The Sharwani collaborator slumped in a chair, fur over the cheekbones trimmed, tissue around the eyes puffy. He didn't watch us aliens come in. He held an herbal cigarette wrapped in brown paper in his left hand, palm against his knee, and stared at the coal. His eyes flicked to the right, then he lifted his cigarette to his mouth, closed his eyes, and sucked smoke in.

I sniffed, wondering how strong a drug he had there, and sat down three seats to his right. Beside me was an olive bird, Porphyry, who took the cushions off his chair, put them on the floor to cushion his hocks, and leaned his elbows against the frame as though it were bird furniture. The seat immediately to the right of the Sharwani collaborator was empty. To his left sat a Barcon, half in fur, half shed. Other than the skinny nose and the jaws joined between the chin and jawbone point, if he'd been completely shed, the Barcon might have looked like a black human.

I watched the Sharwan smoke—very odd. He looked over at me, a flash of eyewhite, then lifted his shoulders slightly. He? She?

The Barcon leaned over and whispered in his ear. Tissues around the Sharwan's eyes deflated slightly, and he pulled a stone box out of his tunic and gently stubbed out his cigarette on its top, then put the butt into it. Not much of what he smoked left, I speculated, seeing the care he took with it.

The last of us filed in, all the larger sex in sexually dimorphic species. In the non-dimorphic species, I suspected the bigger of the pair came. The Sharwan looked around at us, then said, in perfect Karst One, "I'm Thridai. You can't think of us as pure enemy."

Porphyry took out an oil box and dabbed a finger into it, the nail thicker than mine, and spread it over his face feathers, rubbing it into his nares. When he'd finished and no one had spoken, he said, "We're more sophisticated than that, but we have these unhappy people in our houses."

Thridai looked around the circle, then said, "Many of my kind feel a need to reduce the complexity of this Universe."

One of the non-sexually-dimorphic skinny fuzzies

said, "To be less complex, the Universe would need less life."

Thridai turned both hands so that his palms faced the fuzzy creature. "But you don't go away." I remembered Karriaagzh saying as much to another species that didn't quite trust the Federation.

Nor could we exterminate, with any certainty, a single space-going species. The Universe was huge and the jumps between its space-times infinite.

I asked, "Is a need to understand everything a neurologically determined trait in Sharwani?"

Before Thridai could answer, Porphyry added, "How much ambiguity can you Sharwani take?"

The Barcon next to Thridai seemed to want to restart this discussion group, but Thridai looked around and saw all of us staring at him. He reached into his pocket as if he planned to smoke, but then brought his hand out empty. "I can manage the Federation's ambiguity," he said, his voice rasping from deep in his throat.

"Tell us about your species' behaviors," the Barcon said. He pulled a tuft of fur off his forearm, exposing more dark skin.

Thridai looked at the bare patch, moved his arm as if he wanted to touch it. He said, "We gather information by touch, sight, hearing. Taste is for pleasure or warning."

The Barcon held his arm toward Thridai and leaned its body away. "Here, then."

Thridai reached out with a finger. I noticed that his nail curled up slightly and the fingerpad seemed swollen. I wondered what precisely had been the significance of the female scratching at the clear restraining wall and tried to remember what her hands looked like. The Barcon sat patiently while Thridai tweaked a bit of Barcon hair between thumb and forefinger.

Thridai leaned back and the Barcon started breathing normally again.

"I'm sorry," Thridai said. "Maybe I shouldn't have

demonstrated touch.'' He leaned back in his chair, hair surging up slightly as he closed his eyes, then opened them, looking around the room. ''The polycarbonate walls are a problem. We can't see properly through them, nor can we feel. Heat images are diffused.''

Porphyry raised his olive feathers until they stood out like a muff around his neck and shoulders. The Barcon asked, ''What restraints do you suggest if we let them out?''

Before Thridai could answer, one of the furrier people added, ''We want them to learn Karst One or teach us your own languages. Common ones.''

We were almost mobbing Thridai. He said, ''Perhaps if I talk to them? Do you know where each pair come from?''

''Off-planet administrators, we think,'' the Barcon said.

I said, ''Mine know some Wrengu. Your people attacked just as we were contacting the planet species. The female seems to be going insane.''

Thridai pulled out his stone box and took another cigarette out of it. The Barcon coughed; Thridai put the cigarette back in the box, but didn't put the box in his tunic pocket again, just held it on his thigh, fingers working over it. He finally said, ''They all have children?''

We all cupped our fingers and brought our hands down. He seemed to recognize the signal for ''yes.'' I felt frustrated. What kind of help was he giving us? He said, ''Let the children get together some. You must.''

''We want them to play with our children,'' I said. ''We have mixed-species nursery groups.''

Thridai's fingers gripped his stone cigarette box. He said, ''I'd like to talk to some of them.''

''Mine,'' I said. ''See if you can help the female.''

Porphyry shook his feathers, then settled them. The others looked around at each other, then the Barcon said, ''Officiators, perhaps some of you can bring your

Sharwani couples to the next meeting.'' He stood up
and spoke in another language to Thridai, who immediately put the stone case in his tunic pocket.

"Red Clay," the Barcon said to me, using my Academy name, "you and Thridai can go right now."

"You and he could stay for dinner," I said to the
Barcon. I wanted another person with Thridai and me.

The Barcon said, "My mate. I have other duties."

Thridai was picking at his tunic sleeve with his broad
fingertips. He stared at the threads, running a nail over
them. Well, then, maybe he was nervous about me, too.
I said, "Thridai, do you want to come with me?"

He looked up from his tunic sleeve and said, "I
will."

"I don't want to be cruel to anyone," I said.

"I am in agreement," he said.

Don't show fear, Warren's voice called from memory. I remembered a yellow dog coming at me on his
belly, snarling and cringing. Sharwani did remind me
of yellow dogs, maybe because of the furred cheekbones. I said, "Do you know the bus system?"

He pulled the tunic back from his wrist to show me
his ID bracelet and transportation pass. "I'm trusted
more than perhaps seems reasonable."

We walked to the elevator. "Did you have the language operation?"

"Yes."

"With the computer?"

"Yes."

"Then we can track you through that."

"So your people aren't foolish." His head bent forward, chin to his neck. The elevator doors slid apart
and we got on. As the doors closed and the machine
began to sink, he asked, "Can they monitor everyone?"

"I think the computer can screen for key words,
maybe test for blood substances, but we've never been
bothered."

He touched his head—not the same spot in the skull where I had my plate—and said, "I feared that they would damage me."

"In your case, they'd try very hard to do every thing right." Was that a tinge of jealousy I felt? Really, I told myself, Barcons never wanted to screw up. But they had when trying to rebuild Warren's personality and brain, a darker part of myself replied.

Thridai said, "I'm honored."

I laughed. He stiffened and said, "What is that noise to you?"

"Amusement."

He made a sound that sounded like big rubber bands twanging deep in his throat—*bo'ing, bo'ing*—and touched my chin. "Good, amusement."

When we reached the ground, Thridai looked around as we walked out of the building. Thin clouds hazed our star, and the temperature was about in the mid-sixties Fahrenheit. Thridai asked, "Heavier or lighter for you?"

"My home planet was bigger, but I don't notice it now."

He said, "Heavier for me. Do you have children here?"

"Yes, a son."

"I should have brought my mate." He didn't say any more about her. We walked out the Academy gates and he asked, "Are they functional?"

"We like to keep the cadets under supervision at first. I suspect one could get out if one wanted."

We waited for a bus that wouldn't require transfers. Around us were cadets and officiators, in feathers, fur, and bare skin of all colors, buying snacks from vendors, waiting for buses, leaving buses. Thridai hunched his shoulders slightly as he looked around. The bus pulled up; we got on and rode through Near-Institute District's weird mix of high-income domestic and commercial architectures from over 120 planets. As we passed a stone building with a rose window, clear glass leaded in lace patterns with green glass diamonds at the perimeter, I heard Thridai make that twanging rubber band sound.

"What's funny?" I asked.

"That building reminds me of home. For a second, I was afraid." He looked at me and I saw that the tissue around his eyes was very puffy. I wanted to hug him— he seemed so small and lost—but instead put my hand on his knee, carefully. He seemed to relax slightly, then stiffened again when we came to the platform houses of the birds, all of them going about their household routines exposed to view and the heights. Karst Sun intensified the shadows as it began to set.

"Aren't they embarrassed?"

"No, they're completely feathered and, see, the toilets are opaque. We get off three parks from home, but they're just small parks," I said. "Are you okay?"

"I think so," Thridai said. "The domesticity bothers me."

I thought I understood. As a bird mother chased down and whacked a youngster about ten stories overhead, we reached the bus stop and got off. Again, the rubber band sound.

We walked into Lucid Moment District, Thridai not saying anything more. At my apartment building, I went into the ground-floor provision shop run by a city Gwyng woman, Awingthin. Thridai stopped at the threshold, then came in the shop himself.

"Hi, Awingthin," I said. "Do you have any extra Sharwani foodstuffs?"

She looked over at Thridai and said in Karst Two, "(Out free) he's allowed?"

Thridai's throat bo'inged again and he said, "Yes."

"Sorry/didn't know you'd had a computer installed. Well, yes, I have food for you. Red-Clay, how is Cadmium?"

"I haven't seen him in a while."

"He should visit soon." Her nostrils clapped and the muscles under her facial wrinkles shifted. "And for you, this." She handed me a slab of plastic-wrapped chocolate.

I gave her my credit card and she subtracted the pur-chases, letting me see the reading before she pulled out the card and handed it back to me. I'd just gotten an-other first-contact percentage from Yauntry duties, about two hundred minimum-wage days.

Thridai and I both reached for the food package, but the Gwyng put it in his hands. When we were on the elevator, he asked, "Don't you have small elevators for the food? You'd never have to go into the shop."

"We enjoy going in the shop," I said. "Awingthin is a friend of ours."

"Are my conspecifics angry?" he asked, his eyes puffy again.

"What behaviors show anger?"

He groaned and asked, "You can't empathize?"

"We're semiotic animals. If we know what a behav-ior means, we certainly can empathize."

"How do you learn what it means?"

"Thridai, it's like your amusement sound. You have to explain sometimes. We're not like lower animals; our empathy isn't innate." We got in the elevator.

As the elevator doors closed, he said, "Language is innate to the Universe."

"What about the Gwyngs?"

He said, as we got out on my floor, "The computer does faster what we could figure out with time."

"Gwyngs claim Karst Two doesn't begin to convey the meaning they can express in their own languages," I said. "We eat in the back room."

"Do you believe that?"

"I can't get into a Gwyng's brain and prove they're lying," I said. As we passed down the south hall going toward the kitchen, I saw people with Marianne across the atrium shaft in the other hall. Thridai didn't seem to notice anything, but I smelled something like a dog's smell. Marianne waved, and she and the people with her joined us in the kitchen.

Then I saw the lion. Not a lion, but maybe a cross between a lion and a large ape, with a bobtail. It stopped and crouched. Behind me, Thridai squeaked.

One of the people with Marianne said to the beast, "No. Okay." I looked up from the beast to the ungainly sort of bipedal ape creature, with motley fur, giving this thing orders.

"Marianne, this is Thridai. He's here to help us with the other Sharwani."

Marianne nodded to him and said, "I'm here alone half the time, so I've hired a Quara. These people are his handlers."

The Quara sat down and nibbled off a claw sheath—huge claws—and then looked back at its handlers as if asking, who do I eat first?

"Can this one leave the apartment?" the handler who'd settled the beast said, pointing to Thridai.

"Yes," I said, thinking maybe this would be better than having Karriaagzh, who'd lusted after even a Jerek, hanging around Marianne.

"This one, smell, memorize. Not like others. Don't control him."

The beast shrugged and padded up to Thridai and snuffed hard at his crotch, then his fingers. Then it said, "Yes."

I said, "How intelligent is it?"

The Quara looked at me, then at Marianne, who said, "His name is Hrif. He's intelligent enough."

Hrif looked back at me and said, "Yes, Hrif-self."

The handlers talked to each other in their own language and then to Hrif. The one who'd been talking said, "Keep the sentences simple."

Hrif said, "Go sleep?"

Marianne said, "Yes."

"Miss you," Hrif said to his handlers.

''Smell this one,'' the second handler said, coming up to touch me. ''He also gives orders.'' Hrif swung around and snuffed at me and then padded back down the hall.

Thridai asked Marianne, ''Why do you think we're so dangerous?''

Marianne said, ''The female tried to claw out a friend's eye.'' She didn't seem too happy about Thridai being here, her arms out from her sides, her legs bent slightly.

''Easy, everyone,'' I said. ''Let's go talk to the Sharwani.''

Marianne said something and Thridai answered her in the same language. She said, ''So I am speaking correctly.''

''Maybe the wrong language for them,'' Thridai said.

''No, I've heard them talking. That's why I got Hrif. I'm not a xenophobe, really, but the female is very angry.''

There was, I realized, a difference between xenophobia and the sane practice of caution around strangers, regardless of species. Thridai nibbled at his fingertips, narrow thin tongue tapping out between his teeth, then said, ''Let's see them, then.''

We walked up the north hall and saw Hrif lying over the threshold of my room, his massive paws out in front like a Sphinx. At the polycarb wall, the three Sharwani strained to see him.

Thridai whistled air against his teeth. The female turned and grabbed her mate's shoulder. They began talking Sharwanisa to him, hands scrabbling against the glass as if they wanted to touch him, the female's wrist cast bumping against it.

Marianne said, ''I hadn't noticed before, but they all have big fingertips.''

''Yes,'' I said. ''They like to touch, and they see infrared. A polycarb wall is sensory deprivation to them.''

Thridai said, "They're only minor officials in the occupation. Why don't you let them out?"

I said, "We can't let them go just on your word."

Thridai talked to them some more. I wondered if we could trust him. He turned back to me and asked, "Won't the guard beast protect you? And you have control bracelets. I wore one before they installed the skull-bone computer."

Marianne said, "They have to learn Karst One."

I thought about being in jail and looked at the female, who quivered, hands pressed on the glass over her head. "Only on this floor," I said, then went to lock the elevator.

As I passed him, Hrif got up, heavy hips swinging from side to side, and padded up. Marianne said, "Stop fast moves."

"Him, too?" Hrif said, gesturing with his head at Thridai.

Thridai said, "I'll accept that."

Marianne said, "Yes."

Hrif said, "Nervous. Dumb." He lowered his haunches first, then his forelegs and shoulders, and peeled another claw. I came back and unlocked the door to the clear wall we had the Sharwani behind.

When they came out, trembling, clutching each other, I felt like a bully. The female said in Wrengu, "Go we outside?"

"We want you to learn our language."

"Your female knows our language."

"Some," Marianne said. She spoke a few words of Sharwanisa then, and the female looked down and stroked her son's back with her fingers.

Thridai said, "Her name is Chi'ursemisa. He is Hurdai. The child is Daiur."

"Why us?" Chi'ursemisa asked in Wrengu.

"We need to understand your species so we can calm it down," I said.

Hurdai said something and bo'inged deep in his

throat. Marianne whispered to me, "He said, 'I told you we are samples.'"

Daiur said, in Karst One, "Where's Karl? I'm hungry."

I was as surprised as I'd been when the guard beast had spoken. Marianne said, "Karl's visiting friends tonight."

"We've got enough for everyone," I said.

Hurdai said something. Thridai translated this time, "He'd like to cook."

"I'd rather he didn't get near the burners," I said. Thridai spoke again in Sharwanisa, then Hurdai said something more and they talked a bit without translating.

Hrif moved his joints and legs again and came after us, head down, muttering about duty, his bobtail swinging like a club. I wondered if his kind naturally knew speech or if a computer translated animal sentiments into speech. He settled by corner cabinets we didn't use that much. Marianne said, "Fine. Good."

"Hungry, too," he said, without raising his head.

Thridai asked, "Is this a standard living quarters layout?"

"Yes," Marianne said. She went out, leaving me with all these people, and brought back Quara food like dog kibble in a plastic can. Hrif ate while she ran water into a bowl for him.

"Shouldn't you feed us first?" Chi'ursemisa asked.

Thridai talked to her and then said, "We're from the same group on Shar. Shar means The Planet, but I expect everyone calls their planet that before space travel."

I wondered if they knew each other before capture.

"Who will cook?" Marianne asked, beyond caring whether the Sharwani knew each other before or just went to the same museums.

"If you'll let me, I will," Thridai said. "We need an oil suitable to us and a shallow pan." He took the food that we'd been feeding Hurdai and Chi'ursemisa, with the same oil, and did entirely different things with it than we'd been doing, crisping vegetables I'd boiled, leaving the meat almost raw, and rolling out their bread into big floppy wafers much like the plastic discs they'd used to pick up their food. When he made tea, he left the leaves in.

Marianne said, just to me, "Obviously, what we've fixed for them has been like prison fare."

Worse, I thought. I wondered what Ahrams or Barcons would have done with corn meal and beans if they'd tried to feed me what I usually ate back in Virginia. Beans baked hard as stones?

Chi'ursemisa took the first plate and touched the food with her fingers, then began babbling to Thridai between scoops of food on her flat bread. He looked at us, hair flaring on his head slightly, then handed Hurdai and Daiur their plates. Chi'ursemisa kept talking.

"What is she saying?" I asked Thridai.

"She's just talking," he said. "Nothing strategic."

"We didn't mean to fix their food wrong," Marianne said.

"I told them you didn't," Thridai said. He fixed his own plate, and the Sharwani all sat on the floor to eat. He looked up at us and said, "The platform you have is too high and not big enough."

He was looking at the table. "Oh," Marianne said. I microwaved some human food pouch stews, and we both sat down on the floor to join them, eating with spoons. Chi'ursemisa kept talking, sometimes articulating when she inhaled.

Marianne finally interrupted and said something in Sharwanisa. Hurdai's eyelids swelled, but Thridai stroked under Hurdai's lashes with his thumb.

Hrif went rigidly alert, utterly silent, his club tail raised off the floor.

Daiur said, "Mother hates us around all the time."

Chi'ursemisa stopped talking and stared at her son.

I wasn't sure whether she understood or not. Thridai spoke Sharwanisa to Hurdai, who spread his fingers and moved his hands at the wrists side to side, a wider movement angle than a human ulna and radius could make against human wrist bones. They both looked at Chi'ursemisa, who put her hands over her eyes, palms against the flesh under the eyes.

Hurdai looked at Marianne and spoke Sharwanisa. She answered him and said to me, "They want to know what we want. I said we can only explain in our common language, so they have to learn that first."

Chi'ursemisa said, in poor Karst One, "Beyond that?"

"We need to learn about you and you about us," I said.

"Jailors," she said in Wrengu.

"You jailed the Wrengee," I told her.

She put her hands back over her eyes and didn't answer, then asked, "Touch I you?"

Marianne said, "The Quara might be nervous."

"Touch, no hurt," Hrif said from his corner.

Marianne and I looked at each other, nervous about who should get touched. Marianne moved her legs around to a kneeling position and sidled up to Chi'ursemisa. Chi'ursemisa's fingertips swelled as she raised her hands and put them on the top of Marianne's head. The fingers rotated slightly as Chi'ursemisa brought her hands down the side of Marianne's face. They stopped at the ears, then the index fingers circled in Marianne's ear canal while the thumbs and other fingers felt around her outer ears.

Marianne giggled slightly as if Chi'ursemisa tickled her. Chi'ursemisa pulled her fingers away from Marianne's ears and began to feel her mouth.

I asked, "Do you need to do this?"

"Curious," Chi'ursemisa said.

"No hurt," Hrif said. He rolled so that his hind feet were under his belly, forepaws in front. He raised his head while Chi'ursemisa opened Marianne's mouth and ran a finger over her teeth, then he dropped his head on his forelegs when Chi'ursemisa pulled her fingers out.

Hurdai asked something. Marianne, now that Chi'ursemisa was feeling her neck, said, "He wants to feel you."

Thridai spoke Sharwanisa to Hurdai, then said to me, "Be careful."

Hrif said, "Only one" and rose to his feet. Chi'ursemisa moved away from Marianne. I said to Hrif, "Now this one." Hurdai quickly felt my head, the fingers moist against my skin. He bent his fingers and caught my beard stubble with his nails. Then Hurdai began probing my joints, testing for tendon insertions when he could.

"Whoa," I said, remembering a Barcon examination that determined my physical exercises. Hurdai looked at me; Hrif growled. Thridai spoke Sharwanisa again and Hurdai made the thrummed rubber band sound in his throat. Then his fingertips shrank, leaving slight wrinkles behind. The wrinkles seemed firm, their equivalent of our fingerprints, a biological friction grip.

Thridai said, in Karst One, "Hurdai wanted to see how your body might fight."

"Yes, I knew." I wondered if we ought to stop this. They began talking in yet another language. That upset Thridai. He tried to interrupt them in Sharwanisa, but they talked even faster.

Then Chi'ursemisa asked me in Wrengu, "Joints different. Same species?"

"Yes," I said. "Different sex."

They made the rubber band sounds again. Hrif said, "Stop." He stretched, back arched, front claws digging into the floor, tail bent forward over his back, then came up to Marianne and butted her with his head. "Touch me."

Marianne began rubbing him around his ears. I saw Chi'ursemisa's fingers swell, then wrinkle again. Thridai began picking up the dinner dishes and taking them over to the sink.

I felt weird, as if I'd been sexually handled, not just measured for range of motion, tendon insertions, and general muscle strength. Those tumescent fingertips. And I realized that before this night, I hadn't seen the Sharwani as themselves, but rather as more human than they were, more dangerous than alien. Marianne looked at me—sexual eyeballing—and smiled slightly. She said in English, "I hadn't really seen them well earlier."

I asked back in the same language, "When do we get to the point where we don't carry human templates around in our heads?" I remembered Mica, the Gwyng I dragged out of a fire and saved for a while, drawing me with human features exaggerated toward the Gwyng norm.

Marianne said, again in English, "Maybe we always have to work on it?"

And, I thought, if you don't revise your mental templates, the Universe will confuse you. I wondered if the Sharwani wanted to make the universe over by their templates and subordinate anyone who didn't fit.

Chi'ursemisa got up and began feeling her way through the kitchen equipment, looking over at us and then at Hrif, who growled slightly. Thridai said to us, "She's teasing you. Look at her fingertips."

They were wrinkled, not puffed.

"Can we put them in their room now?" Marianne asked.

Thridai's eyelids puffed slightly, but he spoke to his conspecifics. Hrif rose and padded over toward them, his thick tail held at an angle to his back. I smelled a musky smell, not really unpleasant, just greasing the air.

Daiur said to his mother in Karst One, "Back to the room, please." Then he said, "I'll play with Karl and the others tomorrow."

Hurdai said something to Thridai and then spread his

hands as if imitating a shrug. Who else shrugs like humans? I tried to remember. Chi'ursemisa's eyelid veins knotted, but she turned and went toward the hall. Hurdai spoke to Thridai, then picked up Daiur and followed her. Hrif, his tail still bent to the side, padded behind them, then Marianne and I went behind him until they went through the clear door. We shut it and locked it.

In the kitchen, Thridai was cleaning up, his shoulders twitching. He turned to us and one eyelid vessel had ruptured. Marianne said, "We try not to be cruel."

Thridai said, "Are you afraid of me, too?"

I said, "No." Marianne looked at Hrif, then raised her hand, fingers cupped, and brought it down fast.

"I know the Federation is right. I came to its cause. But seeing my own caged is shocking," Thridai said. He began wiping the dishes with paper towels, rotary wrist movements, the fingers gripping the paper. "Soon, we must be . . . never the same, but . . ."

"In communication? Not fighting?" Marianne suggested.

"The Universe will swallow us if we try to swallow it," Thridai said. I figured the plate was dry by now and took it from him, but gently.

I realized I was thinking in English—a sign in me of being anxious. Slip it back into Karst One, that's a better map for these sorts of situations, I told myself.

Thridai said, "I have to go."

Marianne asked, "Should we go with you?"

"No, I can find my way. Can I use the strangers' facilities? I saw the space in your front room."

We walked with him to the front and he disappeared for ten minutes into the multi-form toilet and cleaner by the elevator. When he came out, I saw that he'd put masking cream under his eyes. He asked, "May I come back?"

I looked at Marianne to let her answer. She said, "Yes, our code is *R-E-R-E* one-zero-two *A* and *I*," giving him the Karst One equivalents to the first letters of our Academy and Institute names, our home floor designation. "Leave us a message if we're not on terminal."

He pulled out a small keypad and jotted it down.

I said, "Are you sure you'll be all right going back?"

"Yes, I like to be out under such a bright sky. Like an hour after sun disappearance all night long."

"But you're not crepuscular, are you?" I asked, wondering if we had the Sharwani under too-harsh lights.

"Leave them with that illumination," he said, almost in a monotone. He patted his tunic top and pants as if checking to see if he'd left anything, then pulled out his stone cigarette box and lit the last half of the thing he'd been smoking earlier. He made the plucked rubber band sound again, but it was higher pitched than before. "But I personally hate having so many details thrust at me." He pressed the button for the elevator.

Marianne said, "And we wouldn't be social companions, would we?"

He looked straight at her and said, "No." The elevator door slid down; he stepped inside and pushed the ground-floor button.

Hrif came in and asked, "Gone? Sleep?"

Marianne said, "Yes."

He looked around the front room and padded up to the sofa, put his paws on it and moved almost delicately onto it. I was about to protest, but he stared me down.

Marianne said, "Come on, Tom."

We went into Marianne's room on the south hall, farther from the Sharwani and Hrif, and talked about human organs that felt better when they filled with blood, then tested them, giggling half the time.

Lips become fantastically sensitive when the blood's in them. Marianne pulled hers away from me and said, "Poor bastards."

Later, she said, "I was so nervous."

"Still?"

"Not as much. They're more ordinarily alien. Does that make any sense?"

I said, half-asleep, "Yeah. Ones like humans you really have to worry about."

The next morning, I tried to fix plates for the Sharwani the way Thridai did. When I slipped them through the food slot, Chi'ursemisa said, "Hearing is touch. You and female . . . last night." She stopped as if what we'd done was weird, more incomprehensible than vulgar.

Hearing is touch? I thought about the pressure of sound waves against membranes. Inside the jellied coils of my inner ear, tiny fibers bending caused impulses to travel up the auditory nerve. Touch? Sort of, I supposed. I said, "What we did is normal for us."

Marianne came out and overheard that. She said something in Chi'ursemisa's language, then said to me, "They've got very sensitive hearing, but they can detune."

"You're always sex?" Chi'ursemisa cleaned her plate with her fingers, licked them with her thin tongue, then said in halting Karst One, "Will study Karst One language. If we can come out."

Marianne said, "One at a time."

Hurdai asked Chi'ursemisa something and, when she replied, made the rubber band bo'ing sound in his throat. Daiur said, "Start with me."

"You can play with the children anytime," Marianne said.

"Two at a time if one is Daiur," I told Chi'ursemisa in Wrengu. Marianne signaled yes with her cupped hand.

Chi'ursemisa said, "I'll be first."

Hurdai said something slowly to Marianne, who translated, "He wants to have some company in there."

I said to Chi'ursemisa in Wrengu, "I wish I could send you three back."

She said, "I'd never be trusted."

I said, "Let's make the best of it, then," and un-locked the door. In English, I said to Marianne, "Why don't we let all of them out?"

Marianne said, "As long as you and Hrif are here," then said something in Sharwanisa. Hurdai pushed his fingers through the fur over his high cheekbones and shambled out. We went into the front room. Funny how more tired and less dramatic they looked under natural light. Chi'ursemisa went to a window and looked out, stretching. Hrif settled his head down on his paws again.

The elevator door opened. We all turned around. Hrif rose to his feet, tense, eyes on the Sharwani. Karl stepped off the elevator, looked around. Daiur ran up to him and hugged, saying, "Friends now."

Chi'ursemisa's eyelid veins swelled slightly, then she nibbled at a finger and sat down on the couch. We didn't say anything. Karl said to Daiur, "That's great. What's your name?"

"Daiur."

"When you grow up, the Federation will call you after a rock." Karl didn't seem enthusiastic about the prospect.

While Hrif and I watched the Sharwani, Marianne went back to her room for a lap terminal and micro-phone. She plugged in the terminal to the core cable and said to the microphone, "Give me the learner series Sharwanisa and Karst One phonemic and morphemics workups, parallels and disjunctions."

The terminal said, "One, two, three, four," showing one ball, two balls, three balls, finally four on the screen. It then counted the balls in Sharwanisa.

Daiur tried to touch the screen, then counted the balls. Chi'ursemisa said, "One, two, three, four," pointing to the adults.

Karl said the Sharwanisa word for "two."

Marianne said, "Karl, we're teaching them *our* lan-guage."

Hurdai said, "One, two," pointing to the children.

Marianne pointed to the sofa and gave the word for that, with its root in *seating instrument* and its bound morpheme for horizontally long. Then she pointed to the chair and gave the word for that. Chi'ursemisa used both words correctly, murmuring the sofa word's terminal morpheme separately.

After an hour, I began to get bored and went to get my own portable terminal to check on what my cadets were doing. Hurdai looked up at me when I came back and plugged into another fiber-optic cable, my terminal configured with a keyboard. He came over to see what I was doing, his fingers resting on my right shoulder.

Instead of calling up cadet records, I had the screen show a map of our neighborhood, and rotated it, then abstracted out the floor plan of our building. He reached for one of the knobs and turned it this way and that, from more abstract schematics to graphics as detailed as fine-grain color photos.

"Here," he said, pointing to the room we were in. Chi'ursemisa came up and looked, too.

I rolled the scale so that we seemed to be zooming away from the neighborhood, away from the city, off the planet. Then I paused, afraid I'd be giving away military information.

Marianne said, "More work," and they'd both learned that much Karst already. Chi'ursemisa curled her leg under her as she sat, fingers spread on the chair arm, and Hurdai squatted, holding his knees. They looked over and blinked at me, both pairs of eyelids falling simultaneously, as if their minds were linked.

= 4 =

Once Hurdai learned enough Karst One to phrase the thought, he asked, "Why not language operations? Thridai had them."

Why not, indeed? For about a month, the Federation task group in charge of the Karst-bound Sharwani debated whether or not to put the Sharwani captives through the operation. The various Sharwani couples, having heard about the language operations from Thridai, seemed to hope this would be done to them en masse, thus giving them time together.

After the fifth task-group meeting, Thridai came back with me to my apartment. Smoking his herbal cigarettes, he told Chi'ursemisa, "No Sharwani government will accept any of us back."

Chi'ursemisa said, "We thought as much." She leaned over, took one of his cigarettes and lit it, her head hair flared slightly.

So much for the Federation's plans to use some of the captive Sharwani in prisoner trades. Did the Sharwani torture their captives? Or simply kill us as animals? I visualized a bird sapient gut-shot, flopping around in null-gravity, blood vivid red balls.

Thridai said, "We need the language operations."

Hurdai made the thrumming rubber band sound down in his throat, very softly.

We went on living together, trusting Hurdai and Chi'ursemisa a bit more each day. One day, Marianne said, "Could you take Karl and Tracy swimming? I'll be fine with them. Thridai's coming over."

I said, "Don't they have nursery group today?" Tracy was Sam and Yangchenla's daughter. I saw Karl freeze when I looked at him. He'd been sneaking toward the harpsichord Sam left behind. He tried to play it, but would get excited and start banging, which broke the quills over the bass strings.

"Karl and Tracy need to practice human flirting."

That sounded ultraliberal to me, but I said, "Okay."

Yangchenla, in a trench coat and shiny boots copied from a smuggled-off-Earth fashion magazine, brought Tracy over. Tracy, hair ironed smooth, skin the color of the bottom of a biscuit, didn't really want to leave Yangchenla, but swimming was bribe enough. She was a lovely little girl with round black eyes shaded by a trace of epicanthic fold. Again, I thought about having another child, my option this time. Not quite yet.

Karl came out of his room with his gym bag and said, "Why can't Daiur go?"

Daiur came out and said, "I swim, too. Please?"

Yangchenla stared out our windows as if challenging me to make the right decision. She looked both prosperous and slightly absurd in her Western clothes. Marianne just grinned at us. I felt a weird sexual tension building and said, "If it's okay with Yangchenla."

Yangchenla said to Daiur, "If you promise to be good."

Daiur said, "I won't duck and bite."

Tracy looked at me and said, "Will you swim, too?"

I nodded at her Western human style, and went quickly to my room for my suit. We'd swim outside on such a beautiful day, in the pond by the gym. When I came back out, Yangchenla had gone, so recently I could hear the elevator moving.

Daiur said, "We have to wait for the cab to return."

Tracy looked over at him and said, "You're pretty."

I pushed for the elevator, then embraced Marianne as though I wouldn't be back soon, She smoothed my hair back and looked at me as if she wanted to say something, but didn't.

Chi'ursemisa came out then and said, "Daiur, so then you get to go?"

"Yes," he said.

She raised her eyebrow hair, the Sharwani gesture parallel to a single lifted human eyebrow. Then she went over to a table between two chairs, opened a drawer and brought out herbal cigarettes and a gnarly but polished jade slab. As she sat down, her thumb rubbed the stone.

Daiur looked at his mother and crouched down, his arms away from his sides. He whined and Chi'ursemisa looked up at him but didn't move. As we got on the elevator, both Tracy and Karl looked at Daiur, then back at Chi'ursemisa stroking her stone, then Karl said, "Mom, come too."

Marianne said, "I can't. Karriaagzh and Thridai are coming over."

Daiur said, "Karriaagzh broke my mother's wrist. She's still stupid in that hand."

We took a bus down to the Academy. I worried about Daiur, but his little throat bo'inged every time we passed young aliens or a particularly ornate building. I asked, "Are you enjoying this, Daiur?"

"Oh, yes." Being kidnapped and taken off to a

strange planet happened to him young enough to make it seem normal.

"Do you like the nursery group?" I asked him.

He lifted his little hand and signaled *yes*, the fingertips swollen as though he wanted to touch everything. Karl grabbed his left hand and nibbled gently, a game familiar to both of them, it seemed. Tracy sat like a demure steel spring, her legs crossed at the ankles, her eyes forward, moving as she read the street signs and the route sheet over the driver's head. She turned her head only very slightly, not showing the boys much attention. I smiled and she shrugged. Yangchenla's daughter for sure.

Daiur rose up on the seat, fingers splayed over the windows, and said, "Wow, look at that one!"

"It's a Wreng," Karl said.

"I never got to see them when we were there," Daiur said. "They're weird. Think about feeling the scales."

Tracy said, softly, "It might be rude."

Daiur said, "We'd let them feel us."

"I suspect fur is as odd to them," Karl said, shaking his head at Tracy, "as scales and bristles are to us."

Tracy pulled out a reading tablet and began skimming. I noticed tiny loops through her earlobes when she pushed her hair back and began twisting it around her finger.

We got off the bus at the main gate. Daiur didn't want to walk, so I carried him on my shoulders, his hands gripping my head right over my ears. As we went into the gym to change, Karl and Tracy walked around each other as if in attractant/repellant orbits, finally splitting up at the women's changing room. I took Karl and Daiur into the men's changing room.

Daiur wouldn't let us see him naked and changed in a privacy cubicle. Karl whispered to me, "It doesn't hang out. He really didn't want to see yours. I told him it could get as big as Hrif's tail."

"Karl!"

"I haven't spied. I called up human biology."

I was about to ask if the nursery group showed each other the various organs, but suspected that I really didn't need or want to know.

When Daiur came out, he held a towel over his chest. We waited for Tracy outside the female changing room. When she came out, her little non-existent breasts covered, Daiur said, "Can I have that kind of bathing suit?"

When he got to the pond, he dropped the towel and I saw that he had four nipples, two lower ones very much smaller than the first pair up near his armpits.

I remembered a guy in our high school who had extra chestbuttons and felt a wave of sympathy, for both Daiur and the human I hadn't seen in over a decade. Daiur saw me looking and said, "Most of us don't have four."

Karl said, "Nobody cares how many you have, or where, or how they work. I told you that."

Daiur said, dropping his chest under water, "Karst people aren't real people. Most real people only have two."

Tracy said, "We can all talk, so we're all real people. That's the Federation law even when the Federation doesn't offer full citizenship to everyone who can talk." She walked out into the pond until she was chest deep, then slid smoothly into a butterfly stroke, head above water all the time.

Daiur swam out and dived under. He came up, laughing, with a fish in his hands. Suddenly, the fish belly squirted silvery babies. He screamed and dropped it.

"They're alien fish," I told him.

"Do they bite?" he asked, treading water, his hair wet and ruddy.

"Only small things, like fingers," Karl said. "How did you catch it?"

Daiur raised the hand that caught the fish and looked at it. "They bite fingers?"

"Not hard," Tracy said, with her hair still dry.

Daiur went down under again and came up with a

large thing that was either a small alligator analog or a very large near-salamander. His index finger was curled away from the thing, bleeding.

"That will bite," Tracy said. "You oughtn't pick things up off the bottom."

"I know," Daiur said, "but I couldn't let it go."

I swam out, took the creature from him and tossed it out into the pond. "You don't bother them, they won't bother you, Daiur."

His finger stopped bleeding as though he'd consciously constricted the veins. The beast could have bitten him harder than it did. I supposed the non-sapients in the pond got used to weird sapients dragging them out.

Daiur said, "But it bit me. It scared me. I've got to get it out and . . ."

Tracy said, "Must you? Is this urge inborn?"

"I'll take you to the infirmary if you want," I said.

"I want to bite it back."

Karl said, imitating Tracy's voice, "Must you?"

Daiur's eyelids puffed. He said, "You think . . ." The veins shrank back. "No, I can forget it. But who can we catch?"

Karl smiled and began swimming toward Tracy. Daiur rolled under like a diving seal.

Tracy went under, thrashing. Before I could swim out, she surfaced, sputtering.

Karl and Daiur bobbed up just out of reach. "Your hair's wet, Tracy," Karl said. "Now it's going to get all curly."

Daiur made the rubber band sound down in his throat, like a thin rubber band, not the broad thick ones his parents' laugh sounded like.

I said, "Your hair looks nice curly, Tracy."

She turned in the water and swam on her back, watching us. Then she sank and Karl went under.

He came up coughing and then said, "She bit me."

Tracy said, "Not hard."

"Tracy, the water here isn't too clean, so don't open your mouth underwater, all right?"

Daiur swam up to me and said, "I don't want to be grabbed." He clung to me, his legs wrapped around my arm, and shivered.

"Are you cold?" I asked.

"I want my daddy," he said. "Let's go home now."

"Why don't we watch them swim?" I said. He pushed his torso away from me and stared as if suddenly realizing how alien I was. I wondered what sort of noises would soothe him. His body stiffened, then he began sobbing. I didn't realize they cried.

Tracy and Karl stopped swimming and looked at us as I picked Daiur up and waded to shore. I remembered sitting here myself, so terribly lonely, under this tree. I had been almost afraid of the pie-sized leaves with vegetable muscles that rolled the leaves into tubes when the wind blew. I thought about blowing on one to show Daiur, but such alien leaves might be too much.

He sat down beside me, his body posture reflecting mine, staring at the leaves, then at me. "Do those leaves bite?" he asked. As I began to worry about him, I heard the high-pitched thrum in his throat.

"No, Daiur."

"You were looking at them funny. Do they roll up in the wind?"

"Yes."

He said, "We have trees like that." From home, I thought. Somewhere on the Sharwani planet is a place with not much sun, lots of wind, and high humidity.

"Daiur?" Karl called.

"I'm tired," Daiur said.

Tracy said, "I'm tired, too." She swam up to waist level, put her feet down, and began wading out.

Karl said, "Well, I'm not tired. We're not going home soon, are we, Dad? We just got here."

Daiur rolled up in a towel, lay down with his head

against my leg, fingered the coarse hair on it, and closed his eyes. He said, "I'm going to sleep."

Tracy found her comb and tried to keep the frizz from drying in. I asked her, "Why do the curls bother you?"

"Mother doesn't have them. Nobody here has them, not even Molly." She looked at Daiur and said, "He's got weird nipples. I've got weird hair. We're better off with aliens."

I said, "If you were on Earth, you'd see lots of people with hair like yours. And some humans have four nipples, just like Daiur."

Daiur squeezed his eyes tighter shut. Tracy looked down at him and said, "Daiur is so impressed."

When we got back to the house, Karriaagzh and a Barcon medic had Chi'ursemisa's wrist in a portable scanner. The Barcon didn't even look up when Daiur hissed. Hurdai made soothing noises and caught Daiur up in his arms.

Marianne asked, "Enjoy your swim?"

"Sure," Karl said, almost, but not quite, giving his mother a kiss.

Tracy came in and sat down on the couch, her hair a black halo around her head. "Marianne, I need your iron."

"Sweetheart, you look beautiful that way, an *Afro*."

"If any of you teases me, I'll bite," Tracy said.

I looked at Marianne; we both shrugged. Karriaagzh looked through the scanner and murmured in Barc. Chi'ursemisa squirmed in the examination chair, then asked, "What will you do?"

"Ream the blood vessels and regenerate the nerves," the Barcon said. "We can do it at the same time as the language operations."

Karriaagzh moved up close to Chi'ursemisa, on the side with her free arm. She touched his face; he protruded his tongue slightly. "All right," she said.

Marianne said in English, "And we're going to Boston. Karl, too. We're getting leave time at home."

I asked in the same language, "Does he know enough English to enjoy it?"

Karl looked at us and said, "I know *going*. I'm *going*."

Tracy said, "Me, too."

I thought about two seven-year-olds, without a word more of English than "going" between them, loose in Boston. Marianne said, "No, Tracy. You need to be with Yangchenla and your aunts more."

As Karriaagzh went over to the elevator and pushed the button, Hrif rose and padded to block Chi'ursemisa from the elevator, bouncing slightly as if calculating the jump necessary to stop her.

"Why Boston?" I asked Marianne.

Karriaagzh turned around and said in English, "Because."

Marianne and Karriaagzh hadn't arranged a little private vacation. I didn't want contact—we had enough for genetic diversity; the degenerative effects of inbreeding are overrated. We were all fringe people. Why should we leak secrets to Earth? Contact would bring in officials. American officials would put me back in jail. Chinese officials might extradite Yangchenla and her people for their ancestors' crime of helping alien warriors.

The elevator took Karriaagzh away. As soon as Hrif relaxed, Chi'ursemisa began pacing.

Marianne, Karl and I had to take the high-wire car out from Karst to the shuttle, like an elevator cable doing the Indian rope trick, with us riding the cable up in a sealed cabin. The high wires had been raised only recently—all the surface gates were closed now, the gate-space dimensions around Karst mechanically distorted to block Sharwani gates. Yangchenla's brother, Kagyu, who'd become an officer, and two Barcons went with us to crew the intrasystem shuttle.

The cabin stopped at an airlock. We scrambled through into a freight-sized transfer pod that had been refitted with about five hours' worth of life support, a viewport, and some peroxide steering jets. I dogged down the hatch bolts extra tight as though hard vacuum was more dangerous than the extradimensional spaces we usually gated through. A magnetic accelerator pushed us off toward an intersystem shuttle, which was mostly huge tanks of helium-3 with a tiny crew space dangling below the tanks, too fragile to land on a planet. I asked Kagyu, "Let me see if I remember how to steer the pod to it."

It was like pedaling an aerial bicycle to bring the pod inside the shuttle. We keyed the airlock doors closed from inside and checked the gauges through the viewport.

As we climbed out and wiggled up into the living quarters, Karl asked, "How long?"

"In a little bit, honey. A few days."

"I'm bored already," he said.

The shuttle living space felt cramped and distorted, round floors fitted with furniture for acceleration and braking, the wall surface a cylinder with free-fall slings and handholds.

"Primitive, isn't it?" Kagyu said.

I said, "Yes, but I don't think Earth does this well."

"I'm sorry I can't go with you. I'm due for observation time. Did they make you go to bed after sixteen hours awake?"

"Yes."

"When we're only watching, that rule doesn't make sense."

"Maybe we irritate other people?" I also resented the rule when I did watches.

The shuttle's helium drives and fuel storage accelerated us to a constant one G. We held that for a day, then the warning horns beeped and we moved from one floor up the handholds to prepare for retrothrust, braking.

"What's happening?" Karl asked.

I said, "We're going to start slowing down."

"How long?"

"As long as we've been moving."

"This is stupid."

"No friction in space," Kagyu said as we settled down against the new floor.

"Space is stupid," Karl said. He glared at us and added, "When are we going to get there?"

"I used to ask when we would arrive when we rode in yak carts," Yangchenla's brother said.

"I bet it wasn't so boring," Karl said. We were flying above the ecliptic, and except for the slowly drifting star clusters, the space around us was empty. The trip was faster than the time I came in from an outstation with Black Amber, back when I was only twenty, twenty-one, but definitely more boring. Maybe we should have brought a Gwyng or three?

The gravity slacked off. Karl ran up to a wall, jumped and, hitting his feet against it, did a flip. The male Barcon of our pair asked, "Is he too young for beers?"

"Yes," Marianne said.

"Sedation?"

"Do you want to be sedated, Karl?" I said, trying to put as much menace in the words as I could.

"Like what they did to Chi'ursemisa and Hurdai? Drugged? No." He stopped popping off the wall and found a book chip, began reading it, flicking the screen on and off at first, then really reading.

Kagyu said, "One couldn't read in a yak cart."

Surely Karl was going to get lost in Boston, a city thick with child-muggers and rapists. I wished we'd taught him more English. I said, "We love you, Karl."

He looked up and said, "So this trip is dangerous."

Marianne said, "We'll get you toys on Earth that you can bring to play with on the trip back."

"Do we have to go back this slow?"

The Barcon said, "We seriously recommend sedation."

Karl said, "Barcon, if you try to give me anything, I'm going to . . . kiss you. On the mouth." He looked up, satisfied that he'd figured out what would upset a Barcon who feared orally transmitted sapient brain parasites that took over Barcon bodies.

This Barcon was tough, aware Barcon parasites died in human bodies and human diseases died in Barcons. "And I will spank on your . . . naked bottom."

A red flush rose up Marianne's neck into her face. She opened her mouth; I laid my hand on her shoulder. She pushed my hand off and closed her teeth with an audible click, then laughed.

Karl slammed another chip into his reader and said, "Grownups suck gut ends."

"Hey, Karl, you wanted to go."

"You didn't tell me it would be so boring."

At the far station, we transferred into another transport, a two-person oval gate capsule. Karl had to sit on Marianne's lap so I could reach the plastic wing nuts on the right side. The inside of the capsule glowed a blue-green that reminded me of dirty fishtanks. Then Karl sat down on my legs while Marianne tightened us down on the left.

I thought he'd complain about how crowded it was, but he trembled slightly and didn't say anything. We made four transitions—fourteen minutes—and then the arrival diode over the hatch came on.

After the hatch seal popped loose, I looked out and saw not some humano-formed creature but Travertine, beaked, olive and black feathered, totally alien, but English-speaking.

"Hi," he said.

"Travertine, how are you going to manage?" I got out of the transport and looked around. We seemed to be in a basement—cinderblocks, a refrigerator, bare fluorescent lights in shop fixtures, an electric heater, no windows, just a door.

"I've got enough food for your trip."

I was about to ask why he was here, then realized Travertine could never be mistaken for an insane deformed human. If Karriaagzh and Marianne were going to leak gate technology to some human, Travertine could explain—he spoke English—but he was definitely alien. And we'd never have to expose a surgically changed Federation spy. I said, "That's nice, Travertine."

"I would like a television," he said, "so I can keep up with your people."

"Who's he?" Karl asked in Karst One.

"A person who helped us get used to Karst when we first arrived," Marianne said. "He speaks Karst One. Maybe you could stay down here?"

"No. I want to see Earth." He managed to say *Earth* in close to English.

"You can't speak Karst One when other people can hear you," Marianne explained to him.

"And where is this?" I asked Travertine in English.

"A little room off the transit line that I made for myself," Travertine said. "There's solid cement between here and the train tubes, so you'll have to gate to your apartment. We installed a transit receiver there. Here's my phone number for here. And you need coats." He handed us each a jacket.

So the closet door was to a transit unit. Karl, Marianne, and I got in, dogged down the internal seals, and stepped out of another closet, lined now with our transit unit.

The apartment was huge: ceiling-to-floor windows, venetian blinds with real wood slats, burgundy carpets, and furniture in pale, mottled woods. We were in a fully furnished apartment, rented for us by some surgically reformed alien we'd never meet. Marianne said, "We'd better sneak downstairs, then make sure they know we've arrived."

Karl went to the windows and, after a little bit of

fiddling, pulled up the venetian blinds. I looked out and said, in English, "God, it's fall."

We were about fifty or sixty stories up. This window overlooked the Charles River and Cambridge, bridges, boats, park trees with flaming red leaves. I opened the other corner window to the motley look of Greater Boston sprawled beneath us, three parts ultramodern glass and brushed steel and one part antique tiny houses.

"Beacon Hill," Marianne said, pointing to the smaller houses almost at the base of our building.

"Who's paying?" I asked.

We went up and then down. Marianne and Karl went to the manager and told him we'd arrived. When you pay lots of money, the man doesn't check as much. She came back with the key cards and we went out to buy our luggage. I stopped and sniffed the air—human air with petrochemicals and fall odors in it.

And chilly. Marianne asked, "Why doesn't Karst use gates for surface transportation?"

I said, "Security and information density."

She said, "Sounds fishy to me."

"It's harder in areas with lots of information. Someone had to put a lead into that closet." I started looking around Boston—didn't look that much different . . . from what? It was different from anything else that I'd ever seen on Earth—Prudential Center, arcades up in the air over street level.

"Here," Marianne said. Karl echoed her English word, and we went up an escalator to a set of shops inside a glassed-in hall with tropical plants growing under skylights. "They've done a lot for Boston lately."

We had credit cards—I didn't ask if the money was real—and took them out to pay for leather suitcases, three of them that I didn't plan to abandon on Earth. Then I took Karl into a boys store while Marianne went elsewhere.

Karl liked a small, vested suit that cost $495—a bit much for kids' clothes, but I didn't want to argue. The salesman asked Karl, "Hi, son, do you prefer right or left dress?"

Karl looked like he was almost about to talk. I said, "American style."

The salesman seemed to understand that Karl wasn't going to say much, and so just helped him with the fitting with an "Okay?" now and then to which Karl could answer "Yes" or "No."

While the suit was being altered, we bought shoes, socks, and shirts, then went next door for some cheaper clothes for me. After I paid for all of it, Karl and I went down to the end of the mall for ice cream. The end of the arcade overlooked an ice-skating rink.

Karl whispered in Karst One, "I want to learn English. They are all like us. They speak it."

I didn't promise, just felt slightly guilty. Earth meant scrubby to me, low-rent, but Boston didn't seem rundown. I said, "I'll take you on the Freedom Trail later, before we go back."

"Teach me English."

"Your language says things better." I looked around. Nobody looked liked they cared to figure out which language we were speaking.

Karl said, "I want to know what I am."

"You're not a what, you're a who."

"Dad, are you ashamed of being human?"

"No," I said, a bit too quickly, a bit too loud.

"Travertine will teach me English when we get back," Karl said as if saying that determined the matter.

Travertine doesn't trust humans, I thought, because I snubbed one of his kind. And what further impressions of humans would Karl give Travertine? "Okay, Karl, you can learn English. Maybe my first Rector's Person can teach you."

"Dad, you teach me." Imperative familiar mode, with a slight pleading tone.

I nodded. He'd learned that much of our body language and began licking his pink bubble gum ice cream more enthusiastically.

Marianne came out of a phone booth and waved at us, then disappeared into a woman's shop. About five minutes later she came out with two boxes—the fastest human female shopper in the Galaxy.

I said, "I thought I'd take Karl on the Freedom Trail this afternoon or tomorrow."

"We've got to get a television set for Travertine," she said.

I took the television to Travertine by myself. He'd tapped a TV cable earlier and now plugged everything in and turned the channel selector until he found a news show. The announcer, an Oriental woman, said, "The nude body of an unidentified teenage woman was discovered in the pond at the Common this evening."

Travertine asked, "Naked is important?" and turned to a wrestling program. Two huge women in bikinis, up to their calves in clear jelly, struggled to throw each other. "Good light-transmitting qualities in the gel," Travertine said before he flipped to a more regular sports station. Football.

I asked, "Travertine, will you be all right here?" I didn't want to hear what he had to say about football.

"If anyone discovers the space, I'll leave before I'm seen." He nodded at the transport pod that we'd arrived in. "Look, Officiator Red Clay," he said, using my official Federation name, "many species' popular entertainments are embarrassing to the intelligentsia." The Karst One word he used for *intelligentsia* had the same fussy overtones as the English one.

I asked, "What is Marianne planning to do here?"

"Take a vacation," he said, the nictitating membranes flicking in his eye corners.

I took Karl on the Freedom Trail, starting in Beacon Hill, telling him about Louisa May Alcott, whom I'd never read until I got to Karst. We saw Paul Revere's house and the Old North Church, both buried in skyscrapers' shadows.

Karl asked, "Why did you leave?"

I said, "I came from a different part of this country."

"Mother wants to come back more often."

I wondered if I should stop her from leaking secrets. *Oh, Marianne, don't expose me.* "Yes, she likes humans now that she's escaped from them."

"Teach me English. What is the term for 'traffic-way'?" Karst One uses a shorter sound for the generality.

"*Street, road, highway.* Depends on what's on it. Airplanes don't have traffic-ways; trains have *railroads.*"

Karl said, "Oh." He looked at me out of the corner of his eye, then looked at the cemetery we were passing. "They have funny sculpture."

"They're memorial stones. Some of us bury our dead."

"Not burnt?"

"Some humans burn their dead. You know that, though."

"So you don't want Mother to help the humans here?"

"I didn't say that." How could I turn her in? Travertine must know what Marianne was doing. I could go to Berkeley, but Alex, the only alien I could find easily, thought I was a bigot about humans.

All I could do was argue with Marianne.

We took a bus back to the Commons and walked through the brilliant fallen maple leaves. I thought about getting Karl a puppy and a real Frisbee here, taking them back to Karst if Marianne didn't screw up and get us all captured.

I did think about getting captured, but I was less terrified of it than I was back in Berkeley eight years earlier. When we got to the apartment, Marianne was gone. I turned on the television, found a cartoon station, and began translating English for Karl.

Marianne came back about four o'clock and said,

"The bastard didn't want to see me. He's busy. He's giving midterms tomorrow."

What bastard, I did and didn't want to ask. Argue with her? I'd just remind her she'd married a jailbird, a redneck hillbilly. Karl said, in English, "Did you see the streets?"

Marianne looked at him and asked, "How much English do you understand, honey?"

I asked in Karst One, "What about third meal?" If the FBI was tapping this place, they'd be going crazy. A language is better than a code any day for non-contextual sheer incomprehensibility.

"I ate at Brennan's when I was here for a linguistics conference," Marianne said.

I felt a twinge of cognitive dissonance; I'd forgotten she'd had a human life on Earth until she was in her late twenties. Early thirties? I'd never asked Marianne how old she was—always knew she was older than me, but not how much. "Is it formal dress?" I asked.

"Not at all," she said.

We went into a place that had old waitresses who reminded me of country women until they opened their Boston-accented mouths. Karl sat, eyes glistening, watching everyone so intently he almost didn't eat. Marianne ate without saying much. Then, as she folded her potato skin into a messy square, she said, "The man I talked to at MIT is very close. And he was an anthro undergrad. Maybe if you and Karl came with me, we could all talk to him."

"John Amber would kill me," I said. "I don't think this is a good idea." Boy, I had to admire her for bringing up her little plot in such a public place that I couldn't rave at her.

"I was told not to mention the Sharwani."

I thought, this must sound really bizarre to anyone overhearing us. "Why not?"

"We might be thought to be the oppressors. You

know psychology. Big corporation against small innovators. But the Sharwani are why they want us in now.''

We sounded, I decided, like industrial spies. ''I want to stay out of it,'' I said. ''Wait.''

''Tom, you think you'd be in trouble again. You'd be able to do anything you wanted if we made the contact.''

''Like me, John Amber has rank one place, but not among his home folks.'' I liked being the highest-ranking human, even if we weren't regular Federation members and were sometimes snubbed because of our low-tech status. If humans came in as regular members, I wouldn't be special anymore. And I did break parole. I'd only been . . . aw, I'd always used my youth as an excuse. Sitting in Brennan's, I realized for the first time I'd been a coward, too afraid to leave my brother. Aliens had to take me away.

When Marianne began covering the potato skin square with scraps of aluminum foil, I began realizing how anxious she was. I said, ''Let me think about it.''

Karl reached over with his fork, raked the foil aside, speared the skin square, and said, in English, ''I eat.''

The waitress gave us a pitying glance for our retarded son as she gave us the bill. We walked back in the dark cold, surrounded by our own species. When we passed a group of kids Karl's age, he gripped my hand harder. *Oh, don't be a coward like your daddy, please.* Probably, a Barcon pair watched us from the crowd, but I refused to look for them. Somewhere, underground, Travertine watched television and mocked us in English.

''Do you like seeing all these other humans?'' I asked Karl in the morning.

He looked up from the cereal he was eating—one he'd seen advertised on television—and said, ''Sometimes.''

I thought about leaving Karl with Travertine while we went to MIT to talk to the physics researcher the Earth watch team marked as the man most likely to reinvent gate technology. But I wasn't sure Travertine had patience enough to manage a bored seven-year-old human, so Karl, dressed in his little business suit, came with us. We got on the magnetic train and floated over the Charles River into a tunnel and then took the escalators up to the MIT station.

Karl said, "Do we have to walk?"

I looked around and saw the buildings—grey pre-stressed concrete, glass framed by brushed steel, cantilevered decks—and said, "Not far."

Marianne saw me looking and said, "Bauhaus." We began walking toward a building with a second-story deck, the student union. While I bought Karl a Coke, Marianne called the guy again and said, "So, when can I see you? I'm very curious about the article you did in *Physical Review*."

She listened for a minute, then said, "Yes, so I'm an amateur physics student. I do have a Ph.D. in linguistics. My husband has studied physics, too."

The guy spoke; Marianne kept nodding her head, then she hung up and said, "He's going to let us buy him lunch. He's busy, but he is very fond of his *Physical Review* article."

I said, "Where?"

"Here. He'll be over in fifteen minutes."

"Marianne, I don't know anything about his article."

She handed me a copy; it was all in Terran-convention mathematics. I looked at it and tried to remember how my first roommate in the Academy explained the gate dimensions and how we . . . not we, sucker, *they* . . . worked ways to create artificial wormholes. Something about energy problems, related to informational density . . . shit. I began to feel like one of the poor slobs flunked out of this campus. I told Marianne, "It's in Terran math, and besides, I forgot."

She held the paper in front of me and pointed to a plain-English passage that I hadn't noticed in skimming. "He says theoretically one could extract at least ninety percent of the energy when the wormhole distortions are released. The Institute of Physics is fascinated by that."

"Can you explain it?"

She shook her head. "No, Travertine is going to talk to him. All we have to do is get him in the closet and gate him through."

I said, "Why didn't some Barcons just kidnap him?"

She smiled and looked at a big man walking briskly toward us. He wore gold-rimmed glasses tinted bronze and a calculator watch, and, like a football jock, had his arms pushed off his sides by hyperdeveloped chest muscles. Any aliens who tried to kidnap this guy wouldn't be able to deal with him easily. He'd shoot, or bruise his fists on them if he were a non-gun-bearing Yankee.

"Hi, are you Marianne and Tom Gentry?"

"Yes," Marianne said, "and you're Professor Joseph Weiss, right. Our son is Karl David."

Karl said, "Hi," in a small, almost distorted voice.

I said, "And how did you get into anthropology?"

He said, "My dad was in Honduras, married a Miskito refugee, my mother. I grew up hearing a lot about them, spoke three languages. Also met Afghan rebels— Dad had them around the house a lot."

I smiled at Marianne, who grimaced back. Yeah, and how were we Reds going to get this guy into our closet? I said, "Couldn't you have stayed in anthro, worked for the CIA?"

He said, "Physics. Much more interesting. We can eat in the faculty cafeteria. I thought you were students."

He had an electric car, much like the ones used on Karst if you didn't mind the shape being different, boxier. We drove across campus to a new building that still had construction scaffolding along one side. He asked Karl, "And are you planning to study physics?"

Marianne closed her eyes for a second, squeezing the lids shut, then said, "He doesn't speak English."

"What does he speak?"

"An artificial language," I said. Then I said to Karl in Karst One, "Tell the man something."

Karl said, "You remind me of Karriaagzh even if you are a human."

"Hum. You all have strange accents." He suddenly seemed suspicious of us. I saw his hand pat his leg— knife or gun—and he caught me looking.

"We'd like to talk to you about your paper in the *Physical Review*," Marianne said. "It sounds like you're on to something very important."

"To which government?" Weiss said. "I'm just a theoretical physicist, but if the idea has energy applications . . ." He stopped on the stairs going into the building. "What is this about?"

Marianne said, "You're inventing a space drive."

"I don't have time to deal with kooks."

I said, "Do you know Jerry Carstairs in Berkeley?"

"Carstairs, the idiot. Smokes drugs, hangs out with losers. Stopped doing decent work five years ago."

"What if you could find a practical application for your work," Marianne said.

"I'd work with the federal government and not talk to loons like UFO people."

"What if we had a friend who could give you more information?"

He showed the woman at the door his ID and we all went in. "Short orders on the left," he said, steering us that way. "You figured all this out from the *Physical Review* article?"

"My friend said it could work as a space gate."

"And where did your friend get his degree in physics?"

Marianne said, "He wants to move to Boston, but . . . You don't have any biases against foreigners, do you?"

Joseph Weiss started taking us seriously then. "You're Russians? Chinese?"

Marianne looked at me and smiled. Karl whispered in my ear, "I am hungry. Now."

I said, "We'd rather not say, but we're sure of our man's knowledge of physics."

"We'd like you to meet him," Marianne said. "If you could come over to our apartment."

"Where?" Weiss asked.

Marianne named the building on Commonwealth. He said, "At least you've got money behind you."

Karl said, in English, "Food. McDonald's."

We ordered hamburgers and ate them. Weiss kept looking up from his at us, his eyes tracking from Karl to Marianne to me, back to Marianne, and then to his own hamburger for a few more bites. Karl bit the end off a plastic tube of ketchup and squeezed the stuff into his mouth. When I grabbed his wrist, he asked, in Karst One, "So, how was I supposed to eat it?"

Weiss finally said, "Why an artificial language for him? Is he a DNA experiment?"

Marianne said, "He's our son. We'll explain after you talk to our friend."

I said, "Actually, I don't think we should give you this information. My wife wants to. I don't think humans are ready."

"Yeah? What if I reported you to the FBI?"

"Do it," I said. "Marianne thought you'd like to exchange ideas with the guy. I think you ought to figure it out without his help. Maybe you're not really prepared."

"Physics isn't like that. We all believe in sharing."

Marianne said, "That's what my friend believes, too."

"Can I tell people where I'm going and when I'll be back?"

"Sure," Marianne said. "There's a phone in our room or you can—"

"I'll tell them myself in person. And what's your apartment number? Can I come over at eight?"

"Fifty-two sixteen," I said. "Sure."

He whistled and said, "I'll be there at eight. Or earlier."

As we left the campus, Marianne giggled and said, "I almost told him we were Albanians. And you helped more than you wanted."

"How?"

"He's the type if he goes to buy glasses frames and the salesgirl says, 'You might be more interested in the cheaper ones,' he'll buy the highest-priced frames in the shop. Oh, no, Dr. Weiss, your brain isn't quite ready for our superhuman concepts."

"I didn't mean to get him to come. I meant to discourage him."

"I know. That's why it's funny."

We took the train from MIT to Harvard Square and walked around buildings ancient by American standards. Karl didn't say much, just watched, rather like a puppy watching wild dogs. Marianne read the historic markers—worse than Williamsburg. I felt poor; this wasn't my history. Above us, I saw two girls sitting behind a third-floor window. They hardly moved, looking down at us with sculptural faces: immobile but not stiff, cheekbones so angular they reminded me of Sharwani, hair bronze colored, clipped at just below their earlobes. One noticed me staring and moved slowly back into the room.

Marianne said, "Rahd-cliffe wenches, Hah-vahd wenches. Too much."

"Too much what?"

"Money, self-confidence, lack of insight. They're impossible."

I'd never seen her intimidated by anything much on

Karst, so this surprised me. "Did you have a good education?"

"Berkeley doesn't quite . . . it's a social thing."

"Well, let's get away then. These people work for the government a lot when they finish?"

"Yes, a lot."

"Well, we ought to observe them." I felt cockier now that I'd seen Marianne intimidated, too.

Marianne ground her toe against a maple leaf on the sidewalk, reduced it to cigarette-tobacco-sized bits. Karl picked up another leaf and asked in Karst One, "Why don't the trees have colors at home?"

"The air doesn't chill enough," I told him.

Marianne muttered, "University of South Carolina." I wondered what she meant until I remembered her advisor urging her to apply for an opening there.

We went back to Boston. Marianne went out walking while Karl and I watched cartoons. She came back around seven with take-out Chinese: chicken and nuts with vegetable in a fiery hot sauce for us, bean curd and snow peas for Karl.

We heard a knock at seven forty-five and then Joseph, on the other side of the door, said, "I know I'm early. I almost didn't come at all."

Marianne got up and let him in. He looked at us and said, "After you left, it sounded stupid."

I called Travertine's number and spoke in Karst One, "He's here, reluctantly, but I'm going to feel odd luring him into the closet."

Travertine's tongue beat against the receiver—at least that's what it sounded like—then he said, "I'll come there. Seal the closet."

I went to the closet and sealed the pod that fitted inside it, then closed the closet door. About five minutes later, blue light flashed around the door edges, then I opened the closet and unsealed the pod without looking at Joseph. I heard him panting.

"Relax," Marianne told him.

Travertine—unmistakably alien—stepped out of the closet, hocks lifted high. He raised his feathers, then clamped them down against his body.

"So, you're telling me I'm close," Joseph said. "Am I too close, so—"

Travertine said, "I'm here to help."

"You're a scientist?" Joseph said, his right hand slipping under the bottom of his sweater—armed, a very nervous physics professor whose daddy had been military or CIA and whose mamma had been an Indian.

"No, but I can explain the further steps you need to take."

"How can you speak English?" Joseph looked quickly at us, then back to Travertine. "Oh, my God."

"I was taught by people who'd spent time here."

"So you've been observing us—not sharing your technology with us." Joseph eased his hand back out into plain view, but sat down heavily on a couch, his muscles tensed. "So, why now?"

Shit. Marianne looked at me and shook her head slightly. Travertine said, "Because we thought you needed to discover the gate theory and technology for yourself, but the group of people we represent—"

Weiss said, "There's something wrong here."

I realized that more than Marianne and Karriaagzh's charity was involved here. Leaking to nearly developed species was strategic, could block the Sharwani. I blew my breath out hard.

Marianne looked at me and said, "We want to bring Earth into the Federation before another group tries to dominate it."

"So Earth's the stellar equivalent of nineteenth-century Africa, huh?"

"Look, Dr. Weiss," Travertine said, settling down on his hocks and massaging between his eyes. "We don't want to do anything to you other than make sure you don't try to dominate space outside your solar system. We'll keep others from trying to dominate you.

We all try to work together in . . . the best word for it is the *Federation*, but that sounds so space operatic.''

"Strings are attached.''

Travertine said, "No, except that if you use established trade geometries, we do regulate those.''

Marianne looked almost cross-eyed at Travertine. Joseph said, "The British used the idea of free trade against the Ashanti. And your Federation doesn't trust humans enough to send a peer, another physicist. They sent a Terran cultural specialist, didn't they?''

Travertine said, "I hate to think of myself as less valuable than a colleague from the Institute of Physics, but humans are a touchy species, dangerous at times, yes.''

Weiss said, "I know what happens to primitive cultures when superior cultures drag them into outsider quarrels. We'll get run over.''

Travertine's beak went up, slashed down. "You're working in ways we haven't seen before—the energy conservation. Not only do we need that, but it has implications for more accurate non-paired gate generation.''

"Great. When we get out there, we'll discuss it.''

Marianne said, softly, "Joseph, when I worked in linguistics, what was happening to primitive cultures made me very sad, but these people aren't like that.''

Weiss said, "I saw the groups I worked with either assimilate, into the lower classes, or rot of diseases. Miskitos, they weren't stupid people, just caught between the Soviets and us. Like the Tibetans.''

Tibetans. How did he know? I stiffened before I realized he was talking about twentieth-century Terran Tibetans. Marianne sat down. But now I did feel strange about how the Federation treated the Tibetans for four hundred years before I came, only a few families moving into the middle levels of Karst life. Travertine whipped his beak back and forth across one narrow shoulder, then picked at his fingernails. Karl asked, in English, "Why sad?"

Joseph said, "Boy, I hit a nerve there. You're not telling me everything."

Travertine asked, "You can read my body language?"

"No, theirs. They are human, aren't they?"

"We know of Tibetans on Karst," I said. "How they got to Karst is a long story."

Marianne said, "They're Asians who've been on the capital planet for over four hundred years. Rather like Gypsies."

Travertine said, "I wouldn't claim that being part of the Federation is easy, Joseph Weiss. The alternative could, however, be more degrading."

"Did your people make their own discovery of this gate system?"

"Yes. We were disconcerted to find an organization waiting at the edge of our system to take us in."

Weiss said, "I bet. But you did discover it for yourselves. How would you have felt if some featherless biped had come down and handed you the thing?"

Travertine drew his neck down, his feathers rose. "If you don't want it, we won't force it on you." His voice was distorted by the odd position his neck was in, twisted down against his breast.

Marianne said, "But . . . we can't just leave."

Joseph looked at us and said, "Yes, you can. Go back. I'm glad to know it's possible. We'll meet your organization in space, then see if we want to deal and find out what the other organization's options really are."

Travertine said, "You humans will have to live in an alien universe. Not all, however, are as different in appearance as I am. Perhaps you would have been less cold to them?" Travertine's beak gaped open, almost in a food-begging gesture.

Weiss looked at us and gripped his chin with one

hand, thumb behind the left jawbone. Travertine got up and walked to the window, pulled on the blinds cords until he exposed a view. He looked out and then said, "I'd like to be able to walk down there some day, without facing panic and xenophobia, Dr. Weiss."

"May I leave now?"

Travertine dropped the blinds and shut the slats. He looked over his shoulder, the long neck bent so that his head faced directly backward. "Certainly. I'm not a kidnapper."

"I want my own species to do it without getting help from one side or the other. Obviously, we are talking about two sides out there."

"Yes." Travertine opened the closet door, but didn't get in, yet.

Weiss picked his coat up off the couch and said, "Maybe I'll regret not accepting your help, and maybe we are xenophobic, but it is my planet. And if there are two sides, lord, will anyone believe me?"

"The Federation capital planet is my planet now," Travertine said. "Perhaps you will understand some day."

Weiss stood silent a second, then he asked us, "And do they treat you as equals?"

"Yes. There was some teasing about my refugee status as a cadet, but . . ."

"Space cadet? It does sound like a fucking joke."

"That's one way of translating the term," Marianne said. "We do well compared to what we were doing on Earth. Karst is our planet, too."

"Karst, that's the human term for a limestone region—caverns and caves under soluble ground?"

"Perhaps in a metaphorical sense," Travertine said, "but it's just an arbitrary noise that happens to resemble an Earth term."

Weiss said, "I will try to get out as soon as I can."

"It's a great place for . . . well, anthropology isn't quite the right word," Marianne said.

"Alien, can I ask you one question?"

"Surely."

"You have to protect against vacuum?"

"You have to protect against dimensions that don't allow your geometries to exist in viable forms. You're sealing a tiny fragment of your geometry in order to push through the hyperhole and back into time-space again."

"I hadn't thought about the engineering problems," Weiss said. He raised both eyebrows and slid out the door.

Travertine slumped to his hocks and said, "He rejected us. Can I stay with you for some minutes?" His feathers rippled on his back. I wondered if anyone had seen him looking out the window. What might he have been mistaken for, a child's toy?

Marianne looked at me, her face very pale, the incipient wrinkles around her nose and on her forehead almost grooved in now, as if the incident had aged her ten years. She said, "Yes, Travertine, but please don't talk about it. We picked the wrong person."

I said, "Weiss knows it can be done and he heard about the need to protect against hostile environments. How did you fail?"

Karl said, in Karst One, "Can we go home now?"

"I wanted contact now," Marianne said. "I am so lonely for real colleagues, human colleagues." She began crying.

Travertine picked at the thick skin around his nostrils and said, "What if your people chose to go with the Sharwani?"

I remembered when the Wrengee decided to go with the Sharwani rather than the Federation, remembered how rejected I felt. "Travertine," I asked, "can you drink the same type of alcohol that we drink?"

He blinked all four eyelids out of phase and said, "Alcohol is more depressing than we need right now."

Marianne nodded. She said to me, "You talk to him.

I'm going to take Karl out for ice cream." To Karl, she asked in Karst One, "Want some cold treat?"

He said "Okay" in English. I helped her with her coat and squeezed her shoulders. Karl put his coat on, then stuck his hand in hers and said, "Let's go. Let us go."

When I locked the door behind Marianne and Karl, I said, "I didn't think you liked humans."

Travertine, still down on his hocks, said, "You'd be terribly dangerous with the Sharwani."

"Oh, so that is it."

He rubbed his beak again, then said, "No. I want to understand humans. Were you afraid of my countryman Xenon when you two served on the Gwyng's ship? Both you and the Gwyng snubbed him."

"Rhyodolite was. I didn't know any better."

"I don't understand humans," he said. "I don't expect to understand Gwyngs, but you build your languages out of signals. When I close my eyes and listen to you when we talk Karst One, you could have feathers."

I said, "As far as the way I acted toward Xenon, I'm terribly sorry. Stupid, but I was young. Rhyodolite was following Black Amber's attitudes then. He's more reasonable now."

Travertine said, "Perhaps I should go back now." He looked around the apartment, then wiped around his eyes with a knuckle, finger folded at the joint where fine little black scales stopped and the softer palm and digit skin, black and moist, began. I remembered Xenon's hands.

"Do you want to stay in our apartment until we go?"

"I want to, but it would not be best." He rose and added, "I have some sleep medicine in my room. I'll gate back now—so nice that iron survives in so many dimensions." He levered himself up and went into the closet. He leaned against the wall, facing away from me. His head swiveled around 180 degrees again and he said, "I'll send the transit unit back."

"We'll be down late morning."

"Close the door after I seal up."

I did. A second later, I saw the blue flash, then waited until I saw the blue flash of the empty capsule returning.

Marianne and Karl came back with two extra cones. I wrapped one extra cone in plastic wrap and popped it in the freezer. Then we all cuddled in bed together, Karl between us, sucking on ice cream.

Marianne said, "I wonder what happens when we do achieve full contact. I'd be terribly sorry if it does hurt you."

I said, "If a Terran government wants me back in jail, I suspect they'll get me. If they don't, I can stay with the Federation. If a Terran government wants to hire me, it's up to me, but the Federation will probably suspect that I was hired even if I wasn't."

"Karriaagzh said as much to me, except that he didn't say anything about surrendering me to the other humans."

"Thoughtful of him to omit something that might interfere with your mission."

"Oh, Tom, do you hate your own kind so much that you'd rather not see them in the Federation?"

I said, "Travertine's afraid of how nasty we'd be if we teamed up with the Sharwani," and felt mean. I patted Karl's back as he lay between us. So I was selfish—I liked being unique, the Federation's highest-ranking human, no jail threats.

As we drifted off to sleep, I realized I couldn't be so sure about my rank, as I wasn't sure what Marianne's rank was at the Institute of Linguistics. I felt instantly guilty about not knowing that, about my attitude to humans, and jerked completely awake, listening to Marianne and Karl breathing. Would she leave me if she had a greater choice of men? Finally, I felt my body jerk again—the sleep twitch—and dreamed about prison.

= 5 =

On the long trip back, Marianne and I taught Karl his first official English lessons. I was resigned to eventual contact with Earth. Good for Karl. Good for Marianne, who could show her dissertation director how well she'd done. I'd manage.

When we went back into our apartment, Marianne and I went into her room to read our messages on her terminal. Karl went to his room to get back in touch with his nursery group. I held Marianne's shoulders while she laid her hand on the keyplate. We had two messages.

First: INSTITUTE OF MEDICINE, OFFICER FOR LANGUAGE OPERATIONS. THE ADULT SHARWANI ARE STILL RECOVERING FROM THEIR LANGUAGE OPERATIONS. WILL RETURN TO YOU IN A TENTH YEAR OR LESS.

Next: AGATE AND CHALK, RECTOR'S OFFICE. HRIF'S TRUE OWNER WOULD PREFER THAT YOU BUY A YOUNG QUARA TO BE BONDED TO YOU IF YOU FEEL YOU STILL NEED A PROTECTIVE ANIMAL.

Marianne said, "I'm glad we don't have to deal with Chi'ursemisa right away." She stood up, my hands slipping from her shoulders, went to her bags and began throwing her clothes on the bed. I wondered if I should help her or start unpacking my own things.

Marianne threw her head back and squeezed her eyelids tight. "The Sharwani will capture Earth," she said. "We're too divided among ourselves. Is this the way you felt when the Wrengee didn't want to join the Federation?" She went into her toilet, then came out with makeup remover pads and wiped her eyes.

I never quite understood what makeup did for her eyes—the lashes were dark, her skin not quite as dark as a Mexican's but darker than most white people's. She looked more masked in makeup than more beautiful. Now taking off the makeup made her seem both older and younger.

"Can I have a few days here without any interruptions?" she said.

"Do you want me and Karl to . . ."

"Leave? Don't. I'm sorry." She added in English, "Oh, man, I just feel wounded, s'all. Maybe it's my period coming on."

Menstruation and the mood swings before it sometimes seemed like a female trick. I said, "Didn't the Barcons design a pill for that?"

"Yes, but I . . ." She got up and threw the makeup remover pads in the trash, then washed her face in the bathroom, leaving the door open. When she came out, we went to the front room where she put on a recording of Sam playing Bach's *Goldberg Variations*. We sat huddled on the sofa staring at the speakers. Karl joined us, looked at me, then sat down on the floor, knees drawn up against his body, arms hugging his shins.

Karl finally said, "I've got a package in my room I can't open. And I want to go out and play."

"Get your father," she said.

I was nervous about leaving her alone, but decided

watching her might make her angry, so I nodded to
Karl. We went back to Karl's room and I saw a narrow
crate with Italian printed on it—CAMPAGNOLO, ATALA,
NIPPON—leaning against his bed.

I went back to the kitchen for bone shears and a stout
knife, then cut the plastic straps and pulled the bubble
pack away. Someone had sent him a child's racing bicycle from Earth—nothing saying who it was from, just
the bike and several spare chains, freewheels, and tires.

Marianne came in as I straightened the handlebars
and said, "I bet it was Karriaagzh."

"Or maybe Travertine?" I said. The pedals were in
their own separate bag. I opened it, saw the pedal
wrench packed with them, and fitted them to the crank-
arms.

Karl said, "How fast can I learn?"

I wished I'd thought about buying him human toys
while we were in Boston. Whoever sent him this had
been more thoughtful. "You can learn fast, I'd imagine," then I repeated in idiomatic English, "Pretty
quick, I bet."

He said, "Mother, come watch, please?"

Marianne said, "Sure, I guess." She moved her
back, curling it from the shoulders down, as if it hurt.
"I wanted to take a bath, but . . ." She shrugged like
a Jewish mother. But then she was Jewish, wasn't she,
if the radical life didn't cancel that out. She put her
hand on the small bike saddle and said, "We should
have done more for you on Earth, Karl. Taken you to a
ball game, the zoo."

"It was fun enough," Karl said. "Will you get me
bicycling clothes like yours, shoes with plastic slots?"

"Sure," I said in English.

Marianne said, "Oh, go by yourselves. I . . ."

Karl's face went rigid, then he smiled slightly at Marianne—a scary control in a kid his age—then wheeled
the bike over to the elevator, leaned it against the wall

and pushed the button. I decided not to bring my own bike. He'd need me to hold him up.

When the elevator door closed, I said, "Your mother wanted to have more contact with Earth."

"It was okay, but I missed my friends," Karl said.

"Do you really want to learn English?"

He sighed and said, "You both talk in it to keep me from knowing what you say."

"Actually, we thought you'd grow up better if you learned Karst One first. But you ought to learn something about the planet you come from."

"I'm learning Tibetan from Tracy."

The elevator doors opened and we wheeled the bike out through the lobby. Several of our neighbors were shopping in Awingthin the Gwyng's store. One of them, a Shiny Black named Silver Thirteen, said, "We're breeding." Her husband, one of those equal-sized males that behaves almost like a female and stays mated for life, smiled and smiled at Karl as if he wanted to practice fatherhood on my son.

I said, "Great," as Karl showed his bicycle to another kid who lived in the building, a Jerek girl younger than the Jerek in his nursery group. Her fur was blond with black streaks, and the bare skin across her face at the eyes and down the nose was a shiny brown, not black as in most Jereks. Her parents, Gouge Rock and Slipzone, both light-brown Jereks with bleached forearm fur, came out of the store and stood a second for politeness before taking her away.

The sky was beautiful—blue with stars and the small sun shining through high cirrus. Some leaves had died and fallen, but nothing like a Terran fall. Before I could stop him, Karl stood over the bike and tried to pedal, but fell over.

"Wait," I said. "I'll hold you until you get the hang of it." I grabbed the left crook of the handlebar under the brake lever with one hand and the seatpost with the other, my hand under the quick-release seatpost bolt.

We pushed along until one of two identical olive bird-types, Travertine's conspecifics from the wall-less houses, said, "Lower his seat and he can push and catch himself with his feet."

It was obvious once he'd suggested it: make the thing a scooter. I opened the seatpost lever and slid the saddle down. Karl could reach the ground on tiptoe with the seat run all the way down, but he shoved off down a slight grade, and put his feet on the pedals. Fortunately, they didn't have toeclips—he floundered off, pedaling, oversteering, catching himself.

I asked the bird couple, "How did you figure that out? Can you ride bicycles with your joint configuration?"

"If one has the proper cams in the chainring and pedal, it's like swimming," the one who suggested lowering the seat said.

"It exposes the knee differences too much," the other one said. "We appreciate your thanks, but we've got an errand to run."

As Karl walked the bike back up to me, I realized I'd forgotten that we humans were exotics.

Then I spotted Thridai, our Sharwani defector, walking with his hands deep in his tunic pockets, a hood over his head. Not part of the uniform, hoods. He stopped farther way from us than I would have, a distance that left me feeling slightly estranged. We'd been crowding the Sharwani if this was a polite distance for acquaintances.

"Thridai, how are you?"

"I moved into Lucid Moment. Do you mind?"

"No, come over. Your fellow Sharwani will be back from the language operations soon."

"Not my *fellow* Sharwani." He came closer, nodding his head slightly, but not a threat nod the way it would have been if a Gwyng did it. "How are you doing, Karl?"

Karl said, "I'm learning how to ride a bicycle. You're Thridai, right? You like the Federation?"

Thridai came closer and began feeling the bicycle with his fingertips, not minding the grease, rubbing that between his fingers, also. "It's new."

"Yes, somebody gave it to me—Karriaagzh, I think."

"Ah, yes, the bird who thinks we all belong together." Thridai pulled rough-textured cloth out from his pockets and wiped the grease off his fingers. "You have a good machine."

"Thank you," Karl said.

Thridai said to me, "I hope you don't mind that I moved near your family."

Odd sound to that, I thought. He pulled the hood with his left hand, holding it closed around his chin, covering the fur over his cheekbones.

The day after I talked to Thridai, two Barcons from Control came to my apartment while Marianne was out. One laid a read-out plate over my skull computer while the other took Karl aside.

The Barcon that stayed behind with me pulled out a piece of plastic that looked like a skull bone—someone's language computer—and plugged a lead from it to his own head, then stared at me.

"What are you doing?" I asked.

"Comparing you to what Thridai saw."

"Thridai?"

"He was killed. We're still investigating. Your Sharwani may come back after the investigation."

"What did Thridai see?"

"We're still investigating."

Karl and the first Barcon came back. Looking puzzled, Karl said, "Daddy, we were playing with the bike early yesterday morning, weren't we?"

The Barcons spoke their language, then the one who'd viewed the skull computer record said, "We're going to recommend free time for a week, but stay here."

I was a suspect. *Why?*

At the end of the week, someone in the vast Karst computer net sent us a message: SHARWANI THRIDAI'S MEMORIAL SERVICE BY THE WALLS AT SUNRISE. YOUR SHARWANI ARE COMING BACK IN FOUR DAYS.

Marianne came into my room—I must have made some odd sound. She read the screen and asked, "Do they think our Sharwani know anything about it?"

I entered: DO THE SHARWANI COMING BACK TO US KNOW?

The unidentified creature—probably someone from the Institute of Control—replied: THEY WILL BE TOLD. WATCH THEM.

Marianne said, "You shouldn't go to the memorial service."

I leaned against her, feeling the warmth, and asked, "Why?"

"Don't you remember how numb you were . . ." She didn't finish but meant . . . *for days after Warren killed himself.*

I almost said, *But he's an alien.* "I can take it."

Marianne said, "When did you see him last?"

"The day before he was killed. Karl and I ran into him when I took Karl out with the bike."

We got another message, from our Rector's People, two Jereks who were our supervisors and parents of a Jerek boychild in our nursery group, born a month after Karl. AGATE HERE. IF YOU THINK SHARING SPACE WITH HURDAI AND CHI'URSEMISA WOULD PAIN YOU NOW, LET US KNOW.

I almost said *Yes*, but entered: WE CAN MANAGE. I TAKE IT THAT I'M NOT A SUSPECT ANYMORE. Then I went into the kitchen to fix an herbal tranquilizer tea. As I heated water in the flash kettle, Marianne put a mint tea bag and some alien honey in her own cup. The water boiled; I poured, then she reached across my arm and stirred my tea for me, an odd little gesture.

"Thanks," I said.

We heard the elevator chime. I toggled the intercom and asked, "Who's there?"

"Your neighbors." Gouge Rock, the Jerek woman, I guessed by the voice. And the elevator intercom picked up the sounds of other bodies shuffling, breathing. I opened the door. The whole elevator was full of neighbors and my bird friends Granite Grit and Feldspar with their son Alchir-singra.

Karl giggled when he saw Alchir-singra.

Granite said, "We now live on the eighth floor here."

And Travertine was behind them. He came out of the crowd sideways, stared up at Granite and half-closed his eyelids, squinting to keep from pulling his transparent eye membranes between himself and the larger bird species. He said, "We thought Marianne and you should have company."

The Jereks and the Shiny Black said, "Yes," while the Gwyng female, with her younger pouch kin, cupped her hand and brought it down.

Silver, the Shiny Black female, said, "We thought you should know we trusted you."

"Thanks," Marianne said. "Would it be polite to offer tea? Food?"

The elevator went back down and brought up the rest of our neighbors—creatures who'd lived here for the past seven years, others who were new to the building. I knew some of them—none well—and now they'd come to see us. And then Travertine didn't live in the building. I asked him in English, "Why now?"

He said in the same language, "We thought you might appreciate that you are not alone with your Sharwani."

The Jereks heard him talking in the alien language and lowered their noses an inch, slight challenge faces. I wondered if they were with the Institute of Analytics and Tactics, our alien CIA. I asked, in Karst One, "What does anyone know about Thridai's murder?"

The Jerek female, Gouge Rock, said, "Several Sharwani told us they've been contacted by a disguised Sharwani, given messages in something like your blindcode, *braillee*?''

Travertine looked from them to me as if he'd been the Terran specialist who'd discovered humans used blindcode. *"Braille,"* I pronounced correctly. "Were either Hurdai or Chi'ursemisa contacted?"

"They said they weren't," Slipzone said, "but do we trust them?"

Marianne said, "Are you asking us as neighbors not to bring them back here?" She sat the boiling pot down and looked around at everyone. The Gwyng shopkeeper, Awingthin, her brow hair flaring, went to the window with her males and stared out. The others looked at each other. Granite Grit said, "No, unless you feel . . ."

Gouge Rock lowered her nose at him.

I said, "We felt like we were making progress with them."

Slipzone closed his eyes, the skin over the eyes just as shiny as his eyeballs, and said, "Perhaps they really weren't contacted. And we don't know how good the surgical disguises are."

Karl said, "I like Daiur. I was more afraid of Hrif."

Awingthin, without turning from the window, said in Karst Two, "(Perhaps) Support should have no say?"

Granite Grit and Feldspar hunkered down on their hocks. Alchir-singra said, in the same language, "Perhaps Gwyngs are afraid—"

"Hush, Alchir," Granite said. He grabbed Alchir's scaly wrist and pulled him down.

The Gwyng shopkeeper said, "I feed you. True, doing that supports me as well (but . . . apprehension). (Anxiety) I won't fuss (more)." She walked away from the window and got in the elevator, her pouch kin trailing behind her. She pushed for her shop floor and, as the doors closed, said, "No insult/back with foods."

No one said anything for a second, then Travertine said, "I understand why she might be nervous, but Red

Clay and Ree the Linguist are most likely to have problems.''

"Dealing with xenophobia is our profession,'' Gouge Rock said.

Granite Grit said, "Tom, the Institute of Control gave Feldspar and me lessons in fighting Sharwani. Our bio-structure gives us good leverage over them.''

Plus the fact that he is over seven feet tall, I thought, and can open a creature's belly with his bare toes.

I said, "I should have invited you over more, Granite.'' Did it embarrass me that Granite and Feldspar had witnessed my fights with Yangchenla? Yes. Then maybe I reminded him too much of his own freak-out time when we were cadet roommates? But he was a bird; mental states that didn't lead to action tended to be as forgotten, for birds, as unrealized dreams.

Then I wondered if Gwyngs remembered everything—all language logged to time embedded in it.

Marianne, thinking more of the present than I was, said, "Thank you all. Perhaps we should have neighborhood parties more often.''

The Gwyng shopkeeper and her pouch kin came back with food carts. Everyone chatted at us as though we were going off on a dangerous mission.

Silver took me aside and told me, "The Institute of Control has implanted Hurdai and Chi'ursemisa with stun devices much like control bracelets. You and the Linguist Ree can control them.''

I remembered Chi'ursemisa's fingers splayed over the polycarb and wondered how deep the Sharwani tactile sense might go, if they'd feel the implants. I shook my heads lightly, thinking about plastic temporal bones that housed skull computers. But they wouldn't have that, now—just the biochemical reversal of some language-center cells to the childhood condition. And stun implants.

The computer housing under my skin and scalp muscles, under my left ear, balanced perfectly with the real bone on the other side. Or else I'd forgotten what real bone there felt like.

Karl came up to me and said, "I'm glad you're teaching me English."

"*Yeah,*" I said to him in that language. The Sharwani would know Karst too well now for us to talk privately in that language.

Ersh, my first Wreng contact, and I met as we walked toward the Walls for Thridai's memorial service. The feathers around his ear holes were matted, as though he'd been twirling them the way a girl will play with her hair with her fingers. He was wearing blue with a green cord—officiator for the Rector now. Big belly scales rustled against the tunic when he saw me. I wondered if his eyelids were still tattooed, but he didn't flick those at me. He said, "Red Clay, Tom," as though not sure whether to use my Federation name or my species name at funerals.

"Ersh." I remembered when we'd met Thridai, our informant, smoking his herbal cigarettes.

"I feel awkward."

"Did you talk much with Thridai?"

"No."

An Ahram stonemason, big and sweating in a leather apron, came up with a handheld chisel and hammer—a primitive custom, to memorialize on walls, done with primitive tools. A bear-stock creature with grey and black fur held the gold-leaf book and an adhesive pot on a tray. All the alien plants trembled around us as the Ahram chiseled out Thridai's name on the latest granite slab. Sweat ran down his skull crest, down by his ears and along his massive jaw. I looked around; not many of us were here for Thridai—his Institute of Analytics handler, a couple of olive birds, Ersh, me. Then the bear-type, who held the gold and adhesive pot, swiveled his ears under his head fur. Karriaagzh came stepping up, feathers covered by the Rector's green that glittered with gold threads, alone as always, his beak chipped as though he'd been biting metal.

"Ersh, Tom, good," Karriaagzh said as he settled down, thighs on lower legs, hocks splayed behind him.

I looked at Ersh's cord again, wondering if he were in training to be a Rector's Person. A bit jealous, yes, I was, if Ersh was going to be trained for that.

Karriaagzh looked at me and said, "Ersh works for my office now as a researcher." I felt foolish, caught being out-of-line ambitious.

The Ahram wire-brushed the chiseled-out name and began laying in the gold. We stayed until he'd burnished it. Gold wasn't terribly valuable here, just something that didn't tarnish in the stone grooves.

Having thought my thoughts about Thridai, I waited until someone would leave first. The work crew started out, then Karriaagzh stood up and stretched, reaching his arms up so straight that the tunic sleeves fell down below the scales on his forearms. The tissue around the yellow eyes seemed puffy.

The polycarbonate wall stayed up, but Marianne bought cloth, rings, wooden rods, and carved brackets. We couldn't nail the brackets to the polycarb, so I glued them up while Marianne sewed curtains.

"It's very nice cloth for tactile people," she said. "And I want to give them some privacy."

Two Barcons brought our Sharwani family back to us. Hurdai came out of the elevator first, the fur bristly on his skull behind the ear where the Barcon medics had shaved it for surgery. The scar of the scalp cut was a white welt bordered by pink. A Barcon followed, its arm bent, palm shadowing Hurdai's movements. Daiur came out and ran to Karl. Chi'ursemisa and the other Barcon walked out side by side, not touching, not looking at each other. Chi'ursemisa's fur looked matted, with a cloth patch where Hurdai had his scar.

"All the others watched us come in," Chi'ursemisa said. "Why weren't you also in the lobby?" She had no accent now, but the phrasing seemed a bit awkward.

"We didn't want to embarrass you," I said.

"Back behind the clear plastic?" Hurdai asked. He stopped; the Barcon lowered his hand and looked once at me, once at Marianne.

Marianne said, "We put up cloth, draperies, over the polycarbonate."

Hurdai repeated the Karst chemical-shorthand word that I'm translating as *polycarbonate*. We all went down together to their room.

Chi'ursemisa asked, "Will it be locked?" Fingers splayed, she leaned against the polycarbonate from the outside this time, staring into the brocaded curtain fabric.

"Not as long as you're cooperative," the Barcon who'd followed Hurdai out of the elevator said. Hurdai rubbed his forearm, nails making sounds against the skin and hair.

Chi'ursemisa looked back over her shoulder at him, her blond facial hair along the cheekbones slightly matted as though she'd been sleeping on that side. She pushed away from the polycarb with her fingers and said, "We'd like to go there now, with the cloth . . . draperies closed."

Karl said, "Don't you want something to eat first?"

Daiur looked from Karl to his mother. "Can Karl and I eat together?" he asked her.

She raised her hand, fingers cupped, and brought it down heavily, almost a sign of surrender.

Marianne went toward the kitchen, leaving me with them. I wished then, for a second, that I'd gotten Hrif back, felt bad about that, then remembered that some Sharwan had murdered Thridai. Maybe it hadn't been a Sharwan after all? But Sharwani reported getting messages in tactile code from someone disguised among us aliens.

Chi'ursemisa went into her room and closed the drapes. I heard her hands on them. Then she came out and asked, "Will you lock us in?"

"Will you try to hurt us?" I asked.

"I don't think so," Hurdai said.

"Your people still attack our ships."

"You want to submerge us in your Federation," Chi'ursemisa said. "Lock us in. More honest."

"Maybe at night," I said, visualizing the control box for their neural disruptors. It was in the kitchen, second drawer under the counter to the left of the sink and dishwasher.

Chi'ursemisa put her hand to her head where the Barcons had opened her brains to change her language centers. We locked eyes for more than a second—hers inhuman, yellow with brown rays, no whites. Her pupils contracted as if she wanted to see less.

"Let's go in and eat," I said.

Hurdai said, "The last time we had a meal together, you sent us away for surgery."

"Now we can understand each other better," I said.

"But it's your structure of understanding," he replied as we started down the hall.

I remembered the Gwyngs complaining about being restricted in their thinking, even in their brain development, by Karst Two, their artificial Federation language. Karst One liberated me, but one of the other refugees wanted to die, caught in Karst's linguistic net. I said, "We feel that those who can't master Karst One or Two aren't really sapient."

"No language explains the Universe," Hurdai said. We were in the kitchen by now. Karl and Daiur were eating at a small table while Marianne was cutting up mushrooms.

Marianne must have caught some of our conversation, because she looked up and smiled. Hurdai and Chi'ursemisa began getting their food out of the refrigerator, talking to each other in their own language in bursts of sound. Maybe they thought we'd force them to speak Karst One now that they knew it. Marianne said to me in English, "Relax, they're just talking about the food."

Chi'ursemisa looked at the stove, solid topped with red lines around the electric burners, and asked, "How do you cook something in a vegetable oil?" Her nose crinkled up slightly.

Marianne got out a frying pan and some synthetic olive oil. Chi'ursemisa dipped her finger into the bottle and tasted it, then poured about a quarter-inch layer of it into the pan. My wife turned a burner on to about medium heat and Chi'ursemisa put the pan on it. Hurdai began cutting up meat. Marianne laughed and looked at me—*see, they don't have sexual roles the way you seem to want to sometimes.*

I said, in English, "Well, we are a long way from Virginia." Her lips twitched and she handed me the oil and some vinegar. While Hurdai fried the meat, Chi'ursemisa fixed vegetable plates.

Hurdai tasted the meat and asked, "Where did you get this from?"

"Downstairs," Marianne said.

"From where?" Chi'ursemisa asked.

"Why do you ask?" I said.

"It's from a food animal on our planet," Hurdai said.

"Probably is," I said. "The Barcons cloned milk animals from my planet for the Gwyngs."

"You travel disguised on other planets?" Chi'ursemisa frowned, her wrinkle rolls thicker than on a frowning human.

Hurdai said something in their language.

"Hurdai, don't tell her to shut up," Marianne said. Hurdai ducked his head and began scooping the meat out of the oil. We all fixed our own plates. Karl heated flat bread that the Sharwani preferred to the plastic wafer scoops and handed a basket of it to Chi'ursemisa.

"We don't sit legs dangling," she told me. "I saw a

low table we could use in your other large room." I
signed assent and we left Marianne and Hurdai with the
children and carried the big coffee table back into the
kitchen. She was very able to hold the table in balance
between us—that enhanced tactile awareness, I thought.

She looked at me with her brown-rayed irises and
said, "Your family are refugees," using the slang word
with its root in the Karst One for "castoff."

"Yes, and we're unstable in our relationships with
others, as you are."

"We are only unstable in our relationships with ourselves," she said. "Would you kill if . . ."

I certainly didn't want Karl to overhear this. "I would
protect my family," I told her.

"What protects mine?" she asked. "Don't try an
answer. We found out that humans are a dangerous species, xeno-flips like us." We had the table at the kitchen
door now—odd to have cooperated in carrying it
through that verbal exchange. The table, broader than
the door was wide, went through on its side. On the
counter, food plates sat on heating or cooling trays, a
material like soapstone that soaked up heat or cold in
the microwave or flash cooler, then kept foods hot or
cold for hours.

Chi'ursemisa didn't say more, just curled up against
Hurdai on the coffee table seat and tapped him with her
fingers. Sensing possible code, I stiffened, but what
could I do? The message was passed. If Chi'ursemisa
now feared humans as potential xenophobic sapient
killers, I decided that I could stand our xeno-flip reputation. Then, an instant later, I was slightly ashamed of
myself.

Hurdai said, "Your Federation has teeth."

Karl and Daiur stopped eating and stared up at us as
though grownups were the aliens. "Yes," I said, thinking of the control box in the drawer about ten feet away.

We finished the meal in silence.

* * *

That night, as I sat on her bed and watched Marianne brush her hair, I said, "Maybe if we can get through this, we can become Rector's People."

The brush stopped. She looked at me, first directly, then through the mirror. "You want to become a Rector's Person?"

I wasn't sure of the tone. "Isn't it okay?"

"You're finally getting to be personally ambitious?" She smiled. I felt like I was sixteen again, but perhaps not the sixteen I'd been in those real years. Maybe I'd regressed to what I'd have been at sixteen in a normal life.

I said, "If we can be good with these people, we can be good with anyone."

"And if Earth never makes it, maybe we can be Rector," she said.

That had never occurred to me. "Is that how you're handling Weiss's attitude?"

Rectors had to be from people in the Federation for four hundred years or refugees—settled in or free of planetary politics. Rector. I'd never considered that before; the thought chilled me. There was a farfetched logic to it. I could stand not seeing more humans than the ones we had on Karst now.

Marianne said, "Karriaagzh began his career as a Rector's Person."

I said, "If we can bring Chi'ursemisa and Hurdai to see the Federation terms as good, we will look quite competent." I realized how formally we were speaking, as though we were exchanging vows. An ambition I wasn't sure I should be proud of had hooked me. I got off the bed and hugged Marianne, half little boy, half future leader.

After Marianne was asleep, I went to the kitchen and got the controller, sat in the darkness holding it.

* * *

The next morning, I slid the controller in my tunic pocket when we all—Marianne, the kids, the adult Sharwani—went walking through the back parks.

Chi'ursemisa went ahead, head constantly turning. She knelt so long by a small plant with blue flowers that we had to wait for her; then she came almost jogging up to us. She darted her hand toward the pocket where I had my right hand over the control box. When I clenched my fist harder over it, she said, "I suspect we are not completely free even if we don't have skull computers that double as tracking devices."

Alien thing against my brain—I didn't want to think about it. Chi'ursemisa looked from me to Marianne. We'd both stopped. Marianne looked more upset about the computer than I'd ever been.

"The Federation doesn't trust itself," Chi'ursemisa said.

Hurdai said, "Chi'ursemisa, did you expect them to just turn us loose?"

"No."

We walked on by the bird platform houses, all their family activities outside the toilets open to view.

Chi'ursemisa and Hurdai began looking at each other rolling their feet over so that they walked on the outside edges. Chi'ursemisa asked, "Are you trying to hurt us?"

"What?"

"The long foot travel, the displays of creatures."

"I'm sorry. We can take a bus home."

"If we turn back now, I think we'll be all right," Hurdai said.

Daiur said, "I'm too tired."

Marianne said, "Come on, I'll carry you."

Karl said, "I'm not tired."

Chi'ursemisa and Hurdai moaned a little as Daiur went up to Marianne. She swung him around to her back and said, "Chi'ursemisa, do you need to walk in front of me or behind?"

"Either way."

As we walked back, Hurdai stopped for a second, staring at one of the bear-types, totally furred, about his height. The bear pushed back the hair on his face, cheekbones not so angular as the Sharwani's, and asked, "Hello, Hurdai. Are you looking for someone like me?"

Hurdai said nothing. We were being watched and it both relieved and irritated me.

When we got home, Chi'ursemisa sat down on the floor by the couch and covered her face with her arms, knees up against her belly. She trembled. When Marianne set Daiur down, he knelt by his mother, but did not touch her. Hurdai sat down, took off his shoes, and massaged his feet. He had five toes, but two big toes instead of one, with matted fur on top of them.

"Can we help?" Marianne asked.

"She's stuck," Hurdai said, "between being us and becoming what you are."

Chi'ursemisa pitched backward, knees still bent, catching herself with her hands just before her head smacked against the floor. Daiur crept around to her head and touched her face as if reading the muscles like braille. He said, "Mommy, nobody has hurt me."

She said something in her own language and then told Marianne, "Please don't translate."

Marianne said, "I hate being a jailor." I was afraid Marianne had given Chi'ursemisa a mental trick to use against her.

Hurdai climbed to his feet and said, "Can we set up a television in our room, if your programs are entertaining?"

Marianne said, "Show them a xenophobia holo. I've got Karriaagzh's here. And see if you can get Support to put in a terminal for them."

"Marianne, maybe that holo would scare them?"

"What is a xenophobia holo?" Chi'ursemisa asked.

"It makes the fears seem funny," I said.

Chi'ursemisa sat up and huddled tighter, arms and

feet intertwined. She squeezed once especially hard, then relaxed. "Funny fear of the bird who broke my wrist? I must see this."

Hurdai said, "Perhaps not."

"Yes," Chi'ursemisa said. "I need funny fear."

Marianne set up the holo tank and player head, explaining as she did, "Karriaagzh, when young, was terrified of some mammals' fear of him. So he played with the fear."

I'd seen the holo before, but now, I noticed more: Karriaagzh's head bobbing back, eyes wide open and glossy, his hands picking at his mangled feathers.

"Stop it," Chi'ursemisa said. "Help me stop it."

Marianne flipped the switch on the thing as I reached for the plug. Hurdai said, "Thank you, we've seen enough."

"I don't know if you really saw—"

"Don't you respect pain?" Chi'ursemisa said, not facing any of us. She got up and went into the polycarb-fronted room. Hurdai picked up Daiur and followed her.

Marianne began pacing, then, after several tight circles, stopped and shook her hands as if they were wet. "Marianne, I can get you a controller," I said after we heard the drapery rings hiss across the rods.

"Oh, just let them kill us. Who are they that we've got a right to keep them prisoner?"

"I saw them bomb Ersh's planet."

"They? Chi'ursemisa and Hurdai? Daiur? *Daiur?* If Daiur's responsible for the bombing, maybe I should arrest you for Ku Klux Klan lynchings?"

"They were on Ersh's planet."

Marianne calmed down a bit, then said, "I don't really think either of them would hurt Karl. Beyond that, what would I do if they attacked us?"

"The controller won't kill them. It just disrupts skeletal muscle control."

She said, "I don't, *goddamn it,* want one. Ersh's people let the Sharwani—"

"It was blackmail, terrorism," I said.

"Shut up, or they'll hear us," Marianne said.

"Who started shouting?" I asked. "We're supposed to show them how people can live together."

"And conspecifics can't fight?" She continued in a calmer voice, "If we can't get pissed with each other without threatening the Federation, then the Federation is too damn fragile."

The next morning, Chi'ursemisa came out of the polycarb room, alone. I heard Hurdai and Daiur talking to Marianne. Chi'ursemisa sat down on the floor and said, "I heard you both arguing last night." She looked very alien, vaguely catlike curled up against a chair leg, eyes half-closed. "The muscle-control implants are reasonable. If your Federation had turned us loose with only its language to shape us, that would be stupid. I don't like stupidities based on principles."

I realized I could interpret what Chi'ursemisa had said to mean that she didn't like Marianne, but I decided to leave that implication buried and simply said, "Are you typical of Sharwani? I haven't known that many."

"I'm not typical. Perhaps you should meet more," she replied, rubbing her nails with a little round stone.

I wondered where she got the stone. Maybe she had one of the Barcons rig her up something like her home nail-keeping equipment? "I can meet more. We've got one hundred twenty-seven Sharwani couples and fifty-seven Sharwani children here in various households, plus other Sharwani on other planets."

"And you think there are other Sharwani here, disguised?"

I said, "Yes."

She said, "What do you think my policies, personal policies, are?"

I had no idea. "What were they before Karriaagzh brought you here?" That seemed a good question.

She said, "Complex. Life is always complex. You have a fighting alien here in this building, bird-stock. Granite Grit?"

"He's more than a fighting alien."

She rolled the stone between her two hands, then took off her shoes and began buffing and shaping her toenails with it. Seeing her do that was slightly off-putting.

I asked, "Did you think the Sharwani had a right to dominate Ersh's people?"

"Instead of the Federation dominating?"

I said, "The Federation isn't like that."

She said, "Maureen Ree thinks it is brutal."

Crack her high pointy cheekbones one, a country voice in me said, as if Warren had gone to live in my brain when he died. "Don't try that," I said.

"Violence isn't that alien to you," she said, looking up but still rolling the stone between her hands, her legs spraddled, kneeling. Damn her, she could read humans better than I could read Sharwani.

"So," I said, trying to sound dumb-ass, "maybe we could have some private talks with disguised Sharwani?"

She said, "Perhaps," and caught her little stone in one hand. Did it have a Sharwani code chipped on it— tactile swollen fingertips reading it? Her fingertips were flaccid now. I tried to remember what they'd looked like when she'd been using the stone on her nails. She said, "Perhaps," again, as if she knew what I thought, to stare at her fingers so.

We Sharwani keepers met again at the Institute of Control. When Granite Grit and I came in the room, Ersh was sitting beside another Sharwan. The new Sharwan looked up at me, then at Granite as if memorizing our faces.

I stared at him. One cheekbone was crushed. A huge scar ran from above his right eyebrow down to his chin, which seemed to have crumbled under a blow. The scar skipped across his eyelid, but the skin there looked raw, as though medics had regenerated his eye. A creature mean enough to make the slash wouldn't have stopped to save an eye.

Ersh said, "This one was a friend to my people. His own tortured him."

"I am Drusah, and I was decorated for this." His index finger cut through the air over his scar. *By us?* I must have looked puzzled, because he said, "For bravery by the Uka Sharwanah. My species understands honor. Your attitude contributes to the problem with us." He pronounced the plural more *ah* than *ee*. He wasn't from the same language group as Chi'ursemisa and Hurdai.

Ersh's scales rose slightly, then flicked down. "The Uka Sharwani are savages."

"No," Drusah said, "Sharwani are the most various people in the Universe."

The Barcon Institute of Control officiator leading our group said, "One sees more diversity in species familiar to one." In Karst, "one" is a real distancer.

"We have over a thousand language groups, over two thousand cultural groups, although only ten are dominant."

"Earth has at least that many," I said.

"And do you recognize courage as a virtue even when used against you?"

"Not officially," the Barcon said. "Red Clay, I think understand humans do, or did in the past, but cruelly."

"Marianne would be better able to say." I remembered about headhunters eating their foes' hearts for the courage they'd had, but that wouldn't put humans in a good light. I said to Drusah, "But it looks like someone put your eye out, then replaced it with a new one."

"Yes." Drusah didn't explain. His shoulders seemed

crooked, I noticed, as he drew them up, squaring his body—a usually defensive posture.

"We would do more surgery," one of the Barcons said, "but he says no."

"The new eye I could use," Drusah said. He shuddered slightly as he looked at each of us again.

Then two more Barcons led in a human—no, not quite a human. If I'd seen him on Earth, I would have thought him slightly deformed and not looked further. But he resembled me as if my face had been broken and rebuilt slightly off.

Granite's head feathers raised slightly and he stared at it, then at me. I remembered the Sharwan who challenged us for Ersh's planet had seen other species of us, too. Could they have copied Granite Grit, or one of the completely furred people? The Barcons holding my Sharwani copy said, "We recognized a human and stopped to see if he had a city permit."

I said, "It looks vaguely like me." Granite hunkered down on his legs, shuffling from one side to another as he sat down. He laid his palms flat on the floor.

The Barcon in charge said, "We think this one or another like him killed Thridai. We captured him when he approached the baby Daiur. We will be checking IDs and skull computers in the city."

Drusah spoke to the other Sharwan in a language that I hadn't heard before, then in another language yet. The Sharwan tried to get away from the Barcons, but they lifted him to his toes by his upper arms. Drusah bared his teeth and flicked his tongue over them, then said, "There are others."

I asked, "What will you do with him?"

"Rebuild him to Sharwani shape," the Barcon said. "All of you, don't let anyone near your Sharwani unless you test the individual."

Drusah spoke again to the other Sharwan, and he began wailing. Drusah said, "He doesn't believe you will fully restore him."

"We'll do a better job than his people could do," the Barcon Control officer said. One of the other Barcons reached in his pocket, pulled an injector box out and hit a dose through the imitation of my neck.

"Get him changed back quickly," I said.

"Did he really kill Thridai?" Ersh said.

Drusah said something short, almost melodious. The other Sharwan, my imitation, said, in mangled Karst One, "I kill you." He swayed on his feet.

Drusah said, "I think not."

Couldn't Thridai distinguish me from this thing? What about Daiur? "Drusah, does this Sharwan look like me to you?"

"I can tell the difference. I'm good at identifying individual animals from a distance."

Ersh said, "He was an animal ethnographer."

Drusah said, "I'm still an animal ethnographer."

Thridai thought I killed him. Control believed that I could be so dangerous. I felt sick.

= 6 =

When I got home from the Institute of Control, Marianne was standing in front of the elevator. Her right arm held Karl beside her. She said, "Molly and Rhyodolite are visiting. Molly brought a loom. Maybe she has Chi'ursemisa tamed."

Back behind us in Molly's old room, I heard Chi'ursemisa giggling like a rubber band banjo and Molly's voice murmuring about piqué looms.

It seemed vaguely absurd, but not as brutally absurd as what I'd seen earlier. I said, "The Sharwani made an imitation of me. I can't believe anyone thought it really looked like me."

Marianne waited as if I had more to explain, as I did. "The fake me approached Daiur."

"What about Daiur?" Karl asked.

"That's how the Barcons caught it," I finished. "Karl, can you ask Daiur what the person who looked like me wanted him to do?"

"Now?" Karl asked.

"Yes, now," I said.

Karl started out, but Marianne said, "Karl, I don't want you near Hurdai or Chi'ursemisa alone."

"But I can't understand how anyone, anything could have thought it was me." It struck me then how alien the others were, how we didn't all see alike.

"Don't forget that the species are different," Marianne said, "even if official Federation propaganda says to ignore the differences. I think we ought to get a weanling Quara."

Karl said, "It's all right being different."

"Why don't we get Karl a real puppy?" I said. "A pit bull–Rhodesian ridgeback cross."

Rhyodolite came out then in just a tunic top slit to expose his armpit webs. The webs were slightly damp, smelling of alcohol, and his wrinkles under his nostril slits sagged more than usual. At the tip of his pointed chin was a tiny bald spot as if he'd rubbed the hair away there.

Did Gwyngs see me as an unformed Gwyng with only incipient nostril and mouth grooves, bald faced, white? Did human skin do anything to polarized light? Rhyodolite said, "Threads boring, (both) females smell," and signed to Karl, who shook his head in our human *no*.

"He doesn't know sign," I said.

"And can't hear Karst Two (brain limits)."

"What do I look like to you?" I asked Rhyodolite.

He found a pencil and printer paper, drew me in the rapid photographically real Gwyng style, as if he were tracing a mental image. He'd only slightly distorted me to the Gwyng form.

Well. I said to Marianne, "Which Sharwan should I check on first?"

"Did you get me a controller?" Marianne asked.

"Here," I said.

"It's too serious now," Marianne said as she took the box, small enough to wear under clothes or on a necklace. "Go see Chi'ursemisa first. Hurdai and Daiur are in the room. I locked the door." She seemed a bit ashamed, then shrugged.

I went down the other hall, the women's side, and stood at Molly's door a moment. Molly worked at a table loom, rather more complex-looking than it seemed to need to be, while Chi'ursemisa lolled on the floor and fingered two lace strips, first one, then another. She said, "A continuous fiber in the first, made with one end worked around thread loops. The second is plant fiber, several strands. In our culture, these things are typical of presynthetic touch toys."

Molly, without stopping her weaving, hand automatically going to switch levers and pulling the beater against the made cloth, looked up at me and nodded, then said, "Right. In our culture, we had to invent faster spinning methods and more efficient plowing systems before we made *lace*." She used the English word *lace*. "When we could make these things quickly with machines, nobody craved *lace* anymore." Molly's right hand cranked at the front roller to bring threads off the rollers at the back of the loom. Then she patted each plane of threads with her left palm, adjusting each roller with her right.

Chi'ursemisa lay down on her back, playing with the lace. She murmured, "I crave touch toys."

"I think of lace as an eyeball toy," Molly said.

Chi'ursemisa looked over at me, her head flat on the floor, sharp furred cheekbone pressed against the carpet. "Red Clay Tom, I don't want to talk to you yet."

"Chi'ursemisa, how do you recognize me?"

"The chopped face hair. I think."

I couldn't tell if she were joking or not. "And you like our lace?"

Molly said, "She's very tactile."

Chi'ursemisa slowly sat up and said, "I need touch toys if I'm to be happy here." One hand, fingertips swollen tight, wobbled up and brushed through her head hair.

Okay, drunk on lace. So where did I go from here? Molly said, "Human women are fairly tactile, too. The difference between the human sexes is tense muscles in the male and sensitive touch in the girl."

Chi'ursemisa said, "How sad. Red Clay Tom is crippled by my standards."

I felt as awkward with these two as I had when I came in on Marianne and some of her birth group—but more pissed. I seemed to remember women with thimbles who thumped boy children on the head with them. "Chi'ursemisa, we've got a problem. I do need to talk to you about it, if you . . ."

"I sympathize," she said. She sat up and looked at me, trembling slightly. "But make it easier on me. Not right now, the talking."

I came up to look closer at the table loom Molly was weaving on and asked, "Piqué loom?"

"For the very, very tactile," Molly said, frowning at the threads. She adjusted another roller, then wove in a metal rod, then two regular threads, then alternated rods with pairs of threads for a while. "And this is velvet," she said, running a device like a specialty wood plane over the rods. A blade in the device cut the rods free.

Chi'ursemisa stood up, her fur and clothes covered with short bits of thread, and came over. We both reached out and touched the cut pile.

"Interesting," Chi'ursemisa said. "Can I . . . how can I get some?"

"It's expensive, but I'll give you a bit of this. I was just fooling around," Molly said.

Chi'ursemisa touched my hand gently and said, "How can I become more self-financed?"

Molly stopped weaving and said, "If she supports the Federation, who could sponsor her as a cadet?"

Molly, did you get this creature to defect with your stupid piqué loom? "Chi'ursemisa, is that what you want?'' I said. I'd have thought Hurdai would have been more willing to take the Federation side.

She touched the velvet again as if she hadn't heard. Not ready to talk yet, as she'd told me already.

I left them and went to the kitchen to fix two teapots, one for the Sharwani and one for us. Rhyodolite came in just as I was wondering what he'd want, and folded his arms so that the webs pulled across his chest. He looked tired, wrinkles drooping, nostril slits moving in and out as he breathed. ''Does my face look/seem flabby?'' he asked me.

Yes, but I wasn't going to say so. ''Not particularly.''

''Liar, Clay Dung.''

''A little.''

He oo'ed and said, ''The Weaver tries/tires me.''

''She said she still loves you. Do you love her?''

''Much easier to get along with (most times) than Gwyng female.'' My skull computer sighed in my auditory centers—that must have also been coded in his Karst Two.

I bumped up against him sideways for old time's sake and pity, then gave him the human teapot, saying, ''Could you take it to Marianne?''

He opened the pot and sniffed. ''For Gwyng, this would be (near) lethal. What's for me?''

''I need to talk to Hurdai now. You want to watch us, see if you pick up anything I don't?''

''Bomb-lizards people kill-mode in Karst City.'' He muttered so that my computer barely gave me linguistic coordinates, but I figured he meant the Sharwani were killing people on the street.

''Really?''

''Not just other bomb-lizards people, either,'' he said. ''Need me to scare them honest?''

''Are they scared of you?''

He opened the cooler and found our milk, drained a bottle, then said, ''I'll terrorize them by chilling into coma, waxy inflexible insane alien. Piss me off, hostile attitudes.''

I said, ''Why don't you take the tea into Marianne instead?''

He shrugged, an imitation of Molly's and Marianne's Berkeley shrugs, a huge sloughing off of responsibilities, and took the tea out. I thought about Chi'ursemisa's safety, wondered if Hurdai knew she was becoming more sympathetic to us. Or maybe she was teasing? I trusted Hurdai to be more honest, but . . . it was an odd problem.

Hurdai and Daiur were watching a xenophobia movie with Gwyngs. I tried to figure out whether the Gwyngs were the terror objects or the terrified, then realized it was a new *avant* ambiguous one. Hurdai looked up and said, ''This one is more realistic than usual.''

''In the ambiguity?''

''Yes. Do you know that when Sharwani lie, we shiver?''

Chi'ursemisa had been trembling.

''Are you interested in helping us?''

''No, but I am the honest one.''

Really? Had Chi'ursemisa given herself away earlier, arguing with him in one of the Sharwani languages we didn't know yet? ''Are you afraid of Rhyodolite?''

''Not fear—disgust.''

Daiur looked up from the movie when Hurdai said that, hair erect on his body. I wasn't sure what that meant and wanted to take him up in my lap and cuddle him. ''Maybe Daiur is afraid?'' I said, wishing I could get Hurdai out, but his arm reached out, fingers wrapped around Daiur's wrist.

Daiur said, ''I don't want to kill anyone. My friends say it's nasty.''

Hurdai said, ''Only grownups are allowed to kill.''

I put the tea down and went back to Chi'ursemisa and Molly. Chi'ursemisa sprawled on the bed, her left foot on her right knee, fingering a piece of lace almost compulsively, a faint odor like burnt ashes in the air. I told her, "Hurdai said when Sharwani lie, they shiver."

"It's emotional to shiver. Keep me away from him." She looked at me, pupils dilated as if she'd just been in the dark. They shrank down to pinpoints, then expanded again slightly.

Molly, still weaving, said, "And lower the lights in their rooms. They're crepuscular." She added in English, "Unless you're being deliberately annoying."

"Thridai said . . . How did you find that out?"

Chi'ursemisa said, "I asked her if the brightness was deliberate. To break us."

"Thridai said to leave the lights as we had them. I didn't quite understand." I wondered why Daiur hadn't complained to Karl, say, or why Chi'ursemisa hadn't told Marianne or me. "I'm sorry. Would you like separate rooms?" I asked. "Where would Daiur be?"

"I want him with me, but . . ." Her fingers fumbled on the lace. It dropped on her chest and she shivered, then picked it up and laid it aside.

"Split up a family, the Federation did," Molly said in English. She stopped weaving and picked up a needle, then sewed along the end of the cloth.

"Maybe," I said in the same language, wondering if Karl had taught Daiur English and if he'd taught that language to Hurdai or Chi'ursemisa. I almost backed out of the room and went back to the front. Marianne was drinking tea; Rhyodolite was playing tic-tac-toe with Karl. I told Marianne, "Get another Quara if you want. Or maybe we can get a real puppy."

Marianne said, "Or both."

I used to talk rough enough and country enough for dog fight invites. Could I go home and pick up a pit bull after all these cultural changes? "Are Molly and Rhyodolite staying?"

"Yes, unless you mind terribly."

"Can Chi'ursemisa stay in their room with them? She wants to be separated from Hurdai."

Marianne said, "I'd rather lock her up and let Hurdai out, but Molly seems to get along with her well enough."

"If she hurts them, I'll kill her," I said.

"We're not supposed to use lethal defense," Marianne said. "I asked already. It's like with circus animals—too valuable to kill if they do maul someone. We've got the stunners."

I said, "Maybe we could just stick them back behind the polycarb."

"A big old bitchy Ahram said that they had to turn us loose and trust us, so we have to turn them loose and hope for the best."

As far as I knew, I didn't have a neural disruptor wired to my nervous system. Or did I? Maybe I should go beat on someone and see.

Chi'ursemisa stayed in Molly's room. We put a Gwyng tube sofa for Rhyodolite in the front room, but Chi'ursemisa dragged it back and slept in it when she wasn't reading Karst One texts.

"Where's Rhyodolite?" I asked Molly a few days later. She'd brought in a floor loom and was weaving in the front room, a Bach cantata playing, VCR playing Terran movies.

"Not here," she said, feet moving on the treadles.

"Well, that's obvious."

"He's downstairs with your Gwyng shopkeeper." She jerked the bobbin out of the shuttle and put another one on the rod, then snapped the rod down and sucked the thread through the side slot. "Rhyo and I only do so much for each other. You like that?"

"I just . . ." No, I felt odd about her with him.

"He's going to get beaten up. Cadmium might, just might, come to help. Of course, Cadmium doesn't approve of interspecies sex, either. *Damn* hypocrites, species isn't supposed to be important," she said with an English *damn*.

"You're dealing with a creature who doesn't even understand your basic semiotic system without brainwork."

"Signs were enough."

"I'm sorry."

"I hate the tension here between Hurdai and Chi'ursemisa. But if Rhyodolite's going to be with that *bitch* downstairs, I'm staying." Karst One didn't seem to have curse words strong enough for her today. Her face relaxed as she bent over the weaving, fingers adjusting the old warp thread, then catching the tail of the new one. "And they won't let me use a fly shuttle."

"Who?"

"The inspectors. Handwoven, completely, with handspun." She pointed to a wire with a plastic seal at the edge of the cloth. "One came by this morning, see? I can't use an electric spinner, either. And it has to look slubby, *the pigs*. Like *junkie* spinning. The buyers want handspun authenticity visible from ten *fucking* meters away."

I didn't say anything; she began weaving again. Hurdai came out with Marianne, who held her hand close to her sternum—controller there under her blouse, obviously. Hurdai's face muscles pulled into vertical ridges, then he ambled over to the VCR screen and sat down, watching. He must have trouble seeing the patterns in the lines with his fast eyes, I thought.

"Where's Chi'ursemisa?" I asked.

"In my room. I found out how to lock my door from the outside," Marianne said. Hurdai looked up at her and corrugated his cheek and brow muscles again. I wondered if the two adult Sharwani had faked a quarrel to put us off-balance. If that was the case, then Chi'ursemisa was in no danger.

Marianne said, "Granite Grit and Feldspar are coming down. They said they could take Hurdai and Daiur out for a walk."

Hurdai began opening the controls on the VCR and

sent the picture rolling. He adjusted it back, saying, "I'm very bored." He sounded almost like Hrif, an animal forced into speech.

We stood waiting for Granite and Feldspar, just looking at each other, Molly weaving away, sucking threads every few minutes. I realized I was standing and sat down on the couch, still looking at them all. Marianne was about to sit down herself when the elevator bell finally chimed. She opened the door.

Granite said, "But I saw you in the park."

"Who?" I said, but he'd looked straight at me when he said that.

Granite said, "I must look more closely." He stepped out of the elevator in his gaudy feathers, followed by Feldspar. Both of them circled me, then Granite pulled out a pen-thing and ran it through my hair at the left ear. "You are you."

"Is it a better imitation, then? You said you could tell the other one from me."

Feldspar said to Marianne, "Punch through to the Institute of Control."

Hurdai rolled the VCR picture again, humming down in his throat. His cheeks and forehead rippled again. Marianne went to her room, came back carrying a small portable terminal which she jacked in an outlet in the front room. She said, "Control says to stay on line."

The terminal speaker beeped; Marianne laid her palm on the keyplate in back. Then Karst One letters flashed on the screen: STAY INSIDE.

Everyone looked at me as if it were my fault. The message continued: INSTITUTE OF CONTROL WILL CHECK EACH FLOOR.

Down below on the street, we heard trucks coming in. Chi'ursemisa, locked in the spare room still, began banging on the door.

Hurdai said, "I'd be a fool to hurt her with all this force present."

Marianne seemed to count all of us before she left to

release Chi'ursemisa. Someone on the street was speaking through an amplifier. I couldn't make out the words from up here. Chi'ursemisa and Marianne came out, Marianne talking to Chi'ursemisa about the search.

When Hurdai reached for the VCR controls again, Granite snapped his beak like a book being slammed shut. Hurdai flinched for the first time since I'd known him. His fur over the cheekbones and his head hair slowly rose; Granite's nictitating membranes slid out from his eyecorners, half-covering his eyes.

The elevator door chimed. I opened it, almost expecting to see a gang of my distorted doubles, but Rhyodolite stepped out with three Jereks wearing Institute of Control neural whip insignia on their tunics. Sharwani could imitate Jereks fairly easily, I thought, but couldn't build a fake Rhyodolite.

Unless they can really speak Karst Two. Bird-kinds could have brains that worked both ways. If Sharwani brains were as complex as their eyes . . .

Rhyodolite squeezed his nostrils shut and said, ''Fake Clay imitation out there—you're the real stink-ape.''

One of the Jereks set up a retinal scan, unplugged Marianne's computer, and plugged in the eye scanner. He said, lowering his nose at Rhyodolite, ''The Gwyng was downstairs, but said he'd like to come up with us.''

Rhyodolite said, ''I saw the fake Red Clay—couldn't/ didn't stop (unsure).''

The Jerek put the scan cup over my eye, then said, ''He's Red Clay Tom Gentry; now the others please.''

We were all us.

Hurdai seemed more bored than ever; Chi'ursemisa was more agitated. Their son said, ''Karl, are we going to play with the others soon?''

''What did the man that looked like me say to you?'' I asked.

''You gave me a present for my mother,'' Daiur said. ''I threw it away because it was nasty.''

''What?'' Chi'ursemisa said.

Hurdai said something to her in a language none of the rest of us knew. The Institute of Control people taped their sounds out of our skull computers and told us, "We're sealing your door."

Molly, still weaving, said in English, "What kind of a police state is this?"

This version of me killed two Barcons and another Sharwani defector, then committed suicide.

That shook me more than I could have imagined. I wondered if my duplicate knew about Warren.

The Sharwani did begin imitating Jereks. A real Jerek couple caught one in the slum district. The smell was wrong.

I knew from my own past that we'd get tired of being scared. If one is not paranoid, one does finally stop worrying. At least, if one is human.

Or Sharwani. Chi'ursemisa and Hurdai began to talk in their other alien language when we were with them. All they said went out to the Institute of Control on cable.

I came home one day and the Sharwani weren't in. Marianne was in the kitchen tearing up salad leaves. I came up behind her and kissed her neck.

She said, "Your doubles and the fake Jereks came in on two radar-transparent gliders. Bone tests showed they'd been weightless for a while. Control says all body traces are accounted for. They're screening nearby space for a launch ship."

"And Chi'ursemisa and Hurdai?"

"Control said let them out. They're watching them."

I said, "Oh," and sat down beside her to help. "Isn't Chi'ursemisa afraid of Hurdai anymore?"

"She said they both realized they weren't in positions to affect policy."

I munched on something like a juicier carrot, then asked, "Where are Molly and Rhyodolite?"

"Downstairs. Awingthin was lonely."

Three other Gwyngs wasn't enough. "Maybe we need to see Molly more?"

Marianne said, "And Yangchenla and Sam."

My mouth puckered slightly, gone a bit dry despite the juicy vegetable. "Might be a bit provocative to have us all together."

She asked, "Not both couples on the same evening?"

I laughed, not wanting her to think Yangchenla still made me nervous.

She said, "It's just like Berkeley squared or to the third power. Tom, it is funny how living here becomes the old daily life. I'm even beginning to get used to Chi'ursemisa and Hurdai."

"Maybe we can only take in so much alienness," I said.

Marianne said, "Karriaagzh told me that accommodation, not absolute understanding, was all that's really critical."

"And Black Amber thinks we need to work on knowing each other better." Marianne's face went rigid when I mentioned Black Amber.

During all this, Marianne and I continued our ordinary officers' duties. My memories of Hurdai and Chi'ursemisa living in my house are almost seamless, but my memories of the classes, seminars and trade discussions are fragments, as though my ordinary duties happened at another time.

Shards and fragments of being ordinary:

. . . a young bird cadet gawky in bald skin and mammal clothes reminded me of Granite Grit when we first met. . . .

. . . one afternoon Karl and I walked down to the pond on the Academy grounds. I caught a fish for him so he could see the babies spill like silver coins out of her belly, but none of the fish were that pregnant. I realized that even if he had seen the fish, he wouldn't have known how alien live-bearing fish the size of bass were. . . .

. . . another isolated time, Marianne and I sat in an audience of mostly first-year cadets, their feathers and hair half grown-out. We all listened to Sam Turner playing music fitted to Marianne's and my private pulse beats. Karl wasn't there, he was in a dressing room playing with Tracy and two of her aunts.

When we'd brought him in, Yangchenla's eyes locked with mine, then she looked away and asked Marianne if we wanted Karl to play with Tracy backstage. But, the first memory I always recall of that night is sitting in a dark hall listening to Sam, with Marianne, my arm around her waist, forgetting that the musician was married to my former lover, intently and only a human listening to human music.

About two weeks after we'd heard that all the disguised Sharwani who'd landed in the two gliders were accounted for, a Jerek came to the seminar room as an Ahram and I displayed behaviors we did and didn't have in common. Our cadets, bird and carnivore based, looked at the Jerek, who watched for a second then said, "Officer Red Clay, could we talk?"

I, suddenly terrified for Marianne, came out of the room with him. He said, "Chi'ursemisa and Hurdai fought. Both are safe, back at your house, but Daiur is missing. Perhaps you should finish the seminar so as not to disturb the cadets."

I went back and finished the seminar. As we moved, the Ahram's crest, the skin and muscle over the bone skull ridge, went pale.

After the session ended, I said, "We're having trouble with our Sharwani guests."

The Ahram said, "I could tell you were upset. I was almost frightened of you."

I said, "I'm sorry," and wished I had a faster way home than bus or hired car. Hired car, probably, but the bus would be by soon and I didn't know how quickly a hired car would arrive, unless I could get Black Amber's private car and driver—perhaps not politically correct. I walked quickly out to the bus gate and caught one that came closest to my neighborhood.

Beyond the bus windows, Karst City suddenly seemed more alien, as alien as the day I'd cut classes years ago and spent the day in an almost xenophobic funk. We—on the bus, outside the bus—were all aliens masked in clothes that tried to make us look identical, which made it even easier for the Sharwani to insert their doubles among us. Was everyone on the bus non-Sharwani?

As I got out, I suddenly remembered Thridai's ambush, not far from here, and felt naked under the floppy tunic, my knees disguised—even, almost, the flat shape of my shoulders. I could imagine someone watching me from above, a small blue-clad body with a shaved face, half the visible skin sparsely haired, pointed nose, bushy eyebrows, an ex-brachiator scurrying for cover.

I got onto the elevator with the two Shiny Blacks and looked at them carefully. The female, Silver, took out a small plastic lump and laid it, ticking, over my left ear. She said, "It is Red Clay." She laid the device over her own ear and the ticking continued. "I'm still Silver."

I said, "I think I could have recognized the difference."

"Pays to check. Those who imagine that we do see our friends, not the species, are more prone to self-deception."

That sounded alien to me then. I cupped my hand and signaled assent. They got off the elevator at their floor.

I got off at my own and saw Granite, sitting on his

hocks like a giant nesting bird, staring at Hurdai and Chi'ursemisa. Marianne was sitting beside Rhyodolite's tube sofa where Rhyodolite had so deeply embedded himself that I could barely see him.

Chi'ursemisa's face was bloody—from wounds or rage-burst blood vessels around the eyes, I couldn't tell right away. I looked at Hurdai. He was holding a cloth against the side of his head. When he saw me looking, he pulled the cloth away. Half his ear was missing. I looked down at Chi'ursemisa's hands, which clenched and unclenched slowly, over and over, nails broken but clean, except for possibly blood gone brown under two nails.

Marianne said, "The Barcons will grow him a new ear if he wants."

Hurdai said, "No, thanks."

Rhyodolite, from inside his tube couch, said, "Collaborator (reasonable one) is coming to talk."

I said, "Drusah?"

Marianne nodded.

Chi'ursemisa said, "It's a domestic matter."

I felt sorry for them if it was. Hurdai touched his ear, drew back a dry finger, and threw the cloth on the table. He said, "We need to find Daiur, quickly."

Chi'ursemisa said something in what sounded like a language I hadn't heard before. Hurdai touched his ear again, sniffed the finger, and answered Chi'ursemisa with an alien word almost like a grunt.

The elevator chimed and I asked, "Who is it?"

"Drusah and Barcons," a Barcon voice said.

Marianne said, "Let Granite check them."

Rhyodolite said, from deep in his sofa, "I can smell the difference."

I opened the door. Rhyodolite wiggled up until his shoulders were out of the tube sofa, then he pushed himself the rest of the way out with his hands. His uniform was a wrinkled mess. The two Barcons and

Drusah stared at him as he sniffed around them and said, "They are who they say they are."

The very slightly smaller Barcon said, "And you have to be a Gwyng."

Drusah and the two other Sharwani began talking rapidly in a Sharwani language we couldn't follow. Drusah stopped and said to us, "There's been another glider landing, but Control found the ship and is intercepting it."

More imitations of me? My skin hairs went up.

Hurdai said, "They have Daiur. Drusah, you're dead if the others see you. We know what you are."

The larger Barcon, a hair broader at the hips, less than an inch higher, pulled out a small terminal and plugged it into one of our leads. She scribbled down something with a data pen, then said, "We've sent for a Control Squad."

Hurdai said, "But they'll be gone by then."

Granite said, "Someone would have to stay with Marianne and Chi'ursemisa."

Marianne said, "I can manage Chi'ursemisa."

Chi'ursemisa said, "Wait for Control. And, Marianne, I am not the problem."

Hurdai touched his ear again and made a sound in his throat halfway between a laugh and a hum.

"What about Drusah?" the larger Barcon said.

"I can come with you," he said. "I've fought against my people before."

"No, no deaths," the larger Barcon said. "I can issue stun sticks." She pulled out two things like cattle prods and gave them to Granite Grit and me. "Tom, also bring the controller. Chi'ursemisa, Drusah, if you're in range, the controller will bring you down, too, but we will make you comfortable."

I wished then for a gun that shot lead bullets, big fat ones.

Marianne said, "Tom, I could go instead of you."

I looked at Chi'ursemisa, then at Marianne. "No, you stay with her. You'll be all right."

The Barcon who'd given us the stun sticks said, "A Control Squad will be here soon. We should wait."

"We're wasting time," Hurdai said. "Daiur's life."

Chi'ursemisa said, "Wait for Control." She bared her teeth; I saw a fragment of Hurdai's ear embedded between two of them. Whatever we did, we needed to get Hurdai away from her.

Rhyodolite said, "Let's go then (now)," and that seemed to make up our minds. Granite raised his feathers until they stood on end and shook them, then jerked them flat, clasped down tight.

The smaller Barcon said, "Control will follow us. They can trace. Drusah will stay here."

We looked around at each other—not at all the comprehending eyeball bounce-around of a group coming home from successful negotiations. When I looked into the big female Barcon's eyes, I felt that we were exchanging glances as a stalling technique.

Rhyodolite said, "We could have been gone by now (the elevator response time is quicker than this looking)."

I went over and pushed the elevator call button. The door opened without chiming, empty, and we all got in without speaking. Hurdai, standing next to me, smelling vaguely of wet ashes, raised his eyes and gave me a most alien stare, the muscles in the face tense and immobile.

Rhyodolite said, "You have a distinctive smell." As he had no word developed for *Sharwani* yet, he spoke a sonar code that my computer transformed into an image of Hurdai.

Hurdai, not having the skull computer, asked, "What did he say?"

The small male Barcon said, "He said he can identify your species by its odor."

"Seems animalistic to sense air molecules," Hurdai said.

Rhyodolite's shoulder fur bristled; I heard it rustle under his clothes. The elevator opened on the ground floor and we got out, Hurdai surrounded by the rest of us, all of us not too close together. Rhyodolite walked in front.

Hurdai said, "About three cross-streets away."

We walked down the street—a street broad enough for buses, electric cars, and pedestrians, with no barriers between us. On either side were apartment buildings—*living floors* was English's closest translation to the Karst One term—mostly closed with mirrored windows tinted bronze, green, silver, set in stone or concrete facades, and some smaller buildings of carved wood.

Two electric cars, with plastic egg-shaped bodies and three thin wheels, came toward us as we walked inland. A bus, transparent on top, opaque black below, pulled away from the curb and turned down the first side street. Another car and a bicycle with a bulletlike Vector covering turned left across from us at the second street and went out, passing the two cars at the third street. All of them went as if that third street, where the hostiles waited, was insignificant.

I looked up and saw high cirrus clouds, mare's tails—so much like Earth's, that sky, except for the visible stars. One star cluster almost merged now with the cirrus whisps. The sky was a lighter blue, all the star clusters in the astronomical neighborhood backlighting it. I wondered if I was so aware of all these sky facts because I'd been on Earth not that long ago or because . . .

. . . because these were aliens who couldn't tell me from a Sharwani copy, because we were going out to find Sharwani disguised as me, as Jereks, as . . . And because of all this, my senses, beyond my consciousness, keened themselves up. Glands sluiced my body with adrenaline; muscle fibers cocked themselves in a wave of slight tics crossing my body, rippling down my arms, relaxing.

My eyes turned to each of my companion aliens. I tried to break down my visual maps of these people, tried to see in them their peculiarly individual traits. Granite looked at me as if he were doing the same thing. We should be able to recognize each other in all situations, I thought, because we'd been roommates from cadet days when we were both stripped of hair and feathers. I tried to memorize the color pattern of his feathers before looking at the Barcons. Barcons were always Barcons, never giving names, and these were in full fur, the semi-human faces hidden.

The female Barcon, guessing why I stared so, said, "You've just met us, so there's no disgrace in non-absolute recognition. Identification by skull implant is safer."

Hurdai said, "They're waiting for me there."

I squeezed the control box without activating it and said, "Who are they trying to look like?"

Rhyodolite said, "Tell the one-eared to go first."

The male Barcon said, "They're waiting for you?"

Hurdai stood there, arms slightly akimbo, fingers curled, knees and back slightly bent. The physics of the posture are trans-specific. His head went up and down slightly, gauging distances. I felt my own body sink slightly. My fingers squirmed up over the control box's activator button. Then my hand tightened, still not pushing the button but firmly on it.

Granite said, "Go first, Hurdai." Granite's short femurs, normally parallel to the ground, jerked, ruffling his body feathers, then the femurs bent below their usual parallel as he crouched, bending hips and knees, then the hock joints that I thought of as his knees, really his ankles. *Get your reality maps straight, Red Clay.*

My mental voice sounded like Karriaagzh.

Hurdai walked forward a few steps, then looked over his shoulder at us. The fur on his cheekbones ruffled;

he pressed his lips even thinner. Then he went through the passage between a small wooden building about four floors and a twenty-story building with no windows.

I looked over at the wooden building on my left and saw silhouettes against windows with wire screens, no glass. I was relieved that whatever they were, they could hear us, then wondered if they were the bad guys, watching, listening.

We couldn't see Hurdai when he said, "Come on."

The male Barcon said, "He talked to others in his language." He patched through a recording to Control, then said, "There's a basement under the wooden building, rock foundation."

His mate said, "Who's in the wooden building?"

Big Barcon fingers moved over the communication device, then he said, "Ape stock, not Ahrams, bigger than Red Clay."

People who didn't care about the temperature, I thought. And in the other building without windows, people who preferred light mixed differently than from Karst's sun.

I thought, I'll kill Hurdai if this is a trap. We began walking in. Rhyodolite went first, a Gwyng forcing himself to be the bravest.

Hurdai was with seven Jereks—no, they weren't Jereks, their shoulders were flat like mine, like Hurdai's. Battles with aliens are supposed to happen in deep space, I thought as I dived away, rolling, from the gun pointed at me. I pushed the controller; Hurdai stayed on his feet. One of the Barcons grabbed me and we ran, bobbing and weaving, to the basement of the wooden house.

Rhyodolite and Granite were standing on the wrong side of Hurdai. I kept pushing the controller box button.

Hurdai pointed. Two Sharwani aimed. Rhyodolite threw himself in front of Granite and his head exploded. Granite bounded forward, twelve feet up and at least that forward, hit the fake Jerek with his stun stick and took the weapon, threw it to us. Then he grabbed the creature who'd killed Rhyodolite and tried to pull it apart, arms in one scaly fist, one leg in the other. Everyone else froze—Jereks, us—and Granite bounded sideways, throwing the Sharwan at the others. Then another bound and Granite was with us, staring out of the slits in the basement wall.

"It has to be a suicide team," the female Barcon said. She sounded as though her observation meant nothing to us.

They were crazy, coming in toward us, skins jerking where the Sharwani would normally raise hair, not lowering the nose in the Jerek threat face. Granite said, "They had flat shoulders."

I said, "Yeah, they still have flat shoulders. And the control box doesn't work on Hurdai."

The male Barcon said, "Hurdai told them to kill Rhyodolite because he knew Gwyngs could smell. But we can smell the difference, too. Ashes, not musk."

Granite clamped his feathers down tightly and shuddered. He picked up the Sharwani gun and said, "Can we kill them?" His hand didn't fit in the trigger guard, though, then he threw it down and we watched it turn red.

As smoke rose from the burning gun, the Sharwani rushed us, Hurdai behind. Granite stunned two of them, then I knocked Hurdai down, his throat in my hands. And I was just wringing his neck, screaming in English, "Motherfucker, pig, son of a bitch, fucked up the control box, used your own son, tricked us."

And he died and went limp. More aliens rushed in. I sat up and screamed. Then I realized their shoulders were round and they were our Jereks, Institute of Control. I put my hands over my face and cried. They pulled my hands down and put plastic cuffs on me, as though I were a wild animal myself.

The Barcons bent over Hurdai, thrusting trocars up his neck veins and arteries, but one of the Jereks clicked a stopwatch and said, "Brain death, stop." I saw Cadmium come up, wearing a Rector's Office patch on his uniform. He looked at Rhyodolite lying there, face down, and said to the Barcons, "Save him. Brain reconstruct."

The male Barcon turned Rhyodolite over and we saw the bloody hollow where his eyes and brain had been. Cadmium slowly sank to the ground. The Barcons tried to rouse him, but he was going into protective coma, chilling down, so they loaded him on a stretcher.

One of the Jereks came up to me and checked my skull computer, then asked, "Is it easy for you to kill?"

I said, "He set us up. I tried to stun him, but the box didn't work. Chi'ursemisa . . ." Chi'ursemisa probably tore the control implant out of him—the ear was a sham. I lost it so badly I tried to wiggle out of the cuffs, then realized I looked like a fool.

The Jerek stepped back until I got myself calmed down somewhat. He said, "You can't judge them as you judge your own kind. I think they were very frightened or they would have aimed better and killed all of you. And you had a stun stick."

"Frightened?" I trembled. "Take off the cuffs, please. I'm not a Sharwan."

He laid a testing device against my skull and said, "The Sharwani duplicate blood heat patterns fairly well. How do you know we're not Sharwani ourselves?"

"You have round shoulders and you smell like Jereks."

He lowered his nose. I almost laughed, but didn't. "Why didn't you get here sooner?"

"Why in Mind's essence did you leave with Hurdai before we arrived? And what happened to your stun stick?"

"Hurdai said . . ." We had listened to Hurdai; that seemed stupid now. I was in trouble. I hadn't been in trouble since I cut classes my first year as a cadet. "I dropped my stun stick."

The Jerek asked, "Are you sufficiently calmed down, Red Clay?"

"I think so."

"Come see what you did, then." The Jerek took the cuffs off. The Barcons put Hurdai on a stretcher without covering his face, not being human and followers of that convention. His eyes were bulging, his teeth bared, one hand was flung back and curled, bloody. I felt my neck and brought my fingers away bloody, but didn't feel any satisfaction that I'd been wounded by him.

The male Barcon said, "I'll take you home."

Granite said, "I'll go with him."

We went walking back, the Jereks passed us with their captives, and a couple of the neighbors gawked at us, me bloody. I noticed then that the Barcon male had a bandaged arm.

The day was still the same. We'd been ambushed in the Karst equivalent of a good city neighborhood, I thought bitterly. We'd been stupid, and I'd killed Hurdai. Now I had to face Chi'ursemisa, but maybe someone would have gotten her out before I got home.

No such luck. As the elevator door went down, I saw Molly and Marianne get up from the sofa, Chi'ursemisa get up from a chair. I could barely look at Marianne, who shrieked and came running to me.

"Superficial wounds," the female Barcon said. "Take him back to one of your rooms and clean him up." I couldn't even be there when they told Molly and Chi'ursemisa that Rhyodolite and Hurdai were dead.

When Marianne got me back in the back, she asked, "What happened?"

"Sharwani killed Rhyodolite. I strangled Hurdai. The neural implant didn't work. I couldn't stop him with the disruptor."

"Drusah and Chi'ursemisa fell down." Marianne's facial muscles quivered; her skin was pale. "Control took Drusah away."

I told her, "We should have waited for them. I can't

take having been so stupid, but when the disruptor wouldn't work, I panicked. I'd dropped the stun stick." Or was I too mean to use it?

She hugged me once hard, then got a wet washcloth and soap. "He led you to an ambush," she said as she laid the washcloth against my neck to soak the blood crust loose. "And he tried to kill you." She wiped gently, breaking open a rip in my skin anyway.

"I thought Chi'ursemisa, the ear, was faked." I started to feel better, at least in human terms. "It was self-defense."

A Barcon voice said, "We don't allow lethal self-defense while angry." I looked up; it was the big female.

I felt like hammered shit. Marianne kept cleaning my neck. Chi'ursemisa came in and said, "I'd like to stay here."

"I killed him, Chi'ursemisa. I thought you'd ripped his control implant out."

"I didn't," she said. She looked tired, fur rumpled over the high cheekbones, skin flaking around the mouth. I remembered that she ripped one of Hurdai's ears off—protecting us? In anger?

I said, "Chi'ursemisa, what have we put you through?"

"Much," she said, then she turned around and left the room. I realized I heard Molly crying—distantly. Rhyodolite was dead, bound for the Memorial Walls.

The Barcon female said, "If anything happens to Chi'ursemisa, we will rearrange your brain."

"Get off my case," I said in English.

"You must come in for counseling," she said.

I said, "Rhyodolite's dead."

Her Barcon eyes looked away, at Marianne, then down at the floor. "We're all upset. Sorry. But you still have to come in for counseling."

Then we heard Chi'ursemisa's ululations—a word I'd

never completely understood before—ululations, like a throat with a siren in it.

Molly screamed. We went running out. Chi'ursemisa held Daiur, alive, wiggling, between her knees. Her head went back, her throat bowed, throbbing out wails that sounded almost metallic, then her head fell forward and she gasped, then threw her head back to wail again. Daiur looked terrified, his hands trying to pry her wrists away, his baby fur standing on end.

Molly screamed in English, "Stop the bitch."

"Molly, settle down," I said.

"They killed Rhyodolite."

I said in English, "Look, they've got a low enough opinion of humans here. And Chi'ursemisa lost her lover, too."

Molly sat down, gasping. Chi'ursemisa stopped wailing and looked at her, throat in spasms. Molly said, in Karst One this time, "I wanted to be part of everything. I wanted . . . God, Tom, you think what I had with Rhyodolite was perverted."

Yes, but . . . I didn't say a thing, though.

"You think what I had with Sam was perverted, too."

"I'm not a racist, Molly."

Marianne said, "Molly."

I was about to say, But you left Sam for Rhyodolite. All Sam wanted was to be human. I thought I'd always known that. "Sam's human."

"Do you think I wanted to be human, even on Earth, even before? I . . . I'm no happier being human than you are."

Chi'ursemisa said, "Perhaps Hurdai is best dead, but . . ." She realized how tight she'd been holding Daiur and relaxed her arms. "Where were you?" she asked him.

"Daddy told me to hide." He touched her face.

"Your father is dead." Daiur closed his eyes and trembled. Chi'ursemisa, still cuddling him, said,

"Weaver, Molly, I am tired of being myself, too. My loyalties and disloyalties both are shattered."

I said, "I'm going to miss Rhyodolite." Suddenly, I wondered about Cadmium. "Where's Cadmium?"

The Barcon said, "Black Amber refuses him. Do you want him here?"

I looked at Marianne and then at Molly. Marianne said, "If he wants to stay here, but doesn't he have quarters?"

"He is hibernating," the Barcon said. "Stress reduction. Friends can bring him out quicker. Do you want him out quicker?"

Chi'ursemisa said softly, "Tom, who is Cadmium?"

"Pouch kin of a Gwyng your . . . the Sharwani who attacked us killed."

"We will have to live with each other in small situations as well as large," she said. "I failed with Hurdai."

Marianne flattened her lips, not a smile, and looked at Molly who said, "We can take care of Cadmium. I will." My wife's eyebrows jerked and she looked at me. Molly added, "Rhyodolite was more than a sex partner, and Cadmium isn't Rhyodolite."

Chi'ursemisa stood up, lifted Daiur in her arms, and walked out of the room. The Barcons sighed, then the male wiggled his nose slightly. I said, "If Marianne agrees."

Marianne paused before she said, "Yes, I suppose."

The Barcon male went to my terminal, unplugged it, and plugged in a small hand term of his own. He squiggled his pen on its pad, then said, "We'll bring him up soon."

I remembered that Rhyodolite's tube sofa was still in the front room. "Do you have something to utterly deodorize where Rhyodolite was?"

The Barcons talked to each other in their language, then said, "Don't put Cadmium where Rhyodolite was until we do bring it."

I sat down on the couch and Marianne came up and took my hand. My body felt extremely stiff. The elevator chimed. The Barcons opened the door and Granite stepped out, his nictitating membranes still half-covering his eyes. His face feathers shifted when he looked at me. Did they hassle him about throwing that fake-Jerek Sharwan around?

I said, "They're bringing Cadmium here."

The membranes withdrew into his eyecorners. He sat down, with what were really his ankles pointed behind him. No one spoke. The Barcons went back to Chi'ursemisa's room and murmured to her. She didn't answer. Then they came back and left us.

After a few minutes, Granite stood up, stretched, and put Bach's *Goldberg Variations* on our player.

"Thanks," I said.

= 7 =

The morning after I killed Hurdai, I woke up to find that my hands ached. Was that psychological or had I sprained my fingers on Hurdai's throat? I went to my terminal and read: GO TO RECTOR'S OFFICES AT 10:30 A.M. TESSERACT, RECTOR'S MAN.

For several years now, I hadn't seen Tesseract for more than a few minutes here and there. He was the first Ahram and second alien species that I'd met ever, one of the darker Southern Ahrams I found out later, with a very prominent crest, huge body, jaw like an *Australopithecus robustus*. Weird that he'd counsel me on the killing, I thought, when I haven't kept in real touch with him.

And an odd hour to schedule the meeting—not so soon that I could get it over with and go to the rest of my day. The wait made me nervous, was designed, I suspected, to do precisely that. I ran cold water over my fingers, flexing them.

Then I went in to check on Cadmium, who was

sleeping under a light sheet in a cool room. The Gwyngs downstairs suggested that we let him hibernate at least a week, put time between him and Rhyodolite's shattered skull. Cadmium looked dead, but the biomonitor on his wrist showed he had a temperature five degrees over the room temperature and a pulse of eight beats a minute.

Nothing I can do here, I thought, as I looked down on him, the eyelids slightly open, his blond-streaked hair rumpled, something dark on his head where he fell. Oil maybe, or dirt, not something to wash off right now. Not something that would kill him.

Would the heat from my hand bother him if I touched him? Then I wondered if just being near him I would radiate enough heat to rouse him. By his bed was a heater flagon of olive oil. He'd burn considerable fat coming out of hibernation.

"Take care of yourself," I said softly, then went to the back room for breakfast. Marianne, Molly, and Chi'ursemisa sat eating; the boys were gone. They all looked up at me, and I wondered if being female brought creatures more together than species itself.

"I go in to talk to Tesseract at ten-thirty," I said, giving the Karst One equivalent time.

Chi'ursemisa said, "I need to talk to Drusah."

Marianne spoke to her in Sharwanisa, touched her wrist bone gently.

"I've got a long wait," I said, going to the stove and fixing scrambled eggs and toast. The Federation had not wanted Terran yeast here at first, but we finally got it in so we could bake. I thought about the Tibetans and centuries of no bread. "Tesseract told me I was one test of humans. Yangchenla's family was another. I guess I failed."

"Hurdai," Chi'ursemisa said. Her voice jerked when she said that. "Our lives in your house paralleled the war outside."

I wondered if it would be better for all of us if

Chi'ursemisa and Daiur left. "Sorry," I said. A flash of Rhyodolite's empty skull, face blown away, hit me. Not that sorry, Chi'ursemisa, but . . .

It was the local equivalent of eight-thirty. I wished I had something to plug into my brain to blank me until ten-thirty. I asked, "Chi'ursemisa, do you need to talk?"

"I will."

Marianne said, "Daiur's taking it well."

"Not really," Chi'ursemisa said. "Sorry, Tom."

I wondered what I'd do if Daiur hurt Karl. Karl was bigger, so unless Daiur got his hands on a gun . . . The image was incongruous: fuzzy little golden Daiur with a big black pistol, both his little hands wrapped around it. But not funny. I shuddered slightly, utterly unwilling to admit out loud to envisioning that.

Chi'ursemisa said, "It is terrible to wait."

I felt worse—they'd waited months behind the polycarbonate. I looked up at Chi'ursemisa's yellow eyes. The iris muscles flexed and her pupils expanded. *Don't be happy to see me, Chi'ursemisa.*

"Well, I won't sit waiting around here. I'll walk over there. That should take some time."

"Catch a bus rather than be late," Marianne said.

Molly's lips twisted, then she looked over at Chi'ursemisa and her chin jerked slightly.

"I've got to leave now if I'm going to walk."

Marianne said, "I'll go with you to the elevator."

While we waited for the elevator to come up, I kissed Marianne on the mouth. Her tongue came out a bit but didn't play. We looked at each other, then she kissed me on the forehead the way she kissed Karl. The elevator door slid down, and I, suddenly very lonely, got on.

Today the sky outside was grey. Tonight it would rain, maybe sooner as the weather effects aren't absolutely predictable. I hadn't gotten two blocks before a Jerek and a Barcon stopped me, ran a computer detector against my ear.

The Barcon said, "You really are Red Clay."

"Wiggle your nose," I said to him.

He did—really a Barcon. The Jerek looked at a screen and said, "This isn't the best idea, walking."

"I have a counseling appointment at ten-thirty," I said.

They looked at each other, then the Barcon said, "Take the bus and walk around the Academy."

"You mean I'm not safe here?"

"I haven't accounted for all Sharwani body traces in the last glider," the Barcon said.

"We can walk him," the Jerek said.

The Barcon began pulling his wrist hair. Maybe I should take the bus, I thought, and see if I could talk to Black Amber before I went in to see Tesseract. "Yes," the Barcon said, "we could walk with him."

So we continued down the street. I felt strange, almost juvenile again, caught being bad. The Jerek's face skin wrinkled over his pointed nose when I looked at him.

We were passing the open-floored bird buildings, those of the olive and brown people like Travertine. The landscaping plants looked particularly happy under the clouds, bursting with green sap, huge leaves.

"They get too much light here," the Barcon said.

"The plants?" I asked.

"And the birds. They complain that they never have to raise their feathers."

We walked on through an area with some small shops and music clubs, some on terraces, some indicated with signs. "Wait," the Jerek said. We stopped beside a building with a sunken entrance connected to ground level with a ramp. The Jerek went down the ramp and came back with a sweet roll. That's what it smelled and looked like. "Here," he said to me, "the chemistry suits you and I thought you might like to eat something.''

Because I was nervous. "Thanks," I said. "Do most people like to eat when they're nervous?"

The Barcon said, "Some like to sleep."

Cadmium, I thought. "We should have waited for the Control Squad," I said.

They, being Control, didn't say anything. I felt awkward again, and we walked on in silence by the shops that catered to the Institute and Academy students. I recognized the place where Granite Grit and I had seen our first semi-illegal xenophobia movie. The Jerek saw me staring and lowered his nose slightly, then whistled softly—his laugh. The Barcon wiggled his nose, then rubbed at it with his hand.

We went in through the Academy gates and toward the Rector's Offices. I checked the time—I had to be there in about ten minutes. The little Jerek male sat down on one of the ancient war-melted chunks of wall and said, "Well, you can't take a bus from here, so you'd better hurry." He rubbed his legs and wrinkled his face skin, then said something to the Barcon.

"Thanks for walking with me," I said.

"We thought it would be wise," the Barcon said, and I realized then that they'd been waiting for me, that probably another Control pair had watched the bus, or been on it. I must have looked a bit hurt, because he said, "And we did want to make sure you were our Red Clay."

I said, "Thank you" more formally and hurried away toward the tower that was closest to the Rector's Offices. When I could see the white, tile front and the chrome pillars of the building itself, I slowed down until I was breathing normally and then went in.

Black Amber came down the stairs into the entrance hall with two Barcons as though I'd been announced. She looked old now, stooped, the webs more wrinkled. One eye pupil was slightly greyed. A cataract? She came

up and ran her furred knuckles down my upper arm.
The nails were thick, crumbling like an old woman's
toenails. Had I just not noticed before?

"I'm sorry," I told her.

"The Bird Rector brought the killing to us."

I wondered if she was being paranoid. She and the
Barcons turned to go with me up the stairs. Did Tesseract have the same offices? How many years had it
been since I came here with Granite Grit when we were
both cadets? More than thirteen years. Karl was eight,
almost nine, now. Suddenly, the past shrank behind
me—not a kid anymore, my elders were old. Before I
walked in here, I knew I was thirty-four, but I'd forgotten that I'd spent all of my adult life with aliens.
Fourteen years of good service and now this.

A Gwyng said, "Tesseract and Karriaagzh will see
you now, Red-Clay."

I looked at Black Amber; she'd gone glassy eyed.
Stiffly she turned and went away. The other Gwyng
opened the door into Tesseract's office. Karriaagzh stood
beside Tesseract's desk; Tesseract sat behind it.

Tesseract said, "Well, Tom." He, too, looked much
older. His face had wrinkled slightly and the skin over
the skull crest seemed looser. Had the muscles in the
crest shrunk?

I bowed my head slightly and said, "Rector's Man
Tesseract and Rector Karriaagzh." Tesseract looked first
at Karriaagzh, who settled down on a suede leather mat,
then at me. I realized as I watched his face go impassive
that he had little love for human beings, that I'd been
his charge once and now I'd killed. The Federation
didn't approve of killing sapients, and my kind had a
bad rep for doing precisely that.

Karriaagzh said, "Chi'ursemisa said she would have
had to kill Hurdai if you hadn't."

I said, honestly, "I feel terrible about killing him,
but when the control box didn't work . . . we should
have waited for Control."

Tesseract sighed and put three different tea bags in as many cups, one a bird cup. On the bag he'd taken one out of, I saw a transliteration for *human* and a number code. Would this tea melt the truth out, both what a human was willing to admit to himself and what he lied to himself about? Karriaagzh pulled his head back and looked at Tesseract before taking his spouted bird cup like a miniature teacup. Could, would a Rector be questioned under drugs? What all was this about?

We sat for a minute, letting the brews steep. Then I took my cup and sipped the bitter tea out of it—alkaloids, not as hot as I'd expected. Karriaagzh ruffled his headfeathers, put his cup down, then picked it back up and drained it in one swallow.

Tesseract shifted his gaze to me and sipped his own cup. The cups, made of a heat sink material, had been prechilled just enough to cool the tea after the minute of brewing. I wondered how fast-acting these alkaloids would be.

Man enough to take me. Tesseract had never trusted humans. My fond memories of him were a joke. I looked into Karriaagzh's yellow eyes with the bone ridges over them, then at Tesseract's bone skull crest with the age-atrophied muscles running down across his skull to his jaws. Then I seemed to move out of my body and saw myself sitting there with them, imagined it, perhaps. A small nervous creature who killed. Kills. Like the Sharwani. Tesseract put his teacup down and looked over at Karriaagzh, then pushed a button on his desk.

Karriaagzh was swaying slightly. Another Ahram, Warst Runnel of the History Committee, entered, followed by a young female Gwyng, not Wy'um, Black Amber's now dead lover, but his replacement on the Committee. The Gwyng's feet twisted as she walked.

Tesseract said, "Red Clay, were you furious when you strangled Hurdai?"

I said, "He killed Rhyodolite. I couldn't stop him."

Who was Hurdai? Not *what* was Hurdai, but who inside? We'd captured him, held him prisoner with sensory deprivation—that plastic slab, that bare room. His mate didn't support him; his child was seduced into playing with killer apes. "I feel sorry for him now, but you aren't fair."

How so not? Warst Runnel looked at Tesseract, then back at me, brow wrinkles going at steeper angles than they did on human faces. I remembered Alex in Berkeley, trapped in human form without his skull crest. Once humans made contact with the Federation, we'd turn him over to the humans. It wasn't fair. "You sacrifice us for History Committee goals." But then I left Earth, hostile to my own kind as Alex had pointed out. "I don't know."

Tesseract wrote something on his pad, then said, "Karriaagzh, Black Amber said she would see your position as less hypocritical if we contacted your own people."

"You allowed my former people to turn you down. They were wrong, but . . ."

"Tom, do you know anything about Black Amber's trips?"

"No," I said.

"So you weren't under any special strain," Tesseract said. "She's taken some long normal-space flights recently. Or so we were told. Red Clay, you claim not to know anything about those?"

"No." And why were they asking me?

The new Gwyng History Committee person said, "Red-Clay/Rector Bird/parallel species self-hate (more excusable in Red-Clay). Must cure both."

My belly quivered. Species self-hate, what could the cure be? Karriaagzh's bill gaped open and slammed shut, bounced open again and slammed, like planks slammed together. He put his fingers in his beak corners, then took out his left hand to massage between his eyes until his nictitating membranes retracted.

Tesseract and Warst Runnel stared at each other, then both big creatures shrugged—unwinding muscles, cocking muscles? I felt like a child who'd suddenly realized adults weren't perfect. But then I decided that for all the squalid politics, I basically believed that Karriaagzh was right—Mind needed to contact all of itself, even if the thoughts were ugly sometimes. I said it out loud, "Karriaagzh, you're being inconsistent if you don't want to bring your own people into the Federation."

He seemed to shrink into himself and said, "It is not consistent with Federation policies to force a contact unless the species is forcing contacts on others."

The Gwyng koo'ed softly. I asked, "Karriaagzh, aren't you a species?" That sounded odd, drugged odd. Karriaagzh pulled his feathers tightly to his body.

Tesseract blew his breath out and wrote again on his data pad, then said, "Tom, would you have let Hurdai live?"

Total confusion. "Where should we have stopped killing him? At the First Contact with Ersh? In my house? I'm sorry." I was sorry, but I honestly felt I was just part of the causes and effects. I wanted to cry, but felt tears would be dishonest, so just rolled my head around on my neck, blinking my eyes.

Karriaagzh said, "You need Tom."

Tesseract's head jerked up and around toward Karriaagzh. He said, "I suppose so."

I said, "What do you mean by that?"

Tesseract said, "Your species is playing with gates."

"Oh, it's too complex already," I said, the drug breaking out waves of self-pity and fear of my own kind. What is that in formal English? *Reverse xenophobia?*

Tesseract said, "Tom, you will meet them."

The Gwyng female said, "Rector's Man, be careful."

Karriaagzh stood up and stretched, then said, "Regardless of what policy I have, you don't have authority to openly contact my people." He walked out of the room before anyone could reply.

Feeling dizzy, I looked at the three aliens remaining in the room and said, "Detox me."

Tesseract said, "No, we have more."

Barcons brought in one of my bad imitations. Tesseract said, "Jereks said the facial and body blood heat patterns seem identical."

My imitation asked, "This one killed Hurdai?"

Tesseract said, "Yes. We're contacting his kind soon."

I asked, "Did you know Hurdai?"

My sort-of double with body heat in the right places said, "We thought Chi'ursemisa . . . Hurdai was good, honest. Ours."

But Chi'ursemisa wasn't. "And you?"

"I . . ."

"He went xeno-flip. At first, we thought he was you, thrashing around too much to lay on a tester," one of the Barcons with him said. The Sharwan trembled. "After your brother . . ."

I interrupted, "Are humans all so monstrous?"

"Yes, I am a monster, now," the Sharwan said. His face reddened. Blush for me, too, I thought. He turned to the Barcon and said, "I will never feel normal again."

"Oh, you'll look just like a Sharwan again, soon," Tesseract said, "with some honor scars."

"Looking isn't what I meant," the Sharwan said. His fingertip expanded and he touched his cheekbones.

"We can build your cheekbones back, even the veins under the skin."

The Sharwan said, "I'll always remember the feel of this, the sight of Hurdai cooling."

In infrared, how vivid, I thought and shuddered. "Now, will you detox me?" I asked.

"Live with it," Tesseract said.

= 8 =

For days at the Earth Oort Cloud station, I watched time-lagged television coming off my home planet. In a three-inch-square window in the upper left of the screen, analogs of instrument needles wobbled as my conspecifics played with gravity, looping it against space-time. Soon, I'd be facing them.

Besides myself, there were five of us officially waiting: Travertine, Granite, a pair of half-shed Barcons, and Wool, who squelched comments on species, especially his. He was a giant creature with thick, blotched skin and a hairy head and shoulders, probably with either Analytics and Tactics or Control. Except for the Barcons, we'd all done in-station waits together before this one. By the second day, I realized the Barcons were Jackie and S'wam from Berkeley, but not de-haired to human norms.

Besides the five of us, Control rotated squads through to familiarize them with humans. Control would be prepared in case of trouble.

One night I watched Japanese gun master digital broadcasts that our own computers cleaned up and projected on flat screens. Figures, ambiguously either sinister or heroic, attacked robots and died speaking Japanese, shot down by factory machines. I identified like crazy with the dying humans. Maybe the official humans would shoot me down? I could imagine humans murderously angry that I defected to aliens—my blood floating in red globs in free-fall. The globs would wobble like giant soap bubbles.

Travertine watched me, still suspicious of humans. Why had I imagined my death in free-fall while he watched? I'd seen Xenon killed in free-fall, and my blood image was too vivid to be merely imagined.

Blood globs in free-fall drift up to cloth and soak in by capillary action, oozing down the fibers as if drawn by gravity, but in all directions, patterned by grease smears that resist blood stains.

Travertine said, "Your face is pale and sweating. Do you need sedation?"

"I'm afraid of what the humans are going to think when they see me with you." I feared human anger more than the xenophobia. I knew how I'd felt when I strangled Hurdai. Now distanced from that killing anger, I was sick of being human if my species innately doomed me to a lethal temper.

But here I was, waiting for a whole planetful of them, all twitchy on the triggers. What was the Federation going to offer them? Sharwani were on the verge of civil war because of the Federation; the Gwyngs sold surplus population on labor contracts; the Yauntry spent all they earned from lithium on education for their young, working furiously to stay in place. This was going to look bleak to the folks who thought space was the final frontier, open range, homesteading, strip mines and all that.

Travertine said, "We are fortunate there are no strong leaders now. Strong leaders seem to drive humans crazy." He plugged in a digital movie player, cutting off the program coming in from Earth, and began watching a collage copy of old Hitler newsreels. Stalin and Hitler grinned at each other, dividing up Poland. Whoever put the images into a digital medium cut in images of death-camp corpses.

"Stop that," I said.

Travertine's feathers raised off his body. "You've been up too long, Tom. Go to bed."

Wool came in, looking unkempt, his face covered with white cream, and said, "Travertine is right. We should put you on twelve-hour shifts."

"What are you doing to your face?" I said.

Wool didn't answer, but wiped with a towel. His face was rose-tan under the hair. The white cream was a depilatory. I looked at his thick skin, mottled grey and brown, and his slit pupils, and thought that de-hairing his face didn't make him look significantly less alien. The grey skin patches along his shoulders and arms seemed slightly moist, with short stiff hairs coming out of them. The other parts of him were more densely furred. The comfortable lies that my brain fed my vision centers lurched and I saw him as a naive human would have seen him: cat eyes, blotched skin that looked diseased, the face so artificially stripped of hair. Then my mental maps skewed back and I felt ashamed of myself. That was Wool I saw as an alien. I looked over at Travertine. Karriaagzh chose us well: tough, very alien. Humans would freak or not. Wool, Travertine, Granite Grit, the Barcons, me—we'd take care of them either way.

"Bed," Wool said again, his oval pupils contracting slightly, not to the slits they'd been in full light, but still like cat's eyes.

"I'd just lie there worrying," I said.

"We'll sedate you. And unsedate if your people come."

I sighed; he sighed back in imitation. We looked at each other, his expression in his dilated eyes, the slight twitch of his nostrils. I pulled up my tunic sleeve and asked, "Will you wear a top when my people come?"

"I have one that breathes properly. Will I look more presentable without face hair?"

I looked at his pupils, then at his muscular lips, the top one that turned down at the sides. He shifted his face muscles and I realized his facial expressions were close to human, bared by the depilatory cream for our reading. "Yes, we'll be able to learn your expressions faster."

"Well," he said, preparing the sedative for me, "I didn't do it foolishly then." He laid the cube on my forearm, but stopped. I guessed he felt a bit embarrassed. "Can you sleep without this?" he asked me.

"Yeah," I said.

"You are tired, aren't you?"

Actually, I was. Seeing how concerned Wool was about being readable by us humans relieved me. "Yes," I said. He stood up and took the cube out with him. I turned on a hologram wall, rain on a jungle, and watched until I saw the scene begin again, twelve-minute repeats. Sometime after the third one, I fell asleep and dreamed of Marianne in a green silk dress, and Karl's sister, who asked me why she hadn't been born yet.

I woke up once, startled, maybe thinking the Americans had come, and lay in the dim light wondering whether the humans would be American, Russian, Chinese, British—whatever. Arabs, maybe. Africans. A huge diverse planet, yet weren't life-bearing planets always that way? How could I represent all human beings to the Federation, much less all the Federation to Earth?

Wool said, "I see light on your eyeballs." He was sitting in the dark, a shadow-form speaking language, but I knew he could see me as well as a cat could have.

"They aren't here, are they?"

"Not yet. You are nervous, which makes us more nervous."

"It's personal," I said.

"You will be quite valuable to them."

"But I'm Federation," I said.

The shape shifted. I heard him suck his upper lip and remembered how he liked to talk after he woke up from one of his short naps. He had no fixed sleeping time. I asked, "Is your home planet's sky bright at night?"

"It varies," he said.

"What happens to Alex when the contact is made?"

"Alex?"

"The blond Ahram with the skull crest cut away, who lives in Berkeley."

Wool said, "The Barcons told me about him. He should have been rotated out. We'll turn him over to your authorities as a goodwill gesture."

"He wanted to know when contact was going to happen. He's afraid of jail."

"Do you think your officials will announce to the general population that we're out here? Contact is sometimes secret among the officiators." He used the Karst One term that I usually translated as *officers*, then said, in English, *"Among the rulers."*

"Is that good?"

"Not unless the rulers are significantly different genetically."

I remembered the Jersey cows among the Gwyng pouch hosts and blood beasts and wondered if the cows had any idea of how far from the Channel Islands they'd gone. "Not the same species?"

"What is species?" Wool said. He got up and left the sleeping room.

I wondered if I'd been asleep long enough and checked my watch. Not quite. Odd Universe to move us around so much, stars whirling planets, planets moving people, people moving animals and each other. Maybe I would be too valuable to be hassled by the FBI or the Virginia law?

Suddenly, I wished I had a banjo, knew how to play

one, almost hearing the Statler Brothers' "Oh, Elizabeth," not a banjo tune, but one of the things the radio played a lot just before I left Virginia with Black Amber and her pouch sons. Then I remembered Bach's harpsichord music as Sam Turner played it, mocking the simple country tune, almost as alien to me as Granite Grit's home planet discs.

If everyone here on this station, including me, could stop thinking of my people as capital *H* Humans, the contact would go better.

But I couldn't stop thinking of myself as a capital *H* Human. Self-defense didn't seem awful, but . . . Did the Sharwani see what they were doing against the Federation as self-defense? Could we ever see around species bounds?

I wondered if I should get up and sedate myself, then turned on a night view of Floyd, the one traffic light blinking through the cycles, cars going by on a five-minute loop. Had it been too boring or too dangerous to stand filming traffic long in nighttime Floyd?

What loop was my brain stuck on to keep throwing me these rhetorical questions?

Lorda mercy, I'm acting like a spooked human, I thought in substandard English. Was I going to revert to mountain dialect when my conspecific officials arrived?

Arrgh, the questions.

I dreamed questions, thinking I was awake, because the room shifted when I opened my eyes. The Floyd holoview was off; the diurnal wake-cycle lights were on. Granite Grit said, "Could you help me oil my feathers?"

"Are they here?"

"Not yet."

"Soon?"

"Soon," Granite said.

"I'd better shave, then I'll fix you up."

"If we have time," Granite said.

I sat up fast, my heart racing.

"Travertine says your fear of humans scares him," Granite said, muscles in the corners of his eyes bunching up. "And the Barcons are no help, talking about being mugged in Berkeley."

What was the right explanation for my fear? There were several socially expedient explanations, none of them precisely and exclusively true. I said, "I'm afraid I'll embarrass them." Well, yes, and the other way around, too.

Wool's voice came in over the intercom, "Get ready."

I said, "Are they here?"

"Not yet, but . . ." Wool broke off. I pulled on my pants and went to the toilet to wash my armpits and shave. Granite came up to me with my tunic top and contacts-and-honors sash. I looked at him and wondered if I'd have time to groom him, too. The electric razor hummed. My pulse was pounding.

After I shaved, I rubbed my fingers over my chin and cheeks to see if I'd missed any stubble, then splashed water on my face. After I toweled off, Granite handed me the rest of my clothes and said, "You can oil my feathers in the common waiting room." He sounded pissed.

"They're more likely to kill me than you," I told him.

"That's not reassuring, Officer Red Clay."

We were on formal terms, were we? "I'm sorry."

He reached out and straightened my sash, then backed out of the toilet cubicle. I suddenly needed to piss and adjusted the urinal to my height. When I came out, Granite was wiping his beak, his nictitating membranes a quarter out over his dark-brown eyes.

"Let's get you fixed up," I said, awkwardly reaching for his shoulder, patting the emerging quills—in moult, no wonder he was edgy.

He flicked the transparent films back into the eyecorners near his nares and rubbed his beak against his arm scales. "You make us more nervous about your people than the Tibetans do."

"Sorry." We started for the common waiting room.

"Make us feel it will go well."

"I'm sure it will," I said. "The Barcons, Travertine, Wool, you, and I all speak English. Wool speaks Russian and Chinese. The Barcons speak Spanish and Portuguese."

"Marianne knows Quechuan."

"Granite, I don't think we're going to have to speak Quechuan any time soon."

"And she knows French, but Karriaagzh wanted her to stay behind."

I thought, I was sent out because I was man enough to take them. We reached the common waiting room. Everyone except for the Ewits and the present Control Squad was there. I supposed that the Ewits were asleep and that we were keeping Control out of sight, but then I saw that the Control Squad leader Pulse sat with Wool. Pulse was a bear-stock creature as hairy as a Barcon, but smaller and thinner, with honey-colored fur. Me and Wool watched an oscilloscope. I started to groom Granite's feathers, my knees on either side of his hocks.

The oscilloscope line went jagged, spikes off the top and bottom of the screen.

"Now," Wool said.

So fast, too soon. My pulse began racing. Granite looked back over his shoulder at me.

Wool began talking in English and Russian, a steady stream of "Don't worry, *nyet boyatsya*, *horoshee ludee*, we've been waiting for you to make contact with us."

"How do you know English?" an American voice, a man, said. Someone in the background murmured Russian, but the accent seemed wrong.

"We've derived your languages from your television broadcasts."

"Bullshit," the American voice said.

"Please meet us. Let us explain what we represent," Wool said.

We heard some other language murmured—Wool and Travertine stared at each other—not any of their languages? Then the American said, "You've trapped us."

Wool said, "Our net kept you from gating into the Sun."

Travertine's beak opened; his face feathers flared; but he didn't contradict Wool verbally. Wool looked over at Travertine and grimaced.

My fingers mechanically oiled Granite's feathers. His beak was open, tongue moving up and down with his breaths.

"May we bring weapons?"

"Sure," Travertine said. He rolled his head on his neck, eyeballs fixed on the radio, then shuddered. "One of my kind was killed by something that looked like you."

"How . . . yes, you've been watching our television. What do you look like?"

"You should first see us live, so we can move our postures to decrease tensions if necessary, make supplicating noises." Travertine rolled his head again and Wool reached over and touched him. Pulse put his hands in his lap and stared at his fingers as if thinking about weapons.

Wool said, "We can lay an airlock over your hatches, but we'll let you do the maneuvering in."

I heard an Oriental language being spoken, a man, then a woman. The woman spoke in Chinese-accented English, "Can one of you come through first? In just a suit?"

Pulse and Wool looked at each other, then Wool said, "No, it's better if we all meet you. We have representatives from several planets, including a refugee from yours."

My head went back as I heard that—*okay, I'm not going to hide.*

Pulse looked over at another screen and said, "They've sent out a laser pulse, coded, but it's obvious what they're saying."

"Yeah," I said.

Wool said to the humans in their transport, "Do you want to know a little about us before we meet?"

"No," the Chinese woman said. I imagined her as looking somewhat like Yangchenla, small and tough, but with a longer, more delicate face. Despite my fears, my cock stirred slightly in my pants, then I was embarrassed.

"We're turning your transport door toward the airlock," Wool told them, his hands working on the grapplers' controls, his eyes on the overhead screens showing the grapplers from five different angles. The airlock tunnel snaked out from the bottom of the middle screen, then showed on all the screens. Sealant gel oozed around the lock's soft plastic rim, then froze as Wool ran a current through the electromorphic gel.

"Okay, now. Bring weapons if you want," Pulse said, scratching the fur over his eyes. Some shed on his fingers and he stared at the blond fuzz for a second before wiping it away on his seat. To us, in Karst One, he said, "Everyone sit down."

I realized, hearing those words, that I'd begun to think in English. Stress affected me that way.

The first one through was a big American black man, wearing a uniform. Travertine's feathers jerked up, then he looked at me. I didn't say anything. The man said, with the voice we'd heard earlier, "Who speaks English?" He had fewer traces of Black English in his speech than Sam did—none: a pure military accent with a tang of West Virginia.

Travertine said, "Wool and I do. Travertine and Wool are our Federation work names. Red Clay, Tom, of course. And two others, but they're asleep now." Travertine's feathers were standing at right angles to his body, quivering as though a wind ruffled them.

Wool said, also in English, "Relax, Travertine."

"I'm Colonel James Cromwell." He looked at me and asked, "Are you human?"

"Yes, sir."

"Red Clay, Tom? The refugee?"

"Yes, sir. My real name is Tom Gentry, my Federation work name is Red Clay."

"Poor boy, I'd guess. What did they do to get you?"

I fought myself back into Standard English. "They educated me."

Colonel Cromwell said, "Send in Chris."

Chris was the Oriental woman. Then I heard another human come through. Joseph Weiss. Cromwell said, "You shouldn't risk—"

"So you are here," Weiss said to me.

"You've met this man before?" Cromwell said.

"And the bird with all his feathers standing on end, I think."

Travertine jerked them flat and said, "So, Dr. Weiss, you changed your mind."

Cromwell raised one eyebrow, then looked at Wool whose dehaired face showed muscles twitching under his cheekbones. Wool said in Karst One, "Red Clay, secret prior information leaks cause one to forfeit contact shares." The Karst phrasing was more direct, but even more formal.

I said, in English, "I'd feel mean making money off my kind." Accent and rhythms straight from the hills—so dumb-ass a sound brought heat to my face.

Cromwell sat down on one of our chairs and stared us all into silence. Weiss slowly turned red, another display of human vascular lability. "Joseph, you said you discovered how to do this all on your own?" The Colonel wasn't exactly asking. His own brown skin was turning a dark rose. Human facial circulatory systems began to disgust me.

"They tried to . . . yes, I knew I was on the right

track or they wouldn't have shown me it could be done.''

Travertine said, "Will you be all right if I stand? I need to—I think your word for it is *slice* or *mute*, in reference to hawks or falcons shitting." He sounded insane. As he spoke, he rose up slowly. Cromwell smiled, then his eyes lost focus, drifted around in their sockets as if the Colonel was trying to figure out maybe whom to arrest. I watched Travertine walk stiffly out of the room. Granite stayed seated.

Wool said, "So, Dr. Weiss, you've already met Travertine and Tom Gentry. Let me introduce you to Granite Grit and Pulse. Tom, what is a Colonel?"

"Lieutenant Colonel, actually," Cromwell said. He suddenly seemed more nervous than he had when he first came in. Weiss began walking around looking at things, his face drooping, his shoulders hunched. He sighed from time to time.

"He's a military leader, more than of a squad, not quite of an Institute," I said.

"We need to make this contact official," Wool said. "Can you help us?"

"Who is this 'we'?" Cromwell said.

"A multi-species Federation of one hundred thirty-four species," Wool said. Travertine came back in now, eyes looking a bit glazed.

"No shit," Cromwell said. "Who's your ranking officer here?"

"I am," Wool said, "but we could also translate what we are as officiators, facilitators."

Pulse asked Wool to translate, then cupped his hand and gestured yes. Cromwell looked from Weiss to Granite to Travertine, then said, "How is this arranged?"

Wool smiled, an expression not natural to his face muscles, which seemed to slip out of place, tendons not grounded on the same bone points. "I leave it to your judgment, but normally, we invite a team of your people here to learn our trade language.''

I said, ''We don't force contact, but if you don't join the Federation, we bar certain gate geometries. It's like a trading union.''

Travertine said in Karst One, ''Why don't you tell them we'll protect them from the Sharwani?''

Wool's features collapsed into one of his true expressions, nostrils flared and tongue slightly protruding. Granite's feathers stirred on his head. Now wasn't the time to threaten my conspecifics with Sharwani. Also, a quick description would sound too melodramatic.

Colonel Cromwell began laughing. The Barcons looked in quickly, and he stopped and said, ''You have more aboard here than you've introduced.''

''They're Barcons,'' I said. ''They look somewhat like black people when they're de-haired.''

Cromwell said, ''You've got to be kidding.''

S'wam said, ''If you aren't in hysterics, Lieutenant Colonel Cromwell, then you don't need us.''

Weiss said, ''I know enough about linguistics not to buy that 'learned your languages from television' line.''

The Barcon who called herself Jackie said, ''Tibetan was the Rosetta stone.''

''Most of the humans we know are descended from Tibetans,'' Wool said.

The Chinese woman smiled. Cromwell looked at her, his trained left eyebrow jerking but not going up in the fine disdainful arch it was educated to make.

Weiss said, ''Tibetans don't call themselves that. And how did they manage in an alien culture?''

Before I could answer, Wool said, ''Some of them are in the Federation Academy now; one is in the Institute of Linguistics; another, I suspect, will be drafted into the Institute of Physics. Others are Free Traders, still others live in ways only half-modified from the life they lived in the Himalayas.''

Cromwell said something in Chinese to the woman.

Wool said something in Chinese himself and explained in English, "Chinese was one of the first non-Tibetan languages we learned."

"We'd like to go back," Cromwell said.

"Why don't you stay?" Wool said. "You're so calm for a human."

"Joe knew you. It makes you seem safer." Cromwell stopped talking as if thinking out more fully the implications of aliens who went around on Earth. "Can we go?"

"Bring everyone in here and wait for an answer to your message. Send more messages. We have plenty of room here. Tom can show you around," Wool said.

"I . . ."

"We can bring in other humans," Travertine said. "The Tibetans are very nice now."

Cromwell shrugged and sat down.

Pulse said, "Of course, if you think you're being held against your will, we would prefer that you leave."

Weiss asked, "Tom, how are your Berkeley wife and little boy?"

I started, not thinking about Marianne just then, and especially not about Karl. "They're fine. Karl's in a multi-species play group."

Cromwell said, "Multi-species play group?"

I shrugged, suddenly aware of how different all my life among the non-humans had been compared to the imaginings about it in human fiction. Yuppie aliens, the feel of a very civilized zoo where we were, as Tesseract tried to explain, each other's keepers. *Am I . . . was I a bad keeper for my brother?* "I have a lot to explain."

Cromwell stared at me a long minute and then said, "I can imagine you must."

My mental concepts clashed—I was Federation, I was human. I was with these people—no, with these others. My body trembled slightly, then I sat down.

"We'll stay," Cromwell said, "if you have room for five more."

Pulse said in Karst One, "I could gate my people out."

Cromwell rubbed his thighs through his uniform and said, "Who'll outnumber who?"

"You will. It's your solar system," Wool said. "You could kill us all and we'd just block you from the established geometries, no more."

"But we'd be out here always," Granite said.

Cromwell said, "We need to send messages."

Wool said, "We can give you a message pod and put it down at the White House, Peking, wherever."

Travertine said in Karst One, "They get suspicious if you try too hard to put them at their ease."

"Oh, Travertine," I said in English, but Cromwell looked like he was indeed becoming more suspicious.

Weiss said, "If they wanted to have stopped us, they would have done something to mislead me."

Chris—how did a Chinese woman get that name?—said, "Gentry, who would have smuggled data to Beijing?" Weiss seemed surprised; I suspected Marianne and Trung, Yangchenla's uncle, but didn't say anything.

"Weiss would have discovered everything independently," Travertine said. "Even Carstairs could have, but he thought Alex knew and kept waiting for answers."

Wool found a message pod. "We can settle all the complexities later," he said. "Now, Lieutenant Colonel Cromwell, you might send whatever message you want."

"I won't know for hours if it arrived."

"We could gate it back. We won't decode it."

Cromwell began to write. Pulse went out then, and the station lights dimmed as the gates drew current to send the Control Squad away. "Bringing in reinforcement?" Cromwell asked, looking up, his skin darker than it had been, slick with sweat, as if describing the situation in writing made the situation more dramatic than when he first saw us.

"No, sending them away," Wool said.

"How many planets again?" Cromwell put his pen down and looked up at Wool when he said that.

"One hundred thirty-four."

"How many didn't join the Federation when you contacted them?"

"About seventeen, and some of those may yet. We're in unofficial contact with about five of them," Wool said.

Cromwell shook his writing hand and clenched and unclenched the fingers, then picked up his pen and wrote more. Then he asked, "Gentry, what is your social security number?"

I felt as if he'd hit me in the stomach.

"You weren't spirited away as a baby," he said. "Or *are* you human?"

I didn't feel human; I felt *too* human. "Sir, I . . . my social security number is . . ." The false one from Berkeley? The real number from Virginia, on my driver's license? I gave him the real one and said, "I was on probation when the Federation found me."

"On probation from what?" Cromwell said.

"Drug charges. I was helping my brother."

"Is he on Earth?"

"No, sir, he's dead. Suicide. We tried to help him." My lips felt stiff.

Cromwell jotted down my social security number and wrote a bit more. Then he held the paper out to me and said, "I'd prefer to take your prints on glass or plastic, but this will have to do."

Wool said, "I'll get you plastic, Colonel, and he's a secretor, so a saliva sample—"

"Prints will do."

I felt . . . not quite betrayed. Isolated. Wool got out the plastic sheet, holding it with a piece of cloth. He handed it to Cromwell, who put his own prints on it and then beckoned me over. I laid my hand on the plastic as if it were a biologic lock, but this print could lock me in, not open doors and computer systems for me.

Cromwell put his report and the plastic in the message pod and asked me, "How old were you?"

"Seventeen. They tried me as an adult."

He looked away, then back at me, and said, "Why?"

Travertine said, "Normally, if a man skips probation and stays out of trouble for three years, the Commonwealth of Virginia drops his case."

Cromwell and I looked at each other and smiled faintly. Didn't Travertine know mine wasn't a normal case? "Do you have other family?" Cromwell asked me.

"Scattered," I said. "Parents died when I was thirteen. Car wreck. My brother raised me, except for a while when he was at the Veteran's right after my folks died." I wondered if he'd see me as poor white trash then.

Cromwell said, "I grew up in Vermont, small town. My parents moved there as kids in the fifties. My father was a pharmacist. Does it bother you that black men could be pharmacists and colonels?"

"No." His people had done better than mine. "Where were your people from originally?"

"Near Spartanburg, South Carolina. Grandfather worked in the Norfolk shipyards, commuted from South Carolina to save money, then bought a metalworking shop in Vermont. 'Got clean away,' he used to tell me."

"That's what I tried to do," I said, but an accident, more than my ambitions, had gotten me to Karst.

"He wanted to see his children just be people," Cromwell said.

"My ex-brother-in-law is like that, too," I said. "Now he's married to a Tibetan woman on Karst and plays human music for aliens. He was black, too. Is black, but on Karst, that's just a skin color."

Cromwell's right eyebrow arched and his face muscles stiffened. He said, "Will you submit to a debriefing?"

Wool said, "He will. We brought him here to give him to you."

I said, "I need to get away now," and, to my embarrassment, stumbled when I'd gotten halfway to the door. No one followed me, which made me feel worse alone. I put on the hologram of New York City and wondered why Granite didn't come in to check up on me.

He didn't. I felt not quite human, not quite not human. Jackie the Barcon finally came in and asked, "Maybe some sedation?"

"Sure," I said.

"Don't be bitter," she said, injecting me at the same time. "We could be surrendered, too, and it will be much more difficult for us if your humans aren't understanding."

"They aren't *my* humans," I said.

"Your genotype tells lies, then," she said, watching my eyelids grow heavy.

"What should I tell them?"

"Be honest always," she said. "You're not trained to lie successfully."

The drug pulled down my eyelids. I dreamed of Karriaagzh and Black Amber arguing over me, scenes in white rooms with views that shifted between Black Amber's beach and a spruce-analog forest.

= 9 =

Humans spoke out beyond my door. I woke up. As I was pulling on my uniform pants, Jackie came in and said, "Fifty-three humans—Marines and linguists— arrived last night."

When I saw the five young Marines pulling the toilet basins up and down, my first thought was that their uniforms were much spiffier than ours. But had I ever been so gawky? Jackie wiggled her nose and said to one, "You wish to guard him."

"Yes, sir," the lieutenant, a beefy redhead, said. I tried to remember how Marine rank went—what was a lieutenant? Why was a lieutenant here?

"Am I leaving soon?" I said.

"Yes," the lieutenant said.

"I'd like to say good-bye to my friends."

The lieutenant's face went rigid. Jackie said, "Granite Grit is this way," and led us through another station door as if the lieutenant had agreed.

I stopped in the doorway, watching. Granite seemed

unperturbed, teaching four linguists the rudiments of Karst One, screens and terminals scattered around the various knees, elbows, and hocks as they sprawled on the floor between two holowalls of alien steppe, a loop with Granite's kind fighting in the foreground.

"Granite," I said in Karst One, "I'm leaving soon. Tell Marianne I'll miss her."

"Tom," he said, "will they want you to tell them your whole life?"

"Probably. Take care. We're xenoflipflops."

"You exaggerate. These people are very interested." In Karst One, *interest* as a verb had strong overtones of involvement, emotional attachment—more so than English. I hoped the humans would become even more interested.

We went on. In a large room that hadn't been used until now, smelling vaguely of ozone and stale grease, Travertine and Wool answered questions in English and Chinese. A Russian sat in the back talking into a small recorder. He looked back at me and scowled as if I should have discovered Russians in space, not Tibetans.

Colonel Cromwell called over the loudspeaker, "Tom Gentry, report to the transporter room." I guessed that he meant the gate room. "Good-bye, Wool, Travertine," I called out in English.

One of the Marines touched my elbow. I said, "I'm coming."

They boxed me in as if I planned to run out into vacuum, but needed Jackie and me to show them where to go.

"We've loaned them a larger transport," Jackie said in Karst One when we all got in the gate room. The transport waiting for us looked like a thirty-foot-long blue egg with white wingbolts outlining the hatch edges. The wings on the bolts were outscale, too, maybe a foot across, two inches thick, slightly ablated from transgeometry wrack.

"Talk English," the red-haired Marine said.

"She said the Federation loaned you the transport pod."

"We're cooperating," Jackie said. "Tom will cooperate. We call him Red Clay, so if someone refers to him by that, we're being formal." She put her fingers over her nose. Were we making her hysterical? She'd lost it once when challenged by Alameda County racists.

"Don't worry about me, Red Clay," she said.

"Stuck inside of human space," the lieutenant said, almost as if he were quoting something, "with the human blues again." Misquoting Bob Dylan?

Colonel Cromwell came in then and looked at the transport's hatch. The Marines saluted him, and he looked up and saluted them back, sloppily with the thumb wiggling. He said to the gate technician, one of the small bears, as if the bear understood English, "You can't put them down underwater?"

Jackie translated from English to Karst One, listened to the bear, then translated back, "The mathematics of water are more fractal than the mathematics of air, just as atmosphere is more complex than low-hydrogen-count space. We're surrendering to you our facilities in Berkeley so you'll arrive there first."

I feared I'd be moved to an underwater station for years of debriefing, a second-to-second replay of my past life. I'd go crazy.

Cromwell said, "If we move him underwater, you can't track him."

"We can track him through his skull computer, but I'll turn it off for you," Jackie said. "Come here, Tom." She held out one of the skull-form plates and a jar of conducting grease.

"Can we take it out?" Cromwell said.

"It's major surgery, and do you have a replacement temporal skull plate ready?"

"No." He didn't sound happy about trusting her to turn my computer off.

I went up to her and leaned my head to the right while she smeared on the grease and laid the plate over the bone. I wasn't aware that anything happened, but I couldn't check unless someone spoke to me in Karst Two. I asked, "Are we leaving now?"

"Yes," Cromwell said. "Dr. Weiss and Academician Wu are staying."

"Is she American Chinese?"

"No, Chinese Christian." Cromwell didn't seem to want to say more. I opened the wing bolts on the transport and opened the hatch. Fresh sealant gleamed on the hatch rim.

"Joint Chinese-American experiments," the Marine said, his back stiff.

"Let's load up," Colonel Cromwell said. Even though the hatch was large enough to walk through erect, I ducked my head as I left. The Marine and Jackie talked briefly, not so loud that I could make out the words, then he came in tailing his squad and dogged down the internal bolts. My job, normally, I thought. In three and a half minutes the transport lurched into Berkeley.

When the Marines opened the hatch, I saw the FBI agent Peter Friese, his hair greying but his shoes just as polished as when he'd come in with another agent to talk to me in Berkeley nine years earlier. He held his computerized attaché case, and his suit jacket swung back enough to expose his handgun.

"We've arrested Alex," he said.

"Did the Federation tell you about him?"

"Were they planning on telling us they'd infiltrated the Berkeley physics department, now, Tom?"

"Yes. How did you find out if they didn't tell you?" I felt very off-balance, flustered, precisely the way Friese wanted me to feel.

"I've been watching him for years. I knew he was some kind of illegal."

I looked at Friese more closely. He looked to be about

fifty. All these years, he'd stayed in Berkeley, never promoted beyond field agent. He'd spotted a real alien, maybe always knew what he'd uncovered, but couldn't speak for fear of being branded crazy. I said, "How's Alex taking it?"

"He's talking a lot," Friese said. I smiled, familiar with this routine from my first bust. Friese frowned and said, "We're taking suicide precautions."

Like a jab to my guts. Cromwell and the Marine lieutenant both looked at me, then at Friese. I said, "He likes humans. He'd always defend them to me."

"Then you aren't human either," Friese said.

"No, I am."

"We'll run DNA checks," Friese said. "That's what we did to Alex. What is his real name?"

I said, "I just knew, know him as Alex." Let's not speak of him in the past tense, I told myself. Then I realized why Friese wanted Alex's real name—I was slow picking that up. I was glad I didn't give Friese this little verbal lever against Alex, but then the Federation was going to turn him over to the human authorities, abandon him to us. "We thought he was turning native."

"And what the fuck did you turn?" Friese asked. He opened his briefcase and faxed my prints out, then said, "Load him, gentlemen." He pulled out the phone jack cable and the attaché case snapped shut.

We walked out of the warehouse in Berkeley, again. The fog obscured the details: trolleys and buses going by with their headlights on, dusk. A grey stretch limo, windows like mirrors, with three different antennas over the trunk, waited at the curb. Friese opened the door and I saw that the same mirror windows blocked off the driver from the passenger compartment, which was huge, big enough for nine sitting on three bench seats in a U around a table. Behind those seats were a bar and a jump seat for the bartender. This was the automotive equivalent of Air Force One.

"Looks like a dealer's car, doesn't it?" Friese said as two Marines got in first, securing the limo's perimeters.

He'd been briefed about Warren. I said, "Warren never had a car like this and he was the only man I knew for a fact was a dealer." I got in, feeling his hand almost touch my head in that cop 'duck the suspect's head' gesture.

Cromwell got in after us. He said to Friese, "Tom was told by his people to cooperate."

Friese said, "They've had us infiltrated for years."

I said, "Spoken like a man who now knows he wasn't crazy."

"Shut up," Friese said.

"Come on, you've been vindicated. You've got an alien anthropologist to torture."

Cromwell said, as we pulled onto an expressway, "Tom, you will have to tell us about Alex."

And the Sharwani, I thought. I was no longer afraid of being shot, but of being interrogated for years, inquisitors probing every detail of my life twice, three times, double- and triple-checking inconsistencies, lapses of memory, the lies I desperately wanted to tell. "Will you let me write my wife?"

"She's a third-generation leftist," Friese said. "And she's a linguist."

I wasn't sure what being a linguist had to do with anything until I realized Marianne's skills could be used for form codes, artificial languages. I wished that we had made up our private language now, that we were together talking in it, away from these people. "I've got a son, Karl David. He's eight."

"What happened to the black musician?" Friese looked at Cromwell and smiled.

"Sapients love human music. He likes playing strictly human music without it being culturally black or white. He left Molly and married a woman named Yangchenla."

"One of the Tibetans," Cromwell said, clarifying things for Friese.

"The Chinese must be thrilled."

Cromwell said, "About as thrilled, Friese, as we'd be if we'd found a bunch of Sea Island blacks out there." Cromwell didn't sound like he thought much of primitives, even of his own race. I was a little shocked, then remembered how the Tibetans had embarrassed me when Black Amber first exposed me to them.

I said, "A village helped a Federation crew once. The language they speak now is about as much Tibetan as French is Latin. Marianne recognized elements of a Buddhist trade language in what they speak. They weren't that isolated or primitive even back five hundred years ago."

Cromwell said, "But the Russians are wishing they had taken Tibet back in the nineteenth century."

I lost interest in their speculations and began worrying about myself as we crossed the Golden Gate Bridge and headed up to Tiburon.

Friese pulled out a black cloth bag from his attaché case and pulled it over my head. Cromwell said, "Hey," but I suspected he was playing the good cop as the bag stayed on until I was loaded in what for a moment I feared was a submarine. But the thing went up and not down.

We flew hours and hours. I remembered the drill for stopping body trembles—pull against yourself. What stance was I supposed to take? Jackie had told me not to lie. Would it be a lie to conceal a hatred of their cop attitudes and suspicions, their xenophobia? Marianne, I thought, would know better how to handle this, more diplomatic with her own kind, my own kind.

And would the cadets I'd been working with miss me?

"Take the hood off his head and let him read something," Cromwell said. "It's a long flight."

Someone slid the hood off without taking any of my

head hair with it. I shook my hair back and watched Friese fold the hood up neatly and put it back in his attaché case.

I expected that the plane wouldn't have windows, but it did. Below us was a dark blank plain with a few lights, the glitter of car lights on trailers. We were flying low, twisting.

"Thanks," I said.

Cromwell offered me a cigarette, but I didn't smoke. One of the Marines came by with canned soft drinks and I took a Dr. Pepper. Funny, after so many years to be drinking a Dr. Pepper. I tried to remember whether I'd been able to buy them in Berkeley. Cromwell said, "We've got magazines."

I almost said, *we get some of them on Karst*, but didn't think mentioning that would be appropriate now.

Clumps of lights passed underneath like the star clusters around Karst in reverse, grounded, not in the sky. Then as we flew into the dawn, I saw a pale, looser cluster behind the Appalachians. The plane turned downward toward a lake.

Friese said, "Weiss said lakes would work almost as well as oceans."

Reality is a set of wave functions with liquid and solid matter being simply more complex vibrations, brains being more complex vibrations cutting reality into standing waves. Yeah, none of this seemed quite real. My body buzzed as if I'd been doing drugs. I said, "Where are we?"

Cromwell said, "Oh, Tom, you aren't supposed to know that." He sounded terribly tired himself.

The pontoons hit the water. Friese pulled the hood out of his attaché case again.

I said, "I was told not to lie."

The Colonel and the FBI man looked at each other and shrugged. Friese folded up the hood and put it away again.

I asked, "Have you announced that we're out there?"

"Not yet," Cromwell said. "We don't want to panic the civilian population."

I could identify with that, not trusting general humans myself.

"Alex's friends organized a defense committee," Friese said. "They want to know what the charges are."

Cromwell looked surprised. Somehow I knew in Berkeley Alex must have been able to find other than Carstairs to confide in, humans who'd accept him for himself.

Friese said, "Tom doesn't seem surprised by that."

I said, "Alex is unorthodox for an Ahram."

"Ahram, Ahram. He never told us what he was. Does he really look like that?"

I hesitated, then remembered I wasn't supposed to lie, and fuck Alex anyway. "He had his skull crest surgically removed, but otherwise that's what he looks like."

"Skull crest?" Cromwell said.

"Their women like them, so it's a secondary sexual characteristic that's been bred for."

"Do they . . . does it . . . ?" Cromwell saw the Marines beginning to giggle and stopped.

I said, "The tissue—skin and muscles—over the crest bone is highly innervated and vascular."

"So you don't like Alex or us," Friese said.

Oh? I shut up. The plane taxied up to a covered dock where another grey stretch limo waited under the roof, surrounded by people with military stances dressed in civilian clothes. I got out and walked toward the car. It had South Carolina plates and a Charleston sticker, but we weren't near the ocean.

"Don't get in that one," Friese said. "The one behind it."

The muddy plates made the green sedan look like a drug dealer's contact junker, but then I realized it was

a Mercedes electric. The roof kept anyone above us
from seeing which car I got into.

As we pulled out, the windows went opaque on the
inside. The driver watched an instrument panel.

"Do you have cars like this on Karst?" Friese asked.

"We have some automatic lanes," I said. I wondered
if they'd shift interrogators on me or if we'd all sleep
for a while next. "Most sapients get bored if the driving
is always done for them."

They didn't say anything. We drove for miles, then
stopped. When I got out of the car, my legs were stiff
and it was completely light outside, traffic noise in the
air—rush hour, about eight-thirty, I guessed. But I
couldn't see anything except tree tips beyond a high
brick fence around three acres of front yard that sloped
up to the fence. In Virginia, the builders would have
put the huge house on the rise—here it was hidden by
a small pond. The house wasn't as huge as a high-class
Yauntry hunting lodge, but it was big compared to most
human houses I'd seen—about three stories, a copper
mansard roof, brick with stone framing the windows.

"The CIA wanted to take you to northern Virginia,"
Friese said, "but no, we had this here and it's surrounded by our kind of people."

The man who came out of the house wore a tweed
country suit like the English advertise in *Country Life*.
He had blond hair, blue eyes, and a long nose. I hated
him instantly, a gut reaction. I remembered a black kid
I knew in high school using *long nose* to mean *white*.
Now I was seeing the ultimate long nose, a true WASP,
one of the right Tidewater people, not one of my kind
of Celtic-Cherokee mountain hybrids. Time to find the
war clubs, time to go on a cattle raid, hide the women.
A monster with eyes that sky shone through was invad-
ing.

He kept coming up to me, inside my personal space,
then just looked at me and stepped back. "Why did

they take you?'' he said. Precisely a Tidewater person—
how astute of them to turn me over to one of those.

"I tried to help one of theirs who was stranded."

"Tried?"

"My brother shot him."

"And you took your brother away to an alien jail?"

"No, we tried to help Warren."

"Tried, again."

"Warren, he killed himself. Nothing in the Universe
could get him off drugs."

The man's thin lips moved into a slight smile. "I
believe you mean that literally."

I shrugged, a human imitation of an alien imitating
my wife's natural shrug.

"I'm James Angleton."

I recognized an old CIA name, obviously now a work
name, and wanted to say, *and you can call me Red
Clay*, but said, "I'm Tom Gentry. I was told to be completely candid with human authorities. I'm a contact
officiator with the Federation of Sapient Planets."

Federation of Sapient Planets sounds better in Karst
languages. In English, the phrase made us all smile. I
felt a little less like a criminal they'd caught.

"And have you officiated for the Federation before?"
Angleton said. "Done it, not just tried."

"Yes," I said. "And one species I helped bring into
the Federation was initially quite hostile." I realized
the implications of what I'd said when I saw Angleton's
thin lips twist slightly, then go rigid. *Yeah, we think
humans are potentially hostile.* "We humans have an
odd reputation in the Federation." *Yeah, I killed another sapient in what I thought was self-defense and was
sent to you for doing it.*

Angleton's head bobbed slightly as if I'd surprised
him with my quick read of his tiny lip flourish. He said,
"And you're bitter over that, yourself." Both of us, I
expected, would strain our face muscles over this interrogation, overriding our natural expressions.

Friese stayed in the car. Cromwell and the Marines got out and began walking toward the house with us. When we were about ten feet from the front door, an Air Force lieutenant and three enlisted men came out of the shrubbery and saluted Cromwell.

I asked, "Is Friese coming back?"

"Yes, but later." Angleton smiled. A stocky man with slightly Asian eyes opened the door as if he'd been watching through a hidden camera. He wore a black suit with long white shirt cuffs showing, and cufflinks. He and Angleton bent toward each other slightly. "This is Codresque," Angleton said. "Show Tom Gentry to his room, Codresque."

Pages of etiquette books flashed before my mind's eye, the human manners Black Amber had forced me to study along with deconstruction and Claude Lévi-Strauss. The books told me that I was introduced this way to servants, but Codresque didn't seem quite like a servant, grey around the temples, face crinkled in a smile, eyes like black beads.

As I followed Codresque through the entry hall, by a staircase all fluted wood and figured carpet, to an elevator, I remembered an anecdote of the American student sent home from the French aristocratic family for not knowing his forks and being too gauche to hide his lack of their kind of polish. Manners in humans cut as well as joined.

When we got in the elevator, Codresque said, "Three." The doors closed and we went up. He added, without my asking, "The elevator only knows my voice."

The upstairs was shabby compared to what I'd seen of the downstairs. He showed me to a small bedroom with thick drapes hanging over the windows. I remembered Karriaagzh checking the windows of his room on Yauntry, when we'd been negotiating with them, and suspected that here, too, the windows were barred, but I wasn't going to look with Codresque watching.

"The aliens sent your measurements. We'll provide your clothes," Codresque said. "I'll bring them up in the morning."

"I need a business suit and a dinner suit if we're going to have any formal meetings," I said, having wondered where my luggage was. "Or I can wear my Federation uniform."

"That?" Codresque said in such a tone that I wasn't sure what his implications were.

"It is a true uniform because it makes all of us more uniform, covers the body shape, the major joints. I have a decorations sash that goes with it for formal occasions."

"Yes, Mr. Gentry, I suspected as much. They sent the sash with your extra tunics and pants." He left, locking my door. I went to the drapes and began to lift them, but not enough to see if the windows were barred or screened. I didn't want to know. I wished Marianne and Karl were with me.

Codresque came back, a nightshirt folded over his left arm. "Here's a sleeping shirt. You will give me that uniform to be cleaned and pressed." He sure wasn't sounding like a servant now. I realized this was a modified skin search, not the strip, lift and spread of jail, but just a little check to see if I'd brought any medium-size weapons. I unbelted the tunic, pulled it off over my head, took off my shoes and socks, then unzipped the fly and pulled the pants off. Codresque turned the pants inside out and said, "The pants are European."

I said, "American. The Federation lets us tailor species cuts around the genitals if we want. The tunic covers that."

"Europeans invented the trousers," Codresque said. I stopped undressing and stood in my briefs, which I'd picked up in Boston last time I'd been on Earth. Codresque stretched out his hand and flicked his fingers back against his palm.

I took off the briefs and said, "Most of us don't really want to see each other's naked alien bodies."

He sighed and handed me the nightshirt. It was like a hospital gown—only to the knees—except that it buttoned down the front. I said, "I'll need a shaving kit in the morning."

"Certainly, Mr. Gentry." He left and locked me in. I opened one of the other doors and saw the toilet with a washbowl standing beside it. The third door was to a closet full of empty wooden hangers. I pulled one off the rod and hefted it in my hand. It might make a weapon against one man. I sighed at myself and put it back.

Who was I here? The teenage criminal assistant dope manufacturer? A decultured human? I closed the closet door and went back to see if the debriefing team had left me anything to read.

Nothing. I sat in a chair by the bed, wondering who I was, and then realized what Karst had made of me: a person who knew the right English, exercised to the physical grace we tended to see more in other species than ourselves. Black Amber said once that grace in a creature worked almost as well as manners. My adult life was formed by Karst, not Camp 28.

A substandard-dialect thought slid into my head: *Yeah, Tom, tell it like you wanna.*

Don't, I said to that thought. I am a contact officiator. Karst made me—not Karst, the Federation made me come here.

I pulled back the sheets and lay down. My last conscious thought was that I should get up and turn out the light, then I dreamed confusing dreams about Marianne and Karl David, Alex accusing me of something.

In the morning I woke up when Codresque brought in an electric razor and breakfast—covered dishes on a tray. As I shaved, he went out for my suit and briefs.

"Thank you," I said when he returned.

"We heat the plates, so it should stay warm," he said.

Right, very proper way to serve food. One book recommended using a microwave. I nodded as if we'd done that all my life in Floyd, then felt ridiculous, but then how would it sound to say, *we have studied your human customs in deacquisitioned library books*?

Codresque smiled. I turned around to pull on the briefs he'd given me and then dressed as if foreigners brought me my clothes every morning. "When will you call me for the interrogation?"

He stopped smiling and said, "At any time."

I sat down and looked at what they'd put on the tray. Eggs, grits, biscuits, coffee—a comment of sorts. I said, "I guess it might be a while before I have *villag* for first meal again."

He nodded as though he knew precisely how Yauntry pseudo-bean jelly tasted and left. I wondered if I was reading too much into the breakfast menu and felt vaguely bad mannered.

After breakfast, no one came for the dishes for what seemed like hours. I finally tried my door to see if it had been locked. Either the knob stuck and then turned, or someone, watching me through a camera I hadn't bothered to look for, unlocked the door as I turned the knob. The door opened, and I walked out onto the landing.

I felt acutely watched and went down the stairs, trying not to act sneaky or hesitant.

Codresque met me at the second-floor landing and said, "There's a bell button in your room."

I said, "I'd like something to read if Mr. Angleton isn't ready to talk to me yet."

"Perhaps you'd like to walk in the garden?"

"No, I'd rather read. I'm still tired from the trip."

Angleton came up to us now, dressed in white shorts and a white knit shirt without any brand insignia on it. "Tennis, anyone?" He said it as if asking was a joke.

I wondered if I wasn't feeling more stiff than tired. "Could you teach me?"

"Humans don't play tennis on Karst?"

"No, James, we play chess and ride racing bicycles."

"Well, let me hit a few balls against the machine, then I'll see."

Codresque said, "He also wants to read."

"Let him have the *New York Times*."

I saw the guards disguised as gardeners moving through the foundation bushes. Codresque, for an instant not at all a servant, smiled at me and went to the foyer. He came back with a small computer screen on a tray and said, "You'd be more comfortable upstairs. I'll bring your tennis things when you've read enough of the *Times*."

Hypertext *New York Times*—I wondered if the UCal Libraries were now on computer this way as I went through all the conflicts involving more than two people, then through the physics news, then through aliens. Not a byte on me—my body more than my brain reacted first, coiling up the belly muscles, running an adrenaline test on the nerves and blood vessels. My mind cycled and recycled—the body's fight or flight proposition was useless.

When Codresque brought me tennis clothes, he asked, "Read enough?"

"So, nobody except the government knows I'm here."

"Perhaps that isn't all of the *New York Times*."

"Are you afraid the general population would panic? That's one reason Karst didn't want to make contact earlier—all the xenophobia movies about alien invaders."

"We did make *The Day the Earth Stood Still*."

I laughed, remembering the Barcons laughing when I proposed that very movie as a defense of human attitudes about aliens. "People out there aren't gods or invaders. And you're not just a servant."

"We are all servants here," Codresque said. His fleshy eyelids hooded his eyes and his lips pulled in, coarse skin around them shifting. I wondered if his stocky body was more muscle than fat. He was shorter than me.

I bobbed my head slightly. Codresque left me then. I dressed and went downstairs. One of the guards, dressed in a white tunic, was dusting. He looked up and said, "I'll take you out to the tennis court."

"Thanks," I said and followed him through the kitchen, which was huge and a bit shabby, paint flaking off the upper cabinets.

"You're going to learn an odd game," Angleton said when he saw us. "The court is clay." He held two rackets in his left hand and balls in his right.

I vaguely remembered having seen asphalt courts and shrugged as if I didn't care. I'd probably never play tennis again. As we walked out, he handed me one of the rackets, handle damp from his sweat. I remembered exercise bars in the Karst gym clammy with cold alien sweat. Somehow, feeling Angleton's sweat on the leather grip made him more a fellow creature to me. I said, "We play with Frisbees and other flying discs on Karst. That's probably the nearest I've come to this."

"Frisbees?"

"The Gwyngs copied them or had something similar."

He adjusted my thumb on the grip and said, "Well, you don't grab; you hit."

"I've seen it on television," I said, "when we were observing."

"Did you like our television?"

"It's gotten better." We were at the court now and I saw the artificial playing machine, white enameled metal the size of a freezer. Arrays of photoelectric cells and sensors glittered as it rolled forward and then backed up to the baseline, squatting on smooth plastic tracks and multi-directional roller balls.

"When are you going to begin debriefing me?" I asked.

"Gee, I don't know," Angleton said as though I was rude to ask. He threw a ball up in the air and hit it. The machine on the other side of the net scooted up, inhaled the ball and blew it back toward us.

I watched carefully to see exactly how Angleton hit the ball, then swung my racket to see how it felt. Okay. Angleton handed me three balls and said, "Serve them. Toss them up and hit them over the net. Keep your wrist bent like this."

First racing bikes, now this. I missed the first ball, hit the second, but out of the court, then got the third one just right. The machine hurled it back to me before I could think. I slashed out and the ball slewed off to the side.

"You want the racket at right angles to ball travel," Angleton said.

So I was a klutz with the racket. I was faster on my feet than Angleton expected.

"You move well," he said after I rushed the net and lobbed one over and straight down into the machine's ball intake, then rushed backwards, jumped and connected, but failed to get the ball in the court.

"It comes from playing at Tenleaving," I said.

"I'm not debriefing you. I'll rally with you a bit." Angleton went to the machine and switched something. It rolled back, then around to the net, stopping and shifting arrays so that it had clear views of both the near and far lines.

We hit the ball back and forth, first with lots of misses on my part, then I began to get better, and this made Angleton seem less intimidating. I realized then that he had been intimidating me.

"Um," he said, "better not do too much of this the first day. You'll be sore."

"Could we go out? I haven't seen a shopping center since Boston."

"Not yet," he said. He put the head of his racket in a cover and zipped it up. "Why you?"

"You mean why did they take me to educate?" He nodded. I said, "They knew that nobody would miss me. Mica, the Gwyng who was stranded here, wrote a good report on me. I wasn't a xenophobe compared to other humans, I suppose."

"Was he really stranded?"

"Two others died. Gwyngs don't set out to die even when they try to be braver than anyone else."

He came over and took my racket and zipped a cover on it, too, sighing as he did. I said, "I'm sorry if you got the wrong impression about the Federation because of what I did as a teenager. I was trying to help Mica."

"You continued to work for your brother after he killed the alien, didn't you?"

"You sound like the judge asking me why I didn't turn Warren in. I'm sorry. My first lover said I didn't ask enough questions."

"We will ask enough questions. Your first lover?"

"Yangchenla, a human descended from Tibetan villagers."

Angleton closed his eyes and shook his head. "Your Federation and the trash it picked up."

I said, "Would you have rather they took you?"

"Why did you ask me that?"

"There's an Institute for Analytics and Tactics. I'm not part of that, but you'd get along with them."

"Alex." He didn't say more.

"If we'd wanted to conquer you, we'd have done it decades earlier."

"You are human."

"It's embarrassing sometimes," I said.

He smiled and said, "Perhaps now your Federation is embarrassed by you."

Shit. Trash person, refugee. Angleton had got me. ''I have a wife, a child.''

''The Berkeley radical sisters Schweigman, the oldest a doctoral candidate dropout, the youngest a hippie weaver on foodstamps. Heiresses both, though the great-grandparents were the last in the family to actually work.''

''Maybe we needed another environment?''

His eyes unfocused. He touched his ear and said, ''I've been told to tell you we suspect this is a test—how we handle you. Nice people, your Federation types. Let's go back to the house.''

We started walking. ''There were wars in the past. Some of the Control Barcons wear things like that in their ears.'' I couldn't see any sign of a transmitter plug in his ear, but I recognized the gesture.

When we got inside, Angleton dropped the tennis rackets on the kitchen table and said, ''Go up to your room and shower, then ring for Codresque.''

I felt watched as I took the elevator up. In my room, briefs, a shirt and an Earth-style suit lay across the bed, with shoes and socks on the floor by the nightstand. I showered and dried off, but still felt clammy as I pulled the clothes on. I didn't know if I wanted an undershirt or not. Would the interrogation be under hot lights?

The tie was under the suit. I tried to remember exactly how to tie it—I'd been schooled in this by Tesseract during the Proper English dialect lessons. The first time, it didn't look right. I suspected everyone was behind the mirror laughing at me, but I pulled the knot apart and retied it, getting it done neatly this time.

My kind of aliens, this time. Why hadn't I realized in the past how complicated First Contacts were? How preposterous to expect newly contacted cultures to simply accept the Federation.

You'll be even more useful to the Federation, I told myself, *if the humans don't keep you prisoner.* But maybe the Federation considered me expendable. Alex had told me that he was.

I rang for Codresque, who seemed to have been waiting just outside the door. He nodded, not speaking, and just as silently, I went with him to the elevator, rode down to the first floor and followed him to a room with a huge mahogany table surrounded by office chairs on rolling castors. Under the windows was a sideboard, and the whole wall on the other side of the room was a giant china cupboard with ten cut-glass doors.

Angleton, Friese, and Colonel Cromwell came in, then a young lieutenant pushing a cart with a recording machine, a VCR, and a monitor.

"Have a seat at the end," Angleton said. They all sat at the other end, Angleton facing me. Another man came in, looked sharply at Codresque and sat down. He looked a bit like Codresque, with nearly Asian eyes, but was taller and almost blond. He and Angleton spoke in some foreign language—Russian, I thought—then everyone looked at me.

"I was told to be completely candid."

"Why did you not make contact with officials when you were back on Earth at Berkeley," the Russian said.

"I felt like I'd been abandoned by people here, so my loyalties were to Karst. To the Federation."

"There's a distinction?" Angleton asked.

"Karst is a planet with a multi-species culture that houses the Federation offices."

"To whom are you loyal? Karst or the Federation?"

I hesitated. "Karst, I think, what the different Federation people have made there. Home planet officials can be a bit suspicious, contemptuous. They rotate people out, or have arm's-length relationships with their conspecifics representing them to the Federation."

Cromwell looked down at his finger. Angleton looked over at him and smiled slightly. The Russian said, "We can have an arm's-length relationship with the Federation?"

"M . . . A . . . D," Angleton said, letter by letter. The Russian looked over at him sharply.

I remembered that the letters stood for *Mutually Assured Destruction*. "Not really, but when a species has all the Universe to hide in, attempting to destroy it is dangerous."

"The Chinese expressed some surprise that the Federation adopted Tibetans," Angleton said to the Russian as if that were a private joke.

Cromwell asked, "What do you know about the Institute of Control?"

"Military, but a bit more restrained than human armies," I said. "We think of the Federation as being like a zoo where we're all each other's keepers. Any species who attacks others, we see them as malignant, but innocent."

"So, we are to be put into a zoo," the Russian said.

"Not just that. We'll help keep order, too. The Federation is trying to bring another species to terms. The Sharwani. They try to conquer other species—"

"Isn't that what the Federation does?"

"No. The Federation is of all the species. The Sharwani bomb and kill."

Angleton and the Russian spoke to each other in Russian again, then the Russian said, "We should ask the Sharwani for their side of the story."

"I killed a Sharwani in what I thought was self-defense, justifiable . . ." I couldn't say *homicide*; I felt so awkward. "Part of the punishment was they sent me to you. He led us into an ambush, but . . . that's how the Federation is."

"So they come in sexes out there," the Russian said. "Did you think he'd turned?"

"But I was supposed to try my utmost to control, not kill, even if I wasn't trained precisely in that. He killed a friend of mine, a Gwyng."

"Are there Sharwani who did turn?" Angleton said.

"Yes."

Cromwell asked, "Have you contained them well enough that we wouldn't be buying dangerous enemies in joining your Federation?"

Angleton said, "Tom, I don't believe you know enough to give us an answer to that."

I felt about ant high. "No, I'm not sure I do. I work out trade and training contracts, help cadets, teach some behavior classes. I'm not in Control or the History Committee."

"Can you draw up an organizational chart?"

I smiled, remembering when Rhyodolite and I faked one trying to impress the Yauntries who'd caught us in their space. A fun memory, yeah? Yauntries killed Xenon, Travertine's conspecific. I stopped smiling. "Bring me a big sheet of paper," I said.

"You're just a little bureaucrat," Angleton said.

"My family's well respected on Karst."

"Okay, a middle-management bureaucrat," Angleton said.

Codresque smiled at me as if tipping me off to Angleton's own status. I said, "So you're a high-level interrogator. How's that not a bureaucratic position?"

The Russian said something to Angleton. He sighed and didn't answer me or the Russian. Codresque laid out a piece of posterboard in front of me, then set down a box of pencils and erasers at my right elbow.

Friese was just listening. After I'd worked a while, I looked up and asked, "How's Alex?"

Everyone smiled slightly except for Friese, who said, "He is not cooperating."

"That's not like Alex," I said. "The Barcons observing with him thought he'd gone native."

"Why are all the Federation contacts with such marginal humans?" the Russian asked, then he muttered to himself, *"Konyesno, pochemutoo."*

"Probably because us marginal types are more open to a variety of experiences."

"Marginal types won't automatically go to the authorities," Angleton said. "And won't be missed if they disappear."

I was about to say, *Marginal types don't get believed when they* do *go to the authorities*, but decided that would be a bit too defensive. "Alex had a lot of friends in Berkeley. Not all of them were marginal."

"All of Berkeley is marginal," Angleton said.

"He was missed when he disappeared. You should have picked up a pair of the Barcons."

"He went against your Federation, I think," Angleton said.

Friese said, "He arranged for a lawyer to serve us with a writ of habeas corpus."

I said, "And you can't kill him and turn him over to his friends?"

"You really think we're that cruel and stupid?"

Suddenly, I felt terror at my own situation. Nobody was filing a writ of habeas corpus on me. "What did he do, set up a Free Alex committee to start proceedings if you picked him up?"

They all stopped talking. That's absolutely what Alex did, I thought. Angleton said, "Codresque, would you arrange to bring us lunch?"

I said, "Does the Free Alex committee know he's alien?"

Nobody answered. I remembered my Berkeley wife organizing the humans on Karst. "Why did you admit to having him?"

"He got word out before we realized he was an alien," Friese said. "We thought he was a traitor like you."

I felt scared again, but said, "We're not at war with you. We've invited you to join us."

"You are a human being, a citizen of the United States of America. They are not human beings," the Russian said.

"Some of us are," I said as one of the soldiers put a place setting in front of me. Lots of forks. The multiple fork custom, Black Amber explained, implied that one's taste was so acute that smears of another food would spoil the dish one was eating, so one used a clean fork for each thing. What mattered wasn't the order of the forks, but the use of the fresh one, except for salad and fish forks. I checked again—no fish fork.

We began with an oyster bisque, then the man serving us brought around something deep fried I thought at first was french fried potatoes. Deep-fried eggplant goes weird in a mouth expecting a potato's resistance. The meat was chicken slices covered with a green-onion sauce.

After lunch, we went out into the library and Codresque served us coffee in small cups. Angleton said, "So all Virginians have some sense of manners."

"My sponsor insisted that I learn both proper English and proper manners."

"You have an alien accent," the Russian said.

"The Barcons rebuilt my speech organs so I could speak perfect Karst One."

"Is there snobbery toward those who don't speak perfect Karst One?" Angleton asked.

"The language operations give us the best chance at learning the language. A species that can't learn Karst One even with the language operations isn't considered sapient."

"No sherry, Codresque," Angleton said. "We must get back to work."

"The table is cleared," Codresque said. "I'll bring tea in at four."

We walked back into the debriefing room. My organizational chart was gone. I sat down. Cromwell said, "Perhaps if you began at the beginning."

Two weeks later in a blur of multiple forks, gallons of coffee by the demitasse, and hot tea without sugar, I'd briefly outlined the most significant things that had happened to me.

On the fifteenth day, before the waiter served us

breakfast, Codresque rolled in a cart piled with tissue biopsy trocars in plastic wrap and stainless steel tissue bottles. He stopped in front of me first and said, "Take off your jacket and roll up your sleeve."

I looked at the others at the table. Angleton was sweating slightly and the Russian looked queasy. They want to make sure I'm human, I realized. After I'd gotten the cloth out of the way, Codresque swabbed my forearm with red antiseptic, and stabbed me with the huge needle. He twisted something at the top of the syringe, then pulled out the needle and put a pressure bandage around my forearm. As Codresque put my flesh sample in one of the stainless steel bottles, Angleton took off his jacket and rolled up his sleeve. As Codresque bent over him, I asked, "Who tests you, Codresque?"

"Angleton, if he's still Angleton."

"I could spot even a Barcon reconstruction," I said. The damn trocar hole was a deep ache.

"But would you tell *us*?" Cromwell said. He took off his uniform jacket and rolled his sleeve up, exposing a muscular, light-brown arm. Codresque pulled the second tissue sample needle out of Angleton, then tore the plastic on the set he would use on Cromwell. Cromwell stared at the needle, maybe wondering if we'd done some weird alien hyper-science on him, turned him into an alien without his knowing about it.

"Colonel, don't look at it," the Russian said.

Codresque seemed a bit gentler with Cromwell than he'd been with me, didn't shove the needle in quite so deep. I said, "Friese, maybe you're an alien and don't know it."

Friese said, "I have been tested earlier, and I assure you I am one hundred percent human."

Cromwell said, "Gentry, don't play that game."

"Sorry, but you all seem so paranoid and it's annoying."

Angleton said, "Your Federation, like all large institutions, is amoral and wants most to preserve itself. We need to know how we, perhaps just as amoral, can best fit into it if we do join it.''

"The Federation is more beneficial than not,'' I said.

Angleton said, "You were sent out as bait for the Yauntries.''

"They educated me. Gave me new cognitive maps.'' I began transmuting the conversation into Karst One in my head and realized I'd been thinking in English for the past two weeks.

"I would not be surprised if your DNA didn't test out human,'' the Russian said. "You seem more alien now. Perhaps from being caught by the trocar?''

"I'm thinking in Karst One,'' I said. What did I look like when I thought in Karst One? How many expressions had I, the sapient ape, borrowed from other cultures?

"Talk about your killing of the Sharwani male in Karst One,'' Angleton said. "We'll set up a tape recorder. Colonel Cromwell will continue afternoon interrogations in English. I'll be away for a few days.''

"We are interested in the blockade of Yauntra,'' Cromwell said.

Codresque finished up with the tissue samples. Angleton went out with him.

After several hours of talking in Karst One to a machine, I felt almost as if I were a holographic projection in a feedback loop. During the afternoons of that week, Colonel Cromwell asked me about the Yauntra blockade, about the time between the average first contact and Federation treaty signings.

Then one rainy morning, Colonel Cromwell took me to a back room with a video player and pushed a disc in. It was a Karst semi-illegal xenophobia movie on human media. Digital, not live, because I was the monster, distorted to ten feet high, killing little Travertines.

"Did you know about this?''

"No. They must have done computer transforms of

my image. Karriaagzh acted in live shots when he was younger. See if you can get his xenophobia movie.'' I talked fairly casually, but I was shocked and hurt. At least, the digital maker hadn't done me killing Shar-wani.

''Why is the Federation smuggling these in to Los Angeles?''

''Should you have told me that?''

''Come on, it's on Motorola media.''

''How widely are they distributed?''

He shrugged. ''They haven't broken in over the air with them. What is the point of them?''

''Okay, there are tensions, xenophobia. Xenophobia movies are a way to make fun of them.''

''It's a pretty confrontive way to let us know that humans make them nervous.''

''Isn't it really a funny way?''

''So, who do you think is making these?''

''Xenophobia movies are semi-illegal, so I don't think anyone will confess to it.'' Sam and Yangchenla walked on, digitalized to giantness, and began arguing with me. *Marianne and Yangchenla did this to me*. Sam and Yangchenla helped the olive birds lay a trap for me.

In the end, Sam and Yangchenla tied me up so Travertine could feed me by hand. Sam said in English, ''Not all humans run amok.''

''It's lack of pigment and excess testosterone,'' Yangchenla's image said in English better than she could really speak. ''Sun and maleness drove him insane.''

I said, ''I've been sent a message by an ex-lover.''

Cromwell said, ''At least, they didn't use the black guy as the villain.''

''Most of the Universe is dark skinned.''

Cromwell said, ''White skin is a cold adaptation.''

''Yeah, your folks ran my folks off into the glaciers about forty thousand years ago and we came back really nasty. That's why the Federation doesn't attack people.

They can hide off in the Universe and come back really nasty forty thousand years later.''

''But they're making you out to be the bad guy.''

''Come on, I'm a bit miffed, but don't you think it is funny?''

''It's not funny that someone is smuggling these visi-discs in.''

''Whoever's doing it, it's semi-illegal. The History Committee would frown at this.''

''I can just imagine getting frowned on by a bunch of weird folks.''

''You almost sounded like a Southern black.''

Cromwell shut up and put in a visidisc showing the famous Karriaagzh-beating-Jereks movie. He watched until Karriaagzh crunched a skull in his beak, then stopped the movie and said, ''It's chaotic out there, isn't it? No discipline in your Federation. Anything can happen, regardless of what you promise.''

I said, ''That's the Universe. Nobody can comprehend it all. Some of us don't understand others of us bare minded.''

Cromwell started the flick again and watched until Karriaagzh burned at the end. ''How did they do that?''

''The flames were alcohol and they used flame retardant on the feathers, too. Karriaagzh is an incredible guy.''

''This wasn't a computer image?''

''I heard he did it live. The birds are less species-bound than us others. I don't think he ever understands xenophobia. It's just cruelty as far as he's concerned.''

''Are all the birds like that?''

''Less xenophobic? I think so.''

Cromwell put both discs up and turned off the disc player, then pushed a call button. When Codresque came in, Cromwell said, ''Take him out, put him on the tennis court, do something with him until lunch.''

''I thought you were supposed to be the good guy to Angleton's bad guy,'' I said.

204 / Rebecca Ore

Cromwell shrugged slightly. The young man who came to help escort me to the tennis machine saluted Cromwell, even though he wasn't in uniform. Cromwell stiffened for a moment, then saluted back and said, "Officially, the uniform salutes the uniform."

Codresque said, "Everyone tested out human, by the way."

When Angleton got back, he called me into the debriefing room alone. He looked excited, face slightly flushed, collar points not lying flat on his collar bones, tie knot off center. I chided myself for being hillbillyish mean about his collar, and remembered that the *Oxford English Dictionary* gave "fighting companion" as one derivation for the *billy* part of that label. Then thought, *too human*.

"The United Nations is going to talk to your people. The Security Council countries decided that we needed to know more. How can we escape over a hundred thirty different species? We can sit back here, interrogating you, but you're obviously biased and don't really know that much. I'm going to be liaison between the UN and the Institute of Analytics and Tactics."

"Are you going to let me go home?"

"To your wife and your semi-upscale apartment? Yes, they're thinking of promoting you, since we swore that you didn't attack any of us."

I laughed, almost out of being hurt. "Sometimes, they don't really understand. They aren't humans, after all."

"I think . . . thank you, Tom."

"For what?"

"For new career opportunities. So, what can you tell me about Lisanmarl, other than she's named for an Israeli rock formation?"

I hesitated. Angleton's face was flushed, and I had trouble not letting my eyes drift down to see if he had more blood than usual elsewhere. "She's a Jerek sterile. Her parents are my present Rector's People, more like counselors than supervisors, controls.

"Lisanmarl is my contact at the Institute of Analytics and Tactics. She reminds me of a woman I saw as a boy in a Hanes hosiery ad, the long nose, the eyes.

"The fur, the slick black facial skin."

"Don't be snide. What faction does she support?"

"The Institute of Analytics and Tactics tends to be conservative, but smart."

"Like us." Meaning, I realized, the Central Intelligence Agency. "Tom, did I tell you the Sharwani contacted us?"

"No."

"It's all right. They're going to join the Federation. I gather that no one trusts them."

"The Sharwani are not a single entity. I mistrusted one I shouldn't have."

"And trusted the one you killed?"

"So, you found Lisanmarl charming?" I wanted to be cruel and tell him more about Jerek steriles, how they were sexual instructors of the young on the Jerek home planet, and how now many of them were sexual entertainers to those who found total body fur a turn-on.

He said, "Yes," in such a simple fashion that I felt crude.

= 10 =

After three more weeks, I felt myself shrinking into the prisoner I'd been at seventeen. Who was there to say otherwise? Just me, in Karst One, Wrengu, Yauntro, but my English more and more betrayed me, slipping back into my old dialect, even with *kh*s, *k*s, dental *t*s and alveolar *t*s mangled sharp and distinct by speech organ operations. Would I ever be free again? Many nights I dreamed myself back to Lucid Moment District. Too often, Marianne and Karl weren't home.

Then one morning I woke up to see Codresque in my room, looking sad, packing my clothes except for the suit he'd laid out across the foot of my bed. He said, "Mr. Angleton wants you to go to Berkeley with him, to help debrief Alex."

I had no choice, so I got out of bed and dressed while Codresque stripped the bed. I remembered the section in my etiquette books on tipping servants and said, trying very hard to speak proper English, "I am sorry all I can do is thank you with words."

He turned his head and made a strange face, mugging almost, lips turned way down, and then said, "No one has quite known how to manage me in America. In Paris and London, people knew." He pressed his lips together.

"Sorry," I said. Maybe prisoners weren't supposed to tip?

He smiled and took my suitcase and said, "We've arranged a gate in the exercise room, so you won't be inconvenienced by an air flight."

And I would never be exactly sure of where I was, either. I followed him through parts of the house I hadn't seen before and into a large room with double doors, weight training equipment pushed back against the walls, a Karst-issue transport pod sitting on gate cables in the middle of the room. "I'm glad I have no transportation stocks," Codresque said.

"Where is this?" I asked.

"Charlotte, North Carolina," he said, smiling slightly. I wasn't sure whether he lied or not.

I got in the pod—just a seat, no internal hatch screws. I heard Codresque's hands tighten the external iron bolts. For about three minutes, I went paranoid. *Am I getting gassed, not transported?* My mind babbled dialect terrors, dabs of reading about convicts staring at the endless Atlantic, in chains, bought for farm help in Virginia. Indentured to the Federation and thrown clean away. Then I heard Angleton talking while he undid the exterior bolts. "Tom told us you used counterfeit money."

Alex stood about ten feet from me, cuffed with disposable plastic cuffs. Friese stood next to him. Alex said, "Tom, you little shit." He looked at Friese and continued, "As a stray, I suppose I'm a ward of the county."

Friese said, "As of twelve tonight, all creatures recognized as sapient by your Federation will be legally considered human here."

I said, "Karriaagzh got us good terms on Yauntra, no retroactive—"

Alex interrupted me. "Can I call my friends?"

"We'd like a list of everyone who knew you were an alien. They should be very helpful when we go public with this," Angleton said.

"I'm going back to get my crest replaced, then I'll be back here. I like humans, most of them."

Friese said, "Why should we let you back?"

Angleton said, "If you give me a list, Alex, I'll call the people who don't know you are not our species, and you can call the ones who do know."

"Jerry Carstairs is the only one who knew," Alex said. "Are you going to tell everyone else?"

Friese said, "You want to return with a skull crest?"

Alex closed his eyes tight and sighed, then looked at me and said, "Well, Tom, here we are, officially."

Angleton's lips thinned and stretched backward at the corners. He said, "I'll be in touch with your friends who were agitating for your release. We have a petition. All of you want to throw a release party? Where do you want to celebrate?"

Alex said, "Thistle and Shamrock."

I wondered how the guys who'd threatened the Barcons in Negro disguise were going to take hearing Alex wasn't human. I said, "No."

"You're a bigot toward your own kind, Tom."

Angleton said, "Oh, I think he's behaved fairly well, considering how brutal he expected us to be. We won't even hold him on parole violations."

I said, "You won't?"

Friese said, "Alex said you asked for valid funds when you were here, and didn't break any local laws."

"Thanks, Alex," I said.

Alex didn't speak, just pushed his hands into his pockets, fists balled, and rocked on his feet, eyes looking to the left of the transport, not focused on anything.

Angleton's mouth made a *tk* sound as if he'd opened

it while dry, maybe to speak, but deciding not to. Friese opened the building door. A blue Oldsmobile waited for us, the driver starting the engine as we walked out. I looked back at the building and saw that it was the same warehouse that we'd used almost a decade ago, that we'd used coming in five weeks earlier, and noticed for the first time how shabby it had gotten in those nine years.

Angleton said, "The public announcement will stress the difficulty of interstellar travel. Your trips were rare events, almost impossible. Large masses can't be moved through the gates."

Lying to the public. Warren told me when the government denied bombing Cambodia, only the enemy wasn't fooled. Alex said, "So you think Tom is right. Humans are xenophobes."

Angleton looked at him, almost as if he were speculating as to whether or not he could handle Alex in a fight, before saying, "Let's see how your friends react when we tell them you're not human."

Alex said, "My friends are tremendously tolerant people."

I said, "Everyone will be surprised, I'm sure."

The Thistle and Shamrock was the same bar, paint over paint on the outside wood, gravel in the parking lot, Guinness signs and neon shamrocks in the windows. I saw Dr. Anne Baseman, in profile, lit by one of the shamrocks that buzzed and spit white light at the stem end. A black guy was with her, dressed in a suit. I remembered a black teenager that Alex had brought to Dr. Baseman's sushi academic party and wondered if he'd grown up into that. Wallie, that had been his name.

Alex got out of the car and said, "I rescued him."

"Wallie?"

"Right. You didn't have to leave Earth to be rescued."

Angleton said, "We thank you so very much."

"Dr. Wallace Vaughn does government consulting," Alex said, "so you should thank me more sincerely."

"I knew some Vaughns in Arlington, from the Tidewater. Perhaps he's related to them, in some way," Angleton said.

We walked in. Alex's friends had tied a banner through the rafters of the bar, over the pool tables. One of the pool table lights was tied to shine up on it: Welcome Out, Alex Murphy.

Murphy's Law. Gresham's Law. I saw Jerry Carstairs flinch when he saw Friese, then grin helplessly at me. I went up to him and said, "Did they give you a hard time?"

"Tom Gresham?"

"I'm really Tom Easley."

Jerry was wearing a user/grower badge, I noticed. He said, "Yes, a crystal-block hard time. I explained if I'd told them Alex was an alien, they would have committed me. Tom, why did Alex do this to me?"

"What?"

"When I knew it was possible and I couldn't figure it out first, oh, man, that killed me."

"You thought Alex would give you clues?"

"Couldn't he have gotten me clues? Even if he didn't have the training himself? Please, I didn't do this to myself, did I, slack off waiting for Alex to help me?"

I almost said, *my wife could have helped,* but remembered that she thought Carstairs was jailbait. "Jerry, I'm sorry, but he was in too much trouble to risk it."

"Alex, yes, that makes sense. I've spent the last two weeks trying like crazy to catch up. I wasn't even . . . fuck Alex." He looked through the crowd and saw Alex. "Fuck you, Alex, you alien mind-fucker."

Alex swayed, then looked away from us. Friese and Angleton darted their eyes toward each other and smiled. Anne Baseman and Wallie began pushing through to us.

Wallie's face and body had filled out, his eyes seemed smaller, tucked back into his face. "Dr. Vaughn, I met you once," I said.

"Yeah." Trace of street still in his speech. He turned to Carstairs and said, "Why are you giving Alex a hard time?"

I realized how stoned Carstairs was then. He shuddered and swayed on his feet, then pushed his glasses back with one finger in that gesture I remembered from years before. If the lights were brighter, I wondered, would tiny lines and cracks show in his skin? I remembered Warren's face before he died and felt my fingers tingle. Carstairs said, "I didn't turn him in. He . . ."

Wallie said, "He helped me."

Carstairs seemed to forget what more he was going to say and that seemed to make him even more angry. Wallie looked at me, the kid he had been showing through his Ph.D. polish. I remembered him saying, *all the language I know are street, street.* In a mean second, I wondered what use the government found with his command of ghetto languages.

Jerry finally said, "Alex is a brain-fucker."

I clenched my teeth and threw my head back slightly, before I could say, "Jerry, he genuinely liked you. Really." *Maybe.*

Wallie looked down at his suit as if he wondered if all his graduate school years had been an alien illusion. I'd had a similar feeling back on Earth this time, wondering if I'd wake up seventeen again and in jail. Wallie asked me as if he didn't know if he wanted the truth or not, "Was, is he really an extraterrestrial?"

"Yes," I said.

"He doesn't even look like that really," Carstairs said. "He's got tentacles, green skin, a beak."

"No," I said. "Alex has just got a skull crest bone, here." I drew my fingers from the back of my head toward my front hairline. "He's bald there and the bone has muscles attached to it, skin over the top of it."

"He's been getting kids out of the flats, how . . . Anne said he picks underprivileged people better than . . ."

"Sometimes, non-humans see us better than we see ourselves," I said.

"No," Carstairs said, "Alex likes to prove humans wrong in their judgments about things." I looked for Alex and saw Anne Baseman looking up at him, talking and touching his shoulder gently from time to time. From here, I couldn't tell if he was crying or not.

Then she took a microphone from one of the waiters and spoke. "Alex, whatever you are, we're happy to see you free. You've helped some of us by our blind spots about our fellow humans. And you've been—can I use the word *human*?—humane enough to seem more like us, fallible, trying, so that I don't think humanity will be seduced into seeing you and others like you as gods come to deliver us."

Alex was crying. I saw the guy with the razor scar across his knuckles, the one who'd threatened the Barcons with a pool cue when he thought they were blacks. He looked bewildered now, getting angry. I went up to Friese—not Angleton, Angleton was too smirky—and said, "Let's talk to that guy, now."

For an instant Friese looked at me as if he wanted a fracas, then he nodded and fell into step with me, pushing through the crowd.

"Remember me?" I said to the man. "Alex's kind helped me."

"You human?"

"Yeah, I'm human. From the Virginia mountains."

"My dad was from Appalachia. I don't know."

Friese asked, "Do you think Alex was using you?"

The man started to get angry again. I said, "Being around humans was, is exciting for him. He must have liked you—he didn't like everyone or every species."

"What is this going to do to us?" he said.

"We don't know yet," Friese said.

"Gonna be like container ships and Korean cars, only worse?"

God, I thought, what will this do to the Japanese? Another major adaptation to deal with in less than two hundred years. "Maybe you can work out in space, getting hydrocarbons from gas giants?"

He almost said something, then looked at Friese. "You official?"

"FBI."

"We supposed to know about this?"

"Contact is difficult to bring about."

The man shook his head very slightly, then turned away from us. Alex's supporters seemed divided, half touching him gently and congratulating him, the others talking among themselves. Alex pushed through the crowd to Carstairs, took Jerry's head in his massive hands and pushed the crown of Jerry's head against his chest—*thud, thud*—in some Ahram gesture I'd never seen before. Then Alex looked at the bar and said, "I need beer."

One bartender shook his head; the other served him. Wallie wandered back over to us and said, "All my life, I thought I knew what was going on."

The man with the scarred knuckles said to Wallie, "He help you and not me?" He looked at us all and moved away, into the crowd, then disappeared. I wanted to tell him how I'd been helped, but realized it didn't matter how many of us the aliens helped if one he liked missed helping him. I wondered then what he did. Work around the dock repairing ship containers? Those scars across the knuckles might be honest work scars.

Alex was calling for another beer. Angleton, smiling, stared at him. Then Alex saw me looking and came toward me. He said, "You think you're bad, don't you?"

As if my fingers were giving me a playback, I remembered how it felt to strangle Hurdai. "I guess we're going to be difficult people to integrate into the Federation. Almost as difficult as the Sharwani."

He put one massive hand on my shoulder and leaned down a bit more heavily than was comfortable. "Tom, you may be a nasty little prick, but the whole human race isn't you." He smelled worse than drunk, fumes of alcohol and rotten meat hitting my face.

I said, "Alex, stop."

He laughed human-style, but the face muscles slid in non-human directions. I remembered noticing that before. He said, "I'm not being very strategic, am I?"

Friese said, "Mainly, you're drunk."

"Ah, Friese, the master FBI hard-ass. Have you ever considered that I'm faking out how badly you got under my skin?"

Friese said, "Did you think everyone was going to love you when they found out you were alien?"

"Anne's pissed."

"But, what she said." I realized after I spoke that sometimes people overcompensate for prejudices and then wondered how far around that could go.

"She . . ."

"Alex fucked her," Friese said.

I sat there, shocked, wondered if he'd bonded to her, why she committed adultery.

"Lot of that going around, Tom," Alex said to me.

I said, "Don't you pair-bond for life?"

Alex shrugged and said, "Humans made me flexible."

Anne came up to us around then and we went dead silent, then she realized what we'd been discussing and said, "Alex, I should have been told. Carstairs knew. Couldn't you have trusted me?" Her lips and jaws worked up and down as if she imagined biting something.

Alex bent his head then, scars outlining where the crest had been amputated. Then he said, "I'm sorry. I wanted to be as good as human for you."

Anne said, "There was always a difference. I thought maybe you'd just been really hurt once, more than physically."

"That's what it was. We overlap with humans, really."

Anne shook her head slightly and said, "You have experiences that I'll never have."

I said, "Do you want to have them?"

She looked at me and said, "Is Marianne doing interesting work?"

"Very," I said, then felt like I was taunting her. In my head, I kept switching between thinking of her as Anne, Alex's lover, and Dr. Baseman, Marianne's mentor.

"Well, my field's suddenly enlarged. Is what I know worthless?" She turned to Alex with that question, but I wasn't sure he knew any more about the Institute of Linguistics than he did about space gate theory.

"Ask Tom."

"Marianne said what she learned from you was valuable."

"I was afraid I'd been turned into an interesting primitive." Dr. Anne Baseman began crying, then she added, in a schoolteacherish voice, "Alex, you're drunk."

Alex said, "You officials, Friese and the other one, why aren't you bullying Tom?"

"They did already," I said.

Angleton said, "Wrong. You were treated very kindly. Alex, we didn't bully him because we knew we could."

Alex said, "You feel less intimidated because you can bully me? I'm a dipshit, gone native."

Angleton said, "The Federation wouldn't have sent a retard here, even if you have been in the field too long, at least by human standards."

Alex found a chair and sat down. Anne said, "Still,

I wish I'd known.'' She reached for his head and rubbed around his scars.

"Must tell you the significance of the crest someday,'' Alex said.

"Do you miss looking like your real self?'' she asked. Friese, Angleton, and I looked at each other. I, for one, felt like an eavesdropper.

Alex said, "I'm scarred. This is my real self now.''

"Why did they leave you in place?'' Angleton said.

Alex, eyes red, tissue around the eyes swollen as if mosquitos had chewed him up there, looked up at Angleton and said, "There was a faction that wanted you to know. You're not that terrible. Tom's problem is that the aliens he first met were unusually xenophilic. Us xenophiles get pissed when you phobes react, but . . .'' He shrugged again and took Anne's hand. She looked like she didn't know if he should have it or not. He said, "It's an informational black hole out there, Angleton. You're going to go nuts if you're not careful. Where's my beer?''

Friese said, "Come on, Alex, we'll take you home.''

Alex stood up, towering over us and swaying. "Getting arrested was bad for my lease.''

Anne said, "To my house, Alex, for now.'' I wanted to ask her what happened to her husband, but couldn't quite manage to say that now.

As we all drove away in our various cars, Angleton asked, "What did he mean by falling into an informational black hole?''

"You know how complex Earth is? Well, you're talking about a hundred thirty-seven or whatever times Earth, plus whatever complexities arise from contact with all the other planets.''

Angleton sighed through rounded lips and said, "Okay. We had an officer who lost it trying to get the absolute facts about who in the Politburo made what decision about Afghanistan in nineteen eighty-seven.''

Telegraph Avenue was still filled with people this late

at night, neon signs and light flats glowing through the slight drizzle. I saw someone who was either deformed or another alien in surgical disguise.

After we'd turned west, Angleton said, "You told us the Gwyngs don't develop all their mental abilities if they didn't learn Gwyng languages, if all they learned was Karst Two. That bothers me."

"I think humans develop more abilities than we'd have otherwise." I wondered if we were going to San Francisco.

"That, also, bothers me."

"Well, Angleton, I hope your informational black hole rotates." We passed a brothel zone and he laughed as though I were saying something that made more sense than I knew. I remembered that he'd met Lisanmarl and that she reminded him of a human woman. Seemed to me that he was projecting his own patterns on aliens. Me, I'd been more confused by the landscapes than by the people.

People, though. I always thought of them as people, except times like when Granite couldn't tell a bad Sharwani surgical copy from the real me. "Angleton, or whatever your real name is, all we can hope for in the Universe is accommodation, not complete understanding."

"Red Clay, you're proof they don't kill helpless people. The Tibetans . . ." He stopped and smiled. "Yangchenla proves they don't kill argumentative humans."

"Yangchenla?"

"The Chinese have been talking to her. In English. Tough bitch, asking about the riot in nineteen eighty-seven."

"I know her. We were lovers for a while."

"She doesn't think much of you, of the Chinese, or the Russians. I think the Dalai Lama wants to talk to her."

I said, "She's not religious, either." Angleton didn't

reply, just smiled, teeth catching another car's head-lights.

Then we started over the Bay Bridge. Bridge wires lit by the cars flickered by like strobe flashes. Angleton said, "I don't expect Yangchenla and her people will cooperate with any Earth humans. But what about our nations? Are we going to be forced into a single human state?" Before I could speak, he waved his hand and continued, quickly, "You don't know enough to answer that."

"There's not one answer to what's going to happen to us. Every individual, much less every species, takes contact differently."

"What we're afraid of is that every nation is going to take contact differently."

I said, "The Federation doesn't allow cadets and officers to bring home wars to Karst. But what you do on Earth, on any species planet, is your business."

"Not yours?"

"I'm Federation. Beyond that, I'm Karst."

"A multi-species culture that feels superior to single-species cultures. A multi-culture species is lower yet."

I almost said, *yes*. We went up a hill and stopped in front of a twelve-story hotel with three uniformed door-men waiting outside.

"Tom, you're not a prisoner, but I'd prefer it if you didn't go out without an escort." As Angleton spoke, three men dressed in suits and mirrored glasses with strange distortions in the lenses came up. It was almost funny to see humans wearing high-tech security garb. One of the doormen took Angleton's car and we all went in together, looking like a minor presidential candidate with his secret service guards.

"What's amusing?" Angleton asked in the elevator.

"I've been through all this before, but with other species. The Yauntries had their media people work on our image. You guys wear the same gear as Barcons, Yauntry guards, walk almost like them. It's kind of neat.'' I sounded a bit adolescent to myself with that last, but one of the security types smiled slightly, too. Then I wondered if he believed me.

Angleton smiled now.

The media team met in the hotel suite. While we drank coffee, Angleton pulled the window shades back. I saw a giant television tower patched and still being worked on by tiny crews so dwarfed by the thing they might have been in space switching freight pods on gate nets.

''Isn't that obsolete?'' I said, thinking about fiber-optic cables.

''Historical monument,'' said the media guy, Rick Sutter, a short stocky fellow with a bald patch at the very crown of his head. ''Sutro Tower. Stars in a lot of media.''

''What are the aliens going to bring us?'' the woman, Nancy Soko, said. She was a skinny, red-haired, leathery 45-year-old with gold chains around her neck and threaded-through holes in her ears. ''Spinal cord reconstruction, retrovirus cures, better birth control?''

Angleton said, ''Sexual entertainers and digital hologram horror flicks starring real aliens.''

An anonymous government man, in a suit the color of an official grey Ford, blinked and frowned.

I said, ''Except for the space gates, mainly faster computers and better medicine.''

''The Japanese and Chinese don't like hearing about extraterrestrial computer improvements,'' the government man said. I remembered my research and wondered if the Japanese would approach the alien technological challenge as intensely as they'd approached the Western challenge in the nineteenth century. Now, not even a whole two hundred years later, aliens brought in laser matrixing, chemical gates responding in gradients to various colored lights, fiber-optic glass that could isolate one photon and wave it to one precise molecule.

"It's our problem, too," Rick said.

"Our surveys don't indicate any sign of public panic, but I'm not sure why," Nancy said. She moved one of her ear chains until a short bar in the chain balanced across the hole.

"Earth wasn't attacked," Rick said. "Why don't we assume nobody's going to hyper-V over aliens? Start showing a more human–looker on talk shows?"

"Then move on to the little warm fuzzies," the government man said. Angleton seemed a bit uneasy.

"They did that on Yauntra," I said. "But people there trusted the alien-looking aliens more. I looked like a slightly deformed Yauntry to them."

"Warm fuzzies? Small warm fuzzies?" Rick asked.

"Does Lisanmarl speak English well enough?" I asked.

"Oh, yes," Angleton said. "Could Yangchenla be bribed to speak positively of how her people were treated?"

"She's a businesswoman," I said.

Nancy frowned slightly. Rick said, "Nancy could talk to her."

"What about my wife?" I asked.

"She's unreliable," the government man said. Angleton twisted his left hand in a gesture that seemed to mean *lighten up*, because the man added, "We haven't talked to her recently. Perhaps she's changed."

"Scholars all love it," I said. "How we work to come to semiotic accommodations, where bare mind fails. The real thing we learn is the meaning of meaning."

"Your wife loves that?" Angleton said.

"I love it. It's like the fantasy of talking animals— intelligences that don't get involved in our species' status games, people who tell us, without being snide, when we're acting like chimpanzees deluxe."

Angleton said, "And who don't really care what your status was among your species."

"Not if you're bright," I said. "Their tests are value free."

"Perhaps," Angleton said, "but they chose to measure certain brain functions and not others."

"I found out on Karst what my real values were, and they weren't Warren's."

Angleton said, "We're not sure you're the most objective witness."

"Back to marketing aliens," Rick said. "Warm fuzzies, shorter than we are, who speak English. Let's get one on 'Night Fringe,' blur the real a bit and poll the viewers."

"Jereks may be short and fuzzy," I said, "but one bit me once."

Angleton said, "You must have deserved it. I'll talk to Lisanmarl. And we'll see what Yangchenla is willing to say and for how much. Maybe Sam Turner could bring in a multi-species jazz trio?"

I said, "Sam plays with humans. On Karst, it's okay to be a merge-humanist musically."

Nancy said, "Warm little fuzzies. Nice, reassuring."

Within the week, Lisanmarl, Angleton, his anonymous colleague, and I were lounging around on broken-down green velvet couches in a television studio ready room, drinking coffee dripped, not perked, from grounds Angleton brought with him. Lisanmarl had bleached her fingers and was afraid that coffee would stain her fur. She stood up, her leathers falling around her knees, and said, in English, "Tom, before the broadcast, come out in the hall with me."

I looked at Angleton, who nodded, and went out. We were waiting to go on the late-night television show after our rehearsal. She said, in English, "I resent this a little." Her leathers, belted at the waist with the groin breasts concealed, covered more of her than usual.

"Why? What?" I said.

"Being treated as if I were harmless."

"We want you to seem non-threatening."

"But don't I threaten even you? Just a little?" She swayed slightly, moving first in an alien way, then moving more like a human woman. One palm rose up, fingers wiggling.

"And how is your health?" I asked, instantly feeling nasty for bringing that up. A side effect of low-grade constant heat is pernicious anemia—Jereks are in heat unless pregnant or nursing, not as insistent as a dog or cat heat, about like human adolescence forever. And being sterile? The Barcons are working on it.

She lowered her nose, then said, "Don't tell James. It would be de-romantic. Dis- . . . unromantic, correct?"

"Maybe he really cares about you?"

"So interesting to have a lover whose hair doesn't insulate his blood circulation patterns." She stopped talking and ran one fingernail around a jewel set in the thick nailbase on her thumb. Her nails were rather more like modified claws than flat like mine; only at the tips were they as thin. I wondered if Jereks filed them to keep their fingers from ending in real claws. She asked, "Are you prejudiced against Jereks?"

"I didn't like Carbon-jet. I like your parents."

"Carbon-jet thought you were really curious enough for our Institute, but you're a coward. Angleton is what I've been looking for."

I just knew that Angleton would read this conversation if he wasn't hearing it right now. Before she said more, a man poked his head out of the Green Room and said, "We need you in five minutes."

"Angleton knows about your feelings?"

"Of course. We are professionals." She lowered her nose at me again.

"But he doesn't know you could come down with pernicious anemia from staying sexy, does he?"

"The Barcons have improved the stabilizing techniques."

"You've got it?"

The man stuck his head out again and said, "Come in, now, don't make us nervous."

We went in. Lisanmarl, eyes fixed on me, slowly moved her nose up, then she swiveled and whistled at Angleton. I thought about Jerek eyes and the usual chill of their environment. Did they see infrared, more complex expressions of the body than we could read ourselves? No Jereks ever put that data in the Federation computer. I wondered if Lisanmarl had slipped.

Was I a coward not to have joined the Institute of Analytics and Tactics? No, I hated Carbon-jet's style.

A light flashed and we went onto the set, cameras on all sides popping up and down out of the floor. Angleton didn't follow us, but stood for a second at the door.

Lisanmarl made a sound like a giggle, a fake human giggle, and began dancing with one of the horn players.

The host, Jake Soko, who was thin and red-haired like his mother, Nancy the media woman, said, "So, Mr. Gentry, aliens like her rescued you from a life of crime?" He sounded just like we hadn't said all of this before.

"Lisanmarl is just one of the many intelligent species out there. They've been good to me."

"You have tapes?"

Yes. We watched a blank wall as if we could see what the optics lines were feeding our homeviewers. A camera popped out of the floor aimed at our eyeballs. "Amazing," Jake breathed. "And that's the beginning of the contact process?"

Well, actually, the broadcast showed tapes of renewed linguistic-team work with the Sharwani, who, like the Jereks, fit the little warm fuzzy bill and were mostly blond, to boot. "Yes, that's how we start with new species, now. The beginning five thousand years ago was different."

"So the Federation is older than recorded human history?" Jake said.

We'd timed it just right in rehearsal. I countered with "But just a microsecond in the Universe's history."

Jake faked a wince as though I'd punned and said, "You say five races built the planet, the base . . ."

"Not base. The trade and information center." We hadn't quite rehearsed this and I was a bit flustered.

"Okay, but I was thinking that maybe this Karst was the planet referred to in Genesis. You said something about a sense that all species reflect one—can I say it?—capital *M* Mind?"

"I'm not sure about Genesis, but yes, there are those who believe that we're all reflections of a universal force too complex to be completely represented in one species." I hadn't liked this when we were discussing it, hadn't liked the flip manipulative way Jake handled it in rehearsal. I wondered if the Gwyngs were right about the Universe being created and destroyed every time a gate opened and closed, because now seemed an odd distortion of the time I'd left behind. Time, not universal deaths and reconstructions, could have distorted this present Earth from my past one, but I wondered if I'd know the difference.

The camera was on Lisanmarl. She finished her dance with the saxophone player and came toward us, cameras sliding up and down on their pistons like weird phallic symbols.

"Lisanmarl," Jake said, holding out both his hands to her.

"Welcome to the rest of the Universe, Jake." It sounded so natural, so slightly sexy. Jake had been afraid to touch her at first.

"Do you find us hairless people odd?"

"No, you're not ugly." This wasn't what we'd planned. Jake stiffened. Lisanmarl continued, "You bare your expressions through more than the face keyhole. Beautiful to see the mind working under the skin."

Keyholes in Jerek country were T shaped, like the bare patch of facial skin across their eyes and down their noses.

"And what do you like best about Earth?"

"The stalactite chimes in Luray Tunnel, Cavern. A love of the enclosed both our species share. Beautiful stone music." She looked at Jake and whistled softly. Jake hadn't believed her when she told us in planning that she was fascinated by our interest in caves.

"So, what does Earth get from contact with all these other species?"

"You get me." Angleton had to bribe Lisanmarl into saying that with emeralds for her nails. Now she said what she'd wanted to say, "You get lessons in arts you never dreamed of, arts that will expand your mental capacities. You will find out what is really your animal past expressing itself, what is shared by all of us."

"Could you and a human man have a child?" Jake threw this in unrehearsed. Lisanmarl gnashed her teeth and I threw back my own head slightly.

"No," she said, without elaborating.

Angleton opened the door between the ready room and the studio and shook his head. Jake said, "Well, I'm sorry if I was rude."

"I accept." Lisanmarl sounded like she wasn't going to forgive him ever.

"Well, folks, you've met the aliens on 'The Jake Soko Show.' Telephone in if you think we're pulling your leg, or if this is real as well as live. And now, a message from our sponsor, who builds cars fit for alien planets, roads or no roads."

A man in the control room cued us that the commercial was running. Lisanmarl turned to Jake and said, "I can't conceive children, a crippling condition for a Jerek."

"Sorry, okay?"

"We had rehearsed so carefully." She was beginning to remind me of Black Amber at her most implacable.

"Tom, are they all like this?" Jake asked.

"No. Isn't the commercial about over?" I said. I'd wanted to add, *Some of us strangle each other with our bare hands,* but that wouldn't be fun television.

The closest camera flashed red. "Tom, did you have a hard time adjusting to aliens?"

"Well, actually, Jake, they were as nervous about me as I was about them. My roommate, now a great friend and a member of the team working out the Earth contact, first thought I was a giant lactating rat."

"He doesn't, now?"

"Now, he knows I'm male and my wife is a giant lactating ape."

"Will we be able to take vacations in space?"

"Jake, the Federation has resorts for people like us. Creatures who like thrill rides generally come from brachiators—tree-swinging people. So the Federation built a resort called Tenleaving with hanging bridges and treehouses, even a rollercoaster."

"So, contact is going to radically expand tourism."

"Right, Jake. We've got worlds of resorts. As soon as the trade treaties are signed, see what your local travel agent has to offer." As I said this, I felt like gagging.

We had, fortunately, decided not to take live calls over the air. Fifteen of the twelve hundred calls threatened the Federation with legal action over abductions; thirty-seven percent believed the aliens were real, thirty-three percent felt this would have been officially announced, and twenty-nine percent had no opinion.

Near the end of the show, after more Jerek dancing and a band that called itself High Warp, Jake read the summary, minus the lawsuit threats, over the air and said, "But we scooped the *New York Times* with this one, folks."

His mother gave us to him. Nepotism, like in southwest Virginia. I hoped that by morning most people would consider Lisanmarl a hoax.

* * *

In the morning, Angleton came in grinning, still dressed in pajamas, smelling of Jerek musk. "Get up, we've got on a wonderful morning show."

I said, "I thought I could lock my door."

"Tom, get up and come watch."

I dressed in pants and a shirt and followed Angleton back into his suite. Lisanmarl sat in a chair, looking almost prim, legs tucked up under her, leathers falling to the floor, nose slightly tucked down as she watched a bank of six televisions, one with colors skewed, really pink, the others adjusted more to normal but wired so that the blues registered as blacks.

"Can't you see blue?" I said to Lisanmarl, not quite focusing in on any set until I saw my own image.

"Easier this way on my eyes." She pushed a button and the blacks turned back into blues. A morning talk show host was interviewing my old teacher from Floyd, the hippie one who'd thought I was so awfully colorful as a renegade hillbilly.

The teacher was greying, beard almost all grey, head hair thinned, bald at the crown, still wearing wire-rim glasses although corrective vision surgery had improved a mile and a half since I was last in Floyd. He said, looking at me as if he knew I was beyond the camera, "Tom Gentry was bright, but he wasn't counterculture and he resented my attempts at friendliness. Maybe he thought I was being patronizing, but . . . well, sometimes, you have to go away from home to find out who you really are. So, now, he's back. I'd like to see him again."

I said to Angleton, "Am I going to?"

"Wait."

My old teacher went on, "He was so loyal to his brother. Misplaced loyalty, we felt, but some of the more conservative teachers hesitated to teach Tom to his full potential. They were afraid they'd only be educating a smarter drug dealer."

"We weren't just dealing it," I said. "We were making it." But we were nobodies to the Atlanta guys.

"Repackagers," Angleton said. He sat on the bed, long skinny frame hunched over, looking tired, not as spruce and utterly High WASP as he had looked when I first met him.

The host said, "Do you think we can trust Tom Gentry?"

The teacher took off his glasses and wiped them with a lens paper he pulled from a pack in his shirtpocket. Then he put them on and said, "I hope so. I wish him well and if the aliens found a better use for him than drugs and jail, then I'm glad they're out there. Maybe they can help more of us."

Lisanmarl said, "We're just here to be here."

"I understand that, darling," Angleton said, almost drawling, "but we've got to avoid panic among the common folk."

Lisanmarl looked at him and tipped down her nose. Angleton got off the bed and said, reaching for her, "Would you bite if I raised your chin?"

She rolled her round shoulder blades and said in Karst One, *"Perhaps we should be panicking to have you humans in."*

Angleton said, "You said what about humans? I'll have to wait until tomorrow."

I said, "She says we make some of the Federation nervous."

"Shush, Tom," Angleton said. "We're missing something really important about you."

On the screen was the deputy who'd gotten his wife to take care of my stock while I was in jail, only now he was sheriff. I realized how much time had passed, how little. This guy hadn't aged like the teacher; he'd become a man, not a young kid deputy. I tried to think about how much time had passed, but Sheriff Deitz was saying, "He almost didn't get tried as an adult. Lots of us were against it. He should have maybe asked for help, but Warren'd worry you worse than a holiness preacher about his rights to Tom when we'd say how he wasn't taking good care of Tom. People here were concerned about Tom, but I guess we shouldn't have gone to Warren about it. No, Warren was quick-tempered and moody, but Tom was always a patient boy.''

I sat up rigid, almost about to throw up. Warren clung to me, then, the way I'd clung to Warren kidnapping him off Earth. And people had tried to talk him into giving me up before we were busted. The announcer said to my teacher, ''Didn't the principal advise that he be tried as an adult?''

''He . . . I don't know if it's fair to discuss this, since the man is dead. Yes, both Warren and Tom scared him.'' I closed my eyes, remembering the principal, scared of knives, teenage boys, and drugs. I used to bring in little broken bits of sharpened steel too small to really call knives, just to bug him. Now, I realized what a little jerk I'd been. The world hadn't simply abandoned me to Warren.

Sheriff Deitz said, ''I'd like Tom to know that I would like to shake his hand if he's been able to work honest and make a family among aliens. It'd have to be a really balanced man to live among so many different alien ways.''

Lisanmarl leaned back and whistled. I remembered Carbon-jet's whistle like that.

That program tailed off and Lisanmarl switched the sound to another picture completely unrelated to aliens or our arrival. Angleton started to reach for the remote control, but she lowered her nose again.

I didn't care. Discovering I'd had a secret life I'd never known about stunned me. I said, ''I want to go back to Floyd.''

Angleton said, ''I was planning to show Lisanmarl more caverns.''

''Carlsbad,'' Lisanmarl said, watching an image of herself, no sound, just her gestures, round shoulders revolving, hands stroking the air, nose circling, eyelids almost clicking open and shut.

"Can't I go to Floyd by myself?"

Lisanmarl looked at Angleton then, her nose half-down, her lower jaw twitching. He smiled at her and said, "No."

"No?"

"Gentry, why drag up that old business?"

"I thought everyone was abandoning me."

"Maybe the sheriff is rerigging his memories so he doesn't look like a nasty redneck on national television."

"I want to find out."

Lisanmarl said, "Everyone might lie. Some might tell this; others tell that."

If the sheriff told the truth, I hadn't been the target of everyone's disdain, but was myself touched with paranoia, that human vice. I felt hideous, Hurdai's killer, suspicious of Chi'ursemisa, rude to Xenon when he was a colleague, a prick to Yangchenla—years of pretending that I wasn't human in the worst ways.

Lisanmarl said, "He should go by himself."

"I need to know the truth."

Angleton got up and took the remote control from her. He turned all the sets off. " 'What is the truth?' Colonel Cromwell goes with him."

"I want to go alone," but as I said that, I realized that I wasn't sure.

Lisanmarl sat, her belly above the leathers' band going in and out slightly, the hair on her shoulders slightly puffed. Then she said, "Tom, take Colonel Cromwell. It will get us all to Karst sooner."

"A military jet will have you both in Roanoke by four this afternoon," Angleton said.

"Are you going, too, Angleton?" I asked.

"No, not to Roanoke."

"But to Karst," Lisanmarl said.

"Oh."

"James is a professional."

Angleton's face jerked toward her. I realized they were each other's greatest professional challenges. Their mutual love of spying made naked skin erotic to the Jerek and a furry belly arousing to the man. And I was outclassed. "I'll go to Floyd with Cromwell, then."

Lisanmarl took the remote control from Angleton and clicked all the sets on again. The screens swirled with our images—human, alien, human, human to human to alien to alien—Lisanmarl, Angleton, me, and now drawings of Gwyngs who favored Jereks, and Granite Grit.

"Is Granite here?" I asked.

"In Washington," Angleton said.

"Could he come to Floyd, too?" I asked.

"No," Lisanmarl said as much to Angleton as to me.

Colonel Cromwell smiled at me bleakly as we carried our own bags off the plane. The government stopped the media for us in Roanoke—no press to greet us, no official car. In the terminal, I spotted Secret Service, FBI, types, black eyeglass frames, ears wired. Cromwell shrugged slightly and found a porter to take our bags and hail a cab. We couldn't have raced for a grey car bristling with aerials; the press would have reacted.

The taxi came; the driver said, "Dispatcher had word to send me." He flashed an ID at Cromwell.

"Hotel Roanoke," Cromwell said as the porter put our bags in the trunk of the taxi. All around us, the dark hills glittered with car and house lights. We went downtown where the tracks had been.

"What happened to the trains?" I asked.

"Underground," the taxi driver said.

"In twenty years?"

"There's the new terminal," he said, pointing at a huge black and grey building about two blocks square.

"They haven't done as much with the airport," I said.

"Mountains are too expensive to move. We've got a maglev connection with Greensboro, anyway, for freight."

"I never expected Roanoke to be so changed."

"Wait till you see Floyd," the driver said. We pulled up in front of the Hotel Roanoke and I looked across the city toward Mill Mountain. The Star wasn't the same, built now of huge gas tube lights, not the incandescents of my childhood. The tubes changed color— green, blue, red, yellow, white—in waves.

As we rode the elevator up to our floor, Cromwell asked, "Have you read Thomas Wolfe?"

"About Asheville and how you can't go home again? But I know I've changed."

"When my father was in his sixties, he went back to his little town in South Carolina. Everyone was so proud, then, of him, and of me." We got out and walked down the green velvet halls looking for Suite 1120.

"Of you?"

"Yes. I flew shuttles."

"Oh."

"That's why I went with Weiss's gate team. I dreamed about space since I was a baby."

I almost said, it should have been you and not me, because I'd never thought about space until I found Mica. Space was for rich kids with engineering degrees. "I'm sorry."

"Don't be. You can help us."

We went inside the suite on top of the hotel. Cromwell pulled back the drapes and we stared out toward Floyd. A glow surrounded Bent Mountain like a small city was hiding behind it. Nothing like that had been in the Floyd I knew as a kid.

I pulled the drapes closed and said, "I miss my mate and child." I hadn't realized I was going to say that until I did. The loneliness that rushed through me with the words startled and appalled me.

Cromwell sighed and said, "What did you say?"

I'd spoken Karst One without realizing it. "I miss my wife and son. Maybe we ought to skip going to Floyd? Maybe?"

"You aren't afraid of those people, are you?"

"Somewhat. And besides, it's changed."

"You've changed, too, but . . ." Cromwell stopped, walked back to the suitcases and began unpacking, hanging a fresh uniform and a civilian suit.

"I'm not as good with humans as I am with others."

"I'm none too fond of self-pity." He looked up from the drawer where he was putting his socks, jaw muscles locking down.

"What if I really could have saved Mica?"

Cromwell looked like he was going to say something quite harsh, then he said, "I wasn't there."

"No, you weren't."

"You're human. That seems pretty inescapable. Do you need to have that be a problem?"

"Sapients . . ." I was going to tell him something I'd learned on Karst, about how flexible all sapients were, how that was the point of developing intelligence. "What is intelligence for, do you think?"

"It makes us better competitors."

"Or more able to come up with win-win games."

"Gentry, if your Federation doesn't play win-win games, I'm personally coming after you. This is unofficial, of course."

I was about to tell him, the Universe is very complex, but decided what would happen would happen. I'd go to Floyd; the human race would go to space; we'd all die with the future holding our grandchildren hostage. "I'll go to Floyd, but I was wondering if the CIA or you guys prompted the sheriff to say what he did."

"You'd like to believe that, wouldn't you?"

I asked, "Would you know if Angleton had rigged it?"

"I don't care. I don't like seeing my kind reduced to

outnumbered primitives in a system that doesn't have to be in the least bit considerate of us. What could the Sharwani do to stop you? Become bullies themselves? We can't refuse to join your Federation, but what will it do to us?"

"What will you be willing to sell off cheap to get dear?" I remembered the Gwyngs constantly building plastic hotels and runways, recycling light degraded plastics into food, waste products into more plastic, always losing something so that Gwyng crews share-cropped gas giants all over the Federation. "The thing is too big to be moral or immoral. I believe we try to work things out so that more creatures gain than lose, but then, the Federation has been good to me."

"So you could overlook what the same Federation did to the Tibetans?"

"It's not as simple as that." Or was it?

"Let's go to sleep."

As Cromwell turned out the lights, he said, "If Angleton were here, he'd ask if you missed your wife's personality or sex? He told me if it came up, but . . ." He clicked his tongue off his velar ridge behind his upper front teeth.

I dreamed Karl aimed a pistol at me.

The next day was cold for May; ice-cored rain, sleet fragments melting on the hired car's windshield. Cromwell went to Route 419 by the half-abandoned mall that was the mall when I was a teenager, too poor and too busy to hang out there myself. Then we turned onto Route 221, going up Bent Mountain beside a light rail line that connected Roanoke to the glow I saw behind the ridge last night.

"Do you know what that's for?"

"I'm not from around here, but it looks like a mag-lev."

"Yeah, guess something's built on top of the mountain."

The train—no, one car—came gliding down. The car had no windows. "Must be from an Ess-cee-eff?"

"SCF?"

"Self-contained factory—shopping center, residences, schools, jobs, all in one. That was a freight car."

"Oh."

"Government sponsored them in areas with high unemployment, lack of job skills."

"Backassward places like Floyd County." I saw some buildings off through the trees, looked like the SCF was about as big as the whole town of Floyd in the late 1980s, maybe about a thousand people.

"We've got seven in Vermont, one in the upper part of the state that's enclosed."

"Where did the energy come from?"

"We haven't been 'backassward' since you left, Tom. We've been tapping some of the minor Jovian satellites."

"I'm not an engineer." What was I good at anyway? Alien small talk?

"Don't underrate your own kind."

"We're the most quarrelsome brachiators in the Galaxy."

"Gentry, you've got a chromium steel attitude problem."

"I'm nervous."

"Well, let's turn around and go back then. I hate driving in this fog."

"No, I'd always wonder."

Cromwell didn't say anything more, just drove by the fog-obscured flame azaleas and mountain magnolias. Then we passed a quarter mile of greenhouses, three of them multi-story helical units like I'd seen on Karst for growing vegetables unable to take raw Karst light and air. Then no greenhouses, suddenly, as if the quar-

ter mile had been projected onto the usual Floyd landscape of cow pastures and handbuilt houses.

"Things have really changed."

"They always do," Cromwell said.

Floyd had grown and on the outskirts were four
streets of foam-metal apartment buildings, like ones I'd
seen the first time in Berkeley. "Pressure space cast-
ing," Cromwell said. "The bubbles strengthen the slabs
as well as make it lighter."

"I saw them in California nine years ago."

"Those were cast on the planet, not quite as solidly
foamed."

At least, I thought, downtown Floyd was the same,
but then I saw that half of the older buildings looked as
if they'd been dipped in plastic. The courthouse, 1930s
modern, had scaffolding up one side, and the steel Con-
federate soldier, who'd worn granny glasses for three
weeks back in 1988, was lying face up in the grass by
his pedestal. Behind the courthouse, where the parking
lot had been, was a new building: stone with bronze
glass windows. On top was a solar collector.

I went in to the old jail with Cromwell. The sheriff
was waiting for us, smiling, while deputies hustled out
some freshly arrested kid who was crying like a mad-
man. I said, "I heard you on television when I was in
California."

"Tom, you've changed. You sound like a foreigner
now."

"Alien, perhaps." I was straining for that educated
English with alien overtone effect. "That kid?"

"Not another version of yourself, Tom. He killed his
ex-girlfriend. We'll send him out for psych-evaluation
tomorrow."

"Oh. You think I should have come forward when I
was having trouble with Warren, then?"

"Tom, it's like this. Your life was a swing thing.
Could have gone good. Could have gone bad. What's a
deputy, some schoolteachers, to do?"

"You could have tried."

"One of the schoolteachers did, didn't he?"

"I thought he liked me being a colorful outlaw."

"We know you wanted to be a good kid. But one of those aliens died because . . ."

"Because I was stupid and scared and because Mica didn't have enough sense to not point a shotgun at Warren. But he didn't want to be officially found out."

"Better that than dead," Cromwell said.

The sheriff's eyebrows slid toward each other, rumpling the skin over his nose. "Tom, lots of Floyd people, before and after your time, have had to go elsewhere to make good. You just seemed to have gone a bit further than most."

"Yes."

"Remember we are proud of you."

"Did you really try to keep them from trying me as an adult?"

"Yes." His accent faded, a funny hissing *yes*, then returned, "But I was only a junior deputy then, Tom, and the principal wasn't a friend of the Gentry boys. Heard about Warren, sorry."

"I wish I'd left him here."

"He tried suicide in the halfway house, too. With drugs, not a man's way of being serious about it."

"He did it with drugs on Karst," I said, faintly comforted that the sheriff had told me this, pissed that he'd implied Warren wasn't man enough to use a gun.

"So, what do you do for your aliens?" the sheriff asked.

"I help coordinate contacts with new species, work with cadets, help negotiate trade agreements."

"Whatever they are, they've been good for you."

"I think so, too," I said, wishing I was away from this man who made me feel like I was a teenager craving adult approval.

"Going back to Roanoke tonight?"

"Not quite yet. I'm going by the school."

The sheriff looked at the deputies standing around and then shrugged slightly. Cromwell's face seemed forced into impassivity.

The woman working on the computer looked up at me and said, "We're happy for you, Tom, but don't go on rubbing our noses in how we misjudged you."

"Now, Helen," the sheriff said, but he was more agreeing with her than not. I heard Cromwell's teeth click together.

"Thanks, Helen," I said and I left that place. Cromwell stepped on out after me. It was beginning to clear off.

"Sorry, Gentry," Cromwell said.

"I'm glad someone was honest."

"How do you know she spoke for many people here?"

"They looked relieved after she said it. Let's go back to Roanoke, back to Karst. What am I trying to prove here? I don't know what you would have done to Mica if I had driven him up to Washington. We can sit here all day hearing 'we woulda, we woulda.' "

"Gentry, you owe us something as fellow human beings."

"No. Bullshit. I owe us all going back to Karst and continuing to be the good officiator there. That makes humans look good."

"Haven't you screwed up with that?"

I gripped my knees and took a deep breath, feeling my fingers digging in as they dug into Hurdai's throat. "I trusted Hurdai. I trusted the neural disruptor to work."

"I have no problem with what you did. Gentry, if you can't defend your friends, it's not that perfect out there."

"Colonel, I'm still learning how to be an officiator and working with you is pushing me more than killing Hurdai did."

He stopped talking and drove me back toward Roanoke. I said, "Let's take the Parkway."

More umbilicaria lichen grew on the rocks than before—the planet cooling, perhaps, to let those black and grey symbiotic shriveled plates spread. Or the road cuts were finally weathered enough. Or I hadn't noticed before. But otherwise, the Parkway seemed the same, except for more houses out beyond the azaleas and rhododendrons.

"Skunk cabbage," Cromwell said. "Didn't realize it grew so far south."

"You don't see it down the mountain," I said. "Don't punish the woman at the jail for being honest. I really don't think anyone was trying to save me for Earth back when I was a teenager."

"You think she committed a breach of security by telling you that you embarrassed them by getting aliens to adopt you? You think we'd go at you that hard? And you think your Federation people are going to trust you after you get back, Tom?"

"Why shouldn't they?" I said.

= 11 =

Back in Roanoke, Colonel Cromwell kept the cab waiting while he made a phone call. I stood in the lobby with my hands in my pockets, wondering when I'd be recognized. Cromwell came back and told me, "Our bags are already down." A porter was trolleying them from the elevator, so when he reached us, Cromwell and I began walking along beside him, back to the taxi.

To the airport, of course. A jet waited for us, pilot standing beside it, drinking coffee in a Styrofoam cup. "Are we going to Washington?" I asked.

"No," Cromwell said. "We're all going back to Karst. Orders. My new duty station, Angleton's also."

"Codresque?"

"I don't know about the Rumanian." We climbed up behind the pilot, and the canopy slid over us.

"Granite Grit?"

"The gaudy parrot on the negotiating team? He's staying here, negotiating. We didn't think you needed to help him."

"Okay, okay."

The pilot began mumbling and shifting his hands over the control display, then the engines ignited and we whirled around and began to move down the runway. I put the earphones on and taped the mike to my throat.

Through the electronics, over the sound of the engine, Cromwell said, "You know how to put on the gear?"

"We're trained in comparative systems," I said. "Any sapient who doesn't force things can generally figure out how to work simple systems."

"Okay, okay to you, too, Mr. Gentry. Why did Granite Grit bring his wife and child?"

"How dangerous is negotiating with humans, anyway? I keep telling them it's damn near lethal, but obviously, Granite thinks I'm prejudiced."

"Shit, you're angry."

"Yes, I was practically told to leave town because I didn't turn out as badly as the whole county expected. You don't let me see Granite Grit. We're sitting here headed up at ninety degrees and bitching about my attitude."

Cromwell said, "You think I'm happy about leaving my wife and kids to go off to some alien planet?"

"Colonel, bring them with you. My kid has lots of friends from his birth group . . . be good to expose them to the way the Universe is going to be."

"Maybe." Cromwell didn't say anything more after that. The plane leveled after a long climb into an almost black sky. I watched the mountains turn to long ridges, then disappear into rolling hills, the Mississippi and St. Louis's arches glinting at the horizon, then closer, over St. Louis at an angle, St. Louis gone, so high the Earth's curve showed.

Then Cromwell spoke. "Granite Grit said he's learned how to tell humans apart. That mean something to you?"

"Yes," I said. "It's just learning to observe more

closely, learning what are significant variables within a species and what are general variables.''

"You ever have trouble telling us black people apart?''

"No. Jereks, though . . . I have trouble with Jereks.''

"Xenophobia? Is it really ingrained?''

"You feel nervous around Granite Grit?''

"We outnumber him here.''

"The closest thing to something that really evokes hard-wired human responses out there are Wrengee, and they're nice once you get to know them.''

"Could I see pictures?''

"Photos don't try to make it easy on you.''

"I'm a flyer. I'm not afraid of any human being going, but . . .''

"You're afraid you'll be afraid?''

"I wish I could order you to help me deal with this. I think there's something in us that can explode . . . and I don't trust you. I think you've all exploded once, there's some terrible initiation. Granite Grit said something about the initial terror.''

"They depilate or de-feather all the new cadets.''

"That sounds freakish.''

"It makes us all alien to ourselves as well as to the others.'' A muscle between my shoulder blades jumped as if his eyeballs pierced me. "It's hard to talk to you when I can't see you and you're right behind me.''

"I'm not going as a cadet. I'm going as a guest.''

"They'll give you a brown uniform, then.''

"Angleton said fucking the Jerek makes this all seem more real, and you . . . those aliens more . . .''

"Accessible? I didn't think it was love between them.'' *Vulnerable* was the word he really wanted to use. "But who's going to get wounded? They're both pros.''

"Angleton started out in Tibet when the Dalai Lama tried to go back. He's a rough enough boy.''

"Thanks for telling me. I'll pass it along. And what kind of wars were you in?"

"Nothing eyeball to eyeball." He cut off the microphone, disconnected in the middle of a sigh.

We began to go down as the Pacific Ocean rolled into view. Bay Area, always in and out of Berkeley. Cromwell turned on his mike and said, "We set up a permanent station on the Farallons."

I remembered seeing, years ago, granite chunks jutting out of the Pacific—weird things. "What about the gate in the warehouse?"

"Closed it down."

We landed and taxied up to a helicopter. Military guys grabbed us and our luggage and threw us in, belted us to the seats. The jet pilot waved at the helicopter pilot, then we took off over San Francisco, the sunset back in Nevada as we'd beaten the planet roll speed.

Then the chopper hovered and bounced like crazy over a landing pad, caught in updrafts. Finally, it settled and a crew ran out to wire the chopper down.

"It's the fringe of the possible for gates, I'm told," Cromwell said as we ducked under the blades and ran to the building.

"It's rather paranoid," I said. "Don't you have gate guard satellites up now?"

"Don't know." We were shivering by the time we got in the building—damp California air comes from beyond the Farallons. "The Audubon Society hates us for taking this stupid rock. The Farallons supposed to be a bird sanctuary."

I looked out the window. It reminded me of the northern part of Gwyng Home: rocks, fogs, wings flapping through. "Are we going now?"

Now, right now. A gate transport with external recessed bolts, fitted to hex keys, waited. I'd have preferred controlling the closures myself, but got in with Cromwell and sat lurching through seven transitions, three minutes each, then out . . .

. . . at a Karst outer space freight station. The bear team who unfastened the bolts looked rumpled, anxious.

"Still practicing security?" I asked in Karst One.

Cromwell sat impassive, staring from me to the bear who answered, "Trying to slow down unauthorized recontacts. Karriaagzh discovered his own people were more alien than . . ."

Another creature—Wool, I realized—interrupted with a word that must have been *hush* in a bear language. He said, in English, "Colonel Cromwell?"

"Yes?"

"We've met before. I'm called Wool." Wool's face was still shaved to expose his expressions. "We'll fly through the planetary system to Karst. We're limiting gate access to Karst surface."

"Security problems?"

Wool didn't respond to Cromwell's question. "You and the other senior humans are scheduled for language operations, unless you'd prefer to learn the language unaugmented."

Cromwell looked at me and asked, "Gentry, did they put you through this?"

"Yes, and my wife and the rest of the family."

He looked at me as if he'd just loved to have panicked if it weren't so unmilitary. "So. Here I am. How long does it take?"

Wool answered, "Seventy or eighty rotations to begin really speaking the language. Days, rotations are about the same."

One of the bears brought in squatty Federation poptop cans, still slightly frosty. Wool offered one to Cromwell, who sniffed after he popped it open and shuddered.

"Doesn't it smell like his planetary beer?" the creature who brought them in asked in Karst One. Cromwell grimaced at the language he couldn't understand.

I said, "That's the problem."

"If he likes things to be really alien like so many of you humans, he'll love Karriaagzh's sister."

"Karriaagzh's sister?"

Wool snapped his teeth, then took a long drink of beer. "Red Clay, get your conspecific ready to fly in. Perhaps we should sedate him now."

I asked in English, "Colonel Cromwell, perhaps you'd like a mild tranquilizer?"

"No," he said. He tasted the beer and put it aside. "I want to remember all of this."

Wool hummed slightly, then said in English, "The trip takes five days. I hope you don't suffer from claustrophobia."

"I've spent five months in an L-5 station, a month setting up the mag shuttle return from the moon."

"Ah, yes," Wool said, trying to put Cromwell at ease, "and at the L-5 station, your people worked out the basics of a space platform rail gun."

Cromwell said, "So do we look like dumb jerks playing with baby toys?"

"No, a space rail gun with non-metallic projectiles got through our defenses to destroy a Wreng city."

I said, "We're starting to fall back into our animals. Cromwell, Wool's only trying to put you at ease."

Cromwell said, "We are not a nasty, brutal species."

Wool said, "I didn't say that."

I said, "I'd like to get home, already, you guys."

Cromwell said, "Where did you get that accent?"

"From my wife, the Berkeley radical."

Wool said, "I apologize if I've broken any cultural taboos. Please relax, Colonel."

"Man, what *don't* you know about us?"

Wool said, "If we hadn't respected your species, we would not have tried to gather so much data. Please." He gestured that we should follow, and began walking through a tube into the straight space-time ship.

Cromwell passed in front of me to follow directly behind Wool. Travertine was second crew on the ship and third was one of Ersh's people. Cromwell asked, "Wrengee?"

"Wreng," Wool said. "Just one. Female."

The Wreng flared scales and jangled rings under her uniform tunic. I remembered her. She'd come to us as a refugee about two years after Ersh. Now, neither Wrengee nor humans would be refugees. I said, "Colonel, don't make her nervous. It's not polite to stare at species differences."

The Wreng said in Karst One, "I'm Ice of Physics, and tell him I won't be able to understand him until later. He's scheduled for the language operation with one of my fellows."

Cromwell said, "She doesn't speak English?"

Wool said, "No, but you're scheduled for the language operation with one of her conspecifics."

"Tom, you made her kind sound scarier."

I said, "Better to be relieved than startled."

"You patronizing little bastard."

"I've been with the Federation since I was nineteen, Colonel."

Cromwell didn't say anything, just sat down in one of the acceleration chairs and stared at Wool, who was setting up the computer. Then he said, "Daddy told me what I was doing couldn't be that much rougher than moving from South Carolina to Vermont."

Ice said, "It's nicer if you bring your family."

Cromwell said, "Lucy's like your wife, Tom, Jewish if you go by her mother." He smiled as if at some private joke. "Her father was military, and black."

I wondered how much more like Molly her mother might have been, then felt guilty, then weird as if I'd always seen Jewish people as radical even though I wasn't sure Marianne was Jewish—certainly not by religion—and here a Jewish girl married a military man. I said, "Every time I commit a stereotype, I get busted. I thought all Jewish girls were radical."

Cromwell laughed. Wool said, "Stereotypes are entropic," and I went *huh*.

"Flesh fights entropy and we're all flesh," Wool said. "Tom, come with me, please."

I followed him to a room behind the main observation deck. He said, "Cromwell may need to admit to fear, so let us have some time alone with him. You are too apt with us."

I felt hurt. Wool's face muscles shifted, then stiffened, then shifted again, sliding over each other just over the jawbone. He had less fat on his face than a human. "We won't isolate you," he finally said.

"I've always wanted to be good at something. Cromwell was successful on Earth."

"Red Clay, Cromwell won't take your aptness away."

"I'm scared, but not of you guys. Of my guys. And not just physically."

"What you were . . . no, I won't let you do that to yourself. So what? You matured into a different language, different culture. We have something for you." He went to a cabinet and pulled out . . .

. . . a Rector's Person's uniform. I stood rocking on the balls of my feet, then my fingers seemed to float through the air to touch the green fabric. I said, "Oh."

"Granite and Feldspar will be the humans' Rector's People. You and Marianne won't work with your own kind."

I looked around for a seating instrument, saw a hassock and sat down. "Thanks, but maybe I can work with humans, really."

"Too embarrassing for them. You can come in and tell them about being totally isolated among aliens as Karriaagzh did to Granite."

I asked, "Can I put it on now?"

Wool laid his hand against my jaw as if he were trying to blind-read my facial muscles. Then he said, "Wait, be obscure during the trip for Cromwell's sake."

"Where's Angleton?"

"Two days ahead of us. He's doing very well. Tom?" He seemed to want to ask me something, then he said, "Your males are not always monogamous, are they?"

"No?"

"The females, are they that much different?"

"Has Marianne cheated on me?"

"This discussion is just theoretical."

"Wool, I hope so." He left me alone then. I grabbed the green uniform and crushed the fabric with both hands, rocking back and forth, remembering the impermanence of those silly vows—for as long as the relationship was convenient. *Now that there were other humans—oh, lord.*

After a while, Ice came in, scale rings fluttering, two beers in her hands. "Hello, Rector's Man Red Clay."

I asked, "Who did my wife share sex with?"

She handed me a beer and said, "Karriaagzh claims he did. Wool felt it would be kinder to deceive you. Perhaps Karriaagzh lied to hurt Black Amber through you."

"Marianne's sister fucks aliens, so maybe I should have expected this."

"You haven't experienced Karriaagzh's own sister."

"What?"

"Black Amber will explain some of this. Karriaagzh will have to step down as Rector. His people are joining the Federation."

"Ice, what did Black Amber have to do with that?"

"She arranged further meetings."

I couldn't imagine how she could dive through her terror, her xenophobia, to contact Karriaagzh's kind. Ice handed me the beer and asked, "May I sit down?"

"Please. Black Amber contacted Karriaagzh's kind?"

"Hate overrides xenophobia sometimes," Ice said. She popped her beer can open and wiped the can against a large unringed scale on her upper arm.

"She's hated him for years."

"But, now she's too old a Gwyng to become Rector."

Poor bitch, I thought. We both opened our beers and sat drinking them in silence. I remembered Karriaagzh's throat spasming over Marianne, couldn't place the time for an instant, then remembered he'd done it when Karl was just newly born. I wondered if Ice were offering me a chance to commit my own out-of-species adultery. I wouldn't give anyone the satisfaction.

The next day, I asked Wool, "Did Marianne do it so Karriaagzh would give me this?" I held out the green tunic with a stiff arm.

"Karriaagzh? Cadmium said he needed you."

"Cadmium?"

"He's going to be the new Rector. And why are you avoiding Cromwell?"

"You told me to leave him alone."

"Sorry, I meant give him some privacy with us."

I was avoiding Cromwell.

Cromwell came up to me when we were passing the ice moon that was supposed to be lucky to see and said, "Ever heard of win-win games?"

"Yes. I'm not afraid you new humans will supplant me. I've had bad news about my family."

"Oh."

"Nothing I want to talk about." I wondered how one got divorced on Karst, then whether I was making too big a deal over it. Maybe Marianne thought I was going back to jail for good? And maybe it hadn't really happened? "Are you getting along okay?"

"I wish we'd finally get there."

I wondered if gating directly to the surface was truly impossible or if we'd taken the space-time way for psychological reasons. "Space is time-consuming. Just as the Federation consumes information."

He stared out at the ice-covered moon with starlight

glinting off it. Some stars were so close we could see their colors. Finally, he asked, "Did they make that planet or is it natural?"

"It's ice they didn't need for Karst's oceans."

"Lord have mercy." He might not speak like most Southern blacks, but he had at least one Southern dialect speaker for close kin. "The very concept."

"Building Karst helped their economies while they stopped killing each other."

"Who were *they*?"

"The five original species: Ahrams, one that's extinct now, the shiny black people, I think Wool's kind, but he never talks about species, and one of the bears."

"Not even that different from each other."

"No, not compared to Ewits, Gwyngs, the bird kinds, and the Wrengee."

"We're just nothing compared to all this."

"All individual species are nothing compared to this. The Federation is like an informational black hole. You can get into it, but never out, and it becomes even denser when a new species adds to it."

"An informational sink. And the information any one species tries to extract from it gives information on that species. Which . . ."

I pictured an infinity of mainframes all compiling information from our skull computers: drug usage monitored by vein taps we weren't told about; our varying blood pressures recorded against the comparative pressures of our companions; the language we used, the languages we heard. And skull computers were just one information source; others were all the questions we asked at our terminals, all the books and records feeding in from millions of years of hundreds of species' histories, all inside the planet Karst in binary electrical configurations. "Yes, lots of information," I said, sounding empty to my own ears as though I'd been stripped of data.

"You did well there."

"What, other than dying, could I have done?"

"I'm sure not everyone gets promoted to Rector's Man."

"I don't know. It's probably like being Colonel."

"One step below General, and I'm still waiting for the full bird."

The ice planet began to slip away from us now. Why anyone thought seeing it was lucky I couldn't figure out. Black Amber saw it after losing Mica; now, here I was seeing it after hearing that my wife cheated on me with my inhuman boss. Former boss. Maybe cheated. Would I believe her if she said she didn't do it?

Did she feel pity for him and if so, was I a pity fuck, too?

"Want to talk about it?" Cromwell asked. "I've been through a lot with my own family."

"Adultery?"

"Yours? Hers?"

"Either."

"If you can't rebuild the trust, you might as well throw her out. Or yourself, whichever."

"Did you rebuild it?"

"When we're together, we're together. And when we're apart, we make sure the base can't gossip."

"I don't want to . . ." I realized saying *I don't want to live like that* would tell him my wife cheated on me. "I don't know what I want. I don't even know for sure that it really happened."

"Obviously, aliens don't save us from human problems."

"They've got their own problems: no pouch for the nymph, sterile children, malfunctioning supplemental lights, brain developmental problems from not learning the right languages in time."

He nodded.

Karst Planet popped out from the bright stars as a half disc, still tiny. Cromwell watched it and read Federation books that Travertine and Tesseract had translated into English. He looked at me and said, "Wool told me we'd be landing on dayside in twelve hours."

The planet filled the horizon, then swung us around to orbit the Karst City lights.

I said, "I came in this way the first time, too."

Cromwell said, "I thought the trip was for psychological reasons as much as security." The others came in then, and he moved easily among them. Wool was growing his facial hair back and scratched it along the jawbone.

I realized we'd be coming in on the day side and Karst City was in the night. "Who's going to meet us? Where are we landing?"

"Black Amber wants to talk to you," Ice said. Her scales rippled her tunic, rings muffled by the cloth.

"Dress for it," Wool said.

I went into my room to change into the Rector's Man's tunic and found a green sash with all my contact and service badges transferred to it, and a new badge for the work I'd just done with my own kind. I switched a wall hologram to the room cameras and stood watching myself, spun myself around so I could see, in slightly delayed pictels, the whole image. I looked like a man of about thirty-five, a real grownup. I watched myself a while before joining the others. Here I was in my life. And the uniform wasn't something my wife had sleazed for me. I wondered if I'd have felt worse or better if she'd had a human lover.

Five minutes beyond Karst City, we came into daylight over empty artificial terrain. Where in all that would my own Rector's Man's place be?

Wool said, "Pull the shells around, everyone," and showed us how to reach back and pull form-fitting shells from behind the seats, a new detail. Inside the general body-shape shells was foam that molded to our contours, moved with breathing. "The foam freezes if you jerk," Wool said, "so breathe easy." The head shell was open at the face and jointed so that it moved like a helmet, but slowly.

Cromwell said, "Seems fine."

"Okay, we're going down."

Air thickened around the ship, lifting it in a long glide down to what was now afternoon. We turned and landed on a runway near the ocean, water glinting between the sea islands. I remembered this now, near the Gwyng History committeeman Wy'um's—no, rather his sister's place. Poor bastard, dead and a male Gwyng. Only aliens gave him positions and houses.

"How long will it take to get to the hospital?" Cromwell asked. His skin looked a bit glossy.

"Too hot?" Wool asked. "The shells can be adjusted."

"No, how long?"

"The atmospheric flight to Karst will take about two-tenths day, that's about four hours, a little more," Wool said. "It's night there now. You'll arrive pretty late."

"Will I be drugged?"

"The language operations are a bit disconcerting."

"So were the centrifuge tests." Cromwell took a deep breath, then watched Wool's hands on the controls as we approached the runway, the sea glittering on beyond us, flat sandy land, like Florida, maybe. I'd only seen photographs of Florida.

And down, a *whump* of braking parachute behind us, wheels squealing, foam tightening around us, then we were taxiing up to the reception building. Ice raised her seat front shell and flicked her scales. "The foam almost sprained my scale muscles," she said in Karst One.

Cromwell said, "It looks like South Carolina. Just like South Carolina." I remembered the cheated feeling I'd had when I saw green grass and blue sky.

"Why not?" Wool said.

"South Carolina doesn't relax me any."

"Oh, it's not really like South Carolina," I said. "You'll see."

Ice got out of her seat while the shuttle was still rolling toward the exit tubes. She arched her back and
rubbed at the base of her scales, catching a fingernail
in one of the scale rings. Cromwell looked at her as if
he wanted to tell her to stay seated until the plane
stopped at the terminal. She wiggled her fingernail free
and stared at it as if inspecting her polish. Her nails
were like human nails, except they were black. When
the shuttle lurched, she grabbed her seat and laughed.
I knew it was a laugh, that fat-frying sound, but Cromwell, who still had his shell fastened over him, turned
his head away, slowly, impeded by the joint connecting
the head portion to the rest of the shell.

Wool swung his shell up and said, "Come on, pull
the tab under the seat rests."

I did and the shell swung up and over me. Cromwell
sighed and did the same. Wool came up and shook him
by the shoulder, like a quarterback to the kicker, then
said to me, "Tom, you've got people waiting for you.
Go out first."

I went out, stumbling when I saw Marianne with
Black Amber. If this had been Virginia, would I have
blasted her down? I remembered my fingers hurting the
day after I killed Hurdai and stood there, body rocking
with my heartbeats. Marianne looked frightened of me.
She finally asked, "Tom?"

My heels sank down and I realized I'd been poised
on the balls of my feet. Black Amber said, "Perhaps
he's heard Karriaagzh's boasts."

Marianne said, "He's a bastard for telling everyone.
It wasn't really like sex for me."

"You did it, then? I'd hoped he was lying."

"He . . . well, it's over. He was just so persistent
and I had no idea. It wasn't . . . Tom, I am sorry. Can
you accept that?"

Black Amber had her thumbs hooked behind her
neck, just wearing pants, her pouch hole uncovered,

head hair matted. She said, in Karst Two, "Non-monogamous is/equals non-monogamous."

I said, "I've never cheated on you, Marianne."

Marianne said, "But our relationship isn't just sexual, Tom, no more than Amber's relationship with Wy'um was."

I stared at them, then said, "Let's get out of here."

Black Amber embraced me, rocked me side to side, then said, "My mind/my aging (agony)."

I said, "Are we going back to Karst now?"

"No, days with me (my final negotiation/request)."

Marianne said, "Black Amber told me you really didn't sleep with her."

I said, "I told you that, too. Let's go."

"You drive," Black Amber said.

"Why, to keep me from screaming at her?" I had been hurt on the trip when I believed Marianne had fucked Karriaagzh, but then half the time, I'd denied it, believed Karriaagzh had lied. Now, seeing Marianne admit it, I was furious.

We didn't speak to each other except when Black Amber gave me directions. As we pulled up to the house, one of Wy'um's younger sisters came out and stared at us. Black Amber wailed—sensing something only apparent to a Gwyng. My skull computer hadn't even squealed. Then Amber said, "I won't outlive the grey bird, but I've made sure he won't stay Rector."

I looked at Marianne as though we were still a team in this. She said, in English, "Black Amber knows she's beginning to become senile."

I asked, "Did you distract Karriaagzh for her?"

"Tom, you aren't even hearing me. Why are you acting like this jealous hillbilly?"

Part of me wanted to strangle her; part of me was crying. "Was it so important to you?"

"What is this, Tom? Be reasonable. You look like you're about to choke."

We were still talking in English. Wy'um's younger

sister, the surviving heir to the house, said, "Not to be rude, but could you stay outside with the quarrel scent until we get a human scent disruptor?" Her nose slits writhed.

I said, "Where's Karl?"

"At Agate and Chalk's."

"How's he taking it?"

"Taking what?"

"Your affair with Karriaagzh."

"Karriaagzh didn't tell any children."

I imagined my little self trying to beat up Karriaagzh, and laughed, then said, "He told people?"

"Yes, he . . . Are you going to hit me or try to beat up him?"

"After all, I am a hillbilly and I strangled Hurdai. Human beings seem to fuck every alien around."

"Tom, I'm not having an affair with Karriaagzh anymore. Listen to me."

I wondered what he did to her, how big his cock was. Cock bird, his sneaky fingers, his frayed feathers spread out over her, obscene images of her breasts, his scaly arms. I said, "I need to take a walk."

"I'll come with you."

I wanted to throw her down on the sand and rape her, smear her with my sweat, jam my seed up her. She looked younger for a second, afraid, maybe aroused, or was I reading myself into her? I walked down the beach and she followed behind me. More humans were coming in; perhaps we should split up, find new people. She could marry another linguist, someone as smart as she was. I could . . . I didn't know. I stopped and said, "Marianne, I need someone who's going to be faithful to me." I heard the desperation in that just after I spoke it and sat down on the sand, hugging my knees, my heart trapped between spine and leg bones, hammering.

She sat down near me, almost as if she knew I could be dangerous to her, and didn't say anything.

I don't want to cry in front of this bitch . . . I don't want to cry in front of this bitch. My eyes began leaking.

She said, "I didn't expect you home so soon. Tom, would you hurt me physically?"

The impulse collapsed. "Oh, Marianne."

"If you're going to be suspicious and jealous forever, then maybe I should move out."

"You make me feel terrible, then you try to make me feel guilty for feeling terrible."

She said, "Let's not hurt each other."

"Woman, I don't dabble around on the side."

"It's okay if you want to."

"Marianne, I don't want to. Have we been drifting apart? Was having prisoners in the house so terrible? What was it?"

"I felt sorry for him. He was so alone. And, Tom, he was persistent. And lonely. And I was the only person who'd bothered to learn his language."

"So you fucked him while Black Amber went to get him conspecific company."

"Even she began to feel sorry for him."

"He horrifies her."

"Not just because he's a bird. Because he was so asocial. She could never understand a creature that alone."

Sob, oh, sob for Karriaagzh. I raised my hands like I was playing a violin. Marianne turned her head toward the ocean. I saw her wrinkles, grey hairs, her skin thicker, really noticed for the first time. Maybe she'd been seeing the aging signs earlier and went to a creature who'd be more fascinated than appalled. I said, "If you don't plan to grow old with me, let's start looking for new partners now."

She burst into tears. I started back toward the Gwyng house, not caring whether she followed me or not, determined to get back home to Lucid Moment District one way or another. The district name now seemed rather ironic.

Black Amber was waiting for me on the porch, standing on the sides of her feet, her hair brushed. "I'm dying," she said.

I stopped, feeling Marianne behind me more than hearing her. "What can I do to help?" I said. Many years ago, she wanted me brainwiped, or was that just hysteria? Then she wanted me to become Mica.

She oo'ed slightly, looking over my shoulder. "Take care of me in an artificial pouch."

I wasn't sure whether she was making trouble for me or not. "Will you be happy?"

Her eyes oiled over as she raised her head and stared out to sea. Swimming until she died was the other option. Marianne said, in English, "Tom, can we talk about it?"

"Do you know what happens to old Gwyngs?" I said to her in Karst One. Black Amber lowered her eyes and sat down, elbows against the ground. She stroked her nostril slits with the fuzzy backs of her fingers.

Marianne said, still in English, "I feel manipulated, Tom."

Black Amber said, "Eye fee mamipoo ated, T'm ."

I said in Karst One, "She's my sponsor. I don't have any living genetic relations except Karl. It's not my fault that every adult on Karst knows you had sex with Karriaagzh."

"Tom, I didn't know it would be so *fucking* important to both of you. Karriaagzh . . ." She sputtered.

Now I spoke in English. "I can't stand another suicide."

"She's manipulating you."

Black Amber said, "The tongue lunge, 'manipullating you.' I forgot the tongue lunge." What she said wasn't exactly an English *l*, but it was close.

Marianne said, in Karst One, "What will you do if Tom won't take care of you?"

Black Amber said, "End me. What are you/Linguist sacrificing if Red-Clay does take care of me? You want him to share your genital skills."

"What happened to Wy'um?" I asked.

"Swam away," Black Amber said. She hugged her knees and rocked sideways. "Red-Clay, Rhyodolite is dead. Did you mourn? Cadmium will be Rector. Will you mourn? I ate my terror—the birds, the birds. Red-Clay, so many birds. While the Rector Bird stole your mate, I forced the other birds . . . ah, Linguist, you can be Rector's People apart from each other."

I'd been wondering about that. Marianne said, "So you want to steal my mate?"

"Are we still mated?"

"Tom, let's not discuss this right now."

"I do not steal genital skills," Black Amber said. She rose to her feet and wobbled, then sucked on her thumb glands. "I ask . . . affection." Affection for the aged wasn't natural for Gwyngs, but I remembered a pouch host beast who'd cared.

"Okay. I'll look like a creep if I say no," Marianne said. She sounded like we still had enough of a relationship that she'd have a say in the matter.

"Well, if Black Amber gets in your way, Marianne, I'm sure now that we have more humans and birds coming—"

"What is this? Just how long do you intend to fuss over what I did? I stopped. We have a son, Tom."

Black Amber said, "Don't say more, Linguist. Your speech etches our brains now (stress)."

Marianne came up and sat down beside Amber and awkwardly hugged her. "Black Amber, why does he want to make me feel so bad?"

Black Amber said, "Don't answer (Red-Clay)/No answer (Linguist)."

I was about to say, if she wanted an answer, *she wouldn't have asked you,* but my mind threw me a sudden memory of Marianne in the elevator with Karl, milk leaking through her bra. "I'm off time here. I need to sleep."

Black Amber said, "Three (of us). On a mat."

Marianne said, "I'm not at all sleepy. I'm going to take a walk."

Black Amber and I went into the house and sat side by side on a mat. I said, "I need to be alone."

"I need not to. I still outrank you." She touched my chin gently. "I did well to sponsor you."

You almost didn't, I thought.

"Cadmium said for me not to split the pair bond with the Linguist if it still existed. He wondered if it would be possible to order you to be reconciled." Cadmium, too, outranked me.

"Give me some time. Don't force it." I bumped my elbow against hers. We were odd people, all us Karst City types. Being alien together, not my mating with Marianne, was the most powerful bond.

= 12 =

Marianne and I didn't quite break up after I got back from Earth, but we insisted on being trained separately as Rector's People. When Black Amber disposed of her household and moved in with us, I bought a tube sofa refitted to keep a senile Gwyng warm and clean. About a week after Black Amber arrived, Marianne invited Alex and Anne Baseman to live with us while Alex healed from his recresting surgery.

It was like a damn zoo. Black Amber lay dying in the heated tube sofa in the living room, Chi'ursemisa and Daiur came back from Chi'ursemisa's skull computer surgery and slept in the room next to mine, now restored to its original solid wall. Karl took the room next to theirs and began to be incredibly rude to all of us. Marianne and her friends had the whole other hall. She and her dissertation director rigged one room up with oscilloscopes, terminals, recorders for esoteric language play.

Alex grumpted around with his bandages and bruised

eyes, then, a month later, he called for the elevator just before we were all going to have supper together. He held the elevator door down with his foot. I was rigging Black Amber's sofa with wheels so I could roll her back to join us in the kitchen. "Tom," he said, "the Barcons were right. I'm a little crazy."

I realized that he was leaving for good.

After the elevator took Alex down, the dinner together fell apart. Anne and Marianne went into their office and stayed for hours. I tried to listen outside the door, but heard nothing, not even breathing, scuffling shoes. When they came out again, I looked inside and saw that they had soundproofed the room sometime when I had been out.

Weeks went by. Then one morning, when Anne, Chi'ursemisa and Drusah had left for the day, Marianne came into the living room where I was feeding Black Amber and said, "If you can forgive Black Amber for wanting to brainwipe you when she first found you, then why can't you forgive me for sharing sex with Karriaagzh?"

"You're not dying," I said. Black Amber lay in her tube couch, the electrically warmed one that she'd had me get for her senility. Her food pump had emptied by now, so I pulled the nipple away from her mouth.

"She collapsed rather fast after you agreed to take care of her until she died."

Black Amber opened her eyes then, milky white, blinded, all those elaborate Gwyng neurons and optical processors either as badly decayed as her corneas and lenses, or trapped under dead tissue. Her nostril slits fluttered. I went over to her and touched her forehead. Her long arm and spidery hand reached out for me. I took her hand and felt the dry skin, the bristly fur on the fingers.

"Linguist," Black Amber said, my skull computer barely able to transform the sounds into Amber's term for Marianne.

Marianne stiffened as if a spider had spoken, then came over to us and took Black Amber's other hand.

"Linguist (no visual)?"

"Couldn't the Barcons fix her eyes again?"

I didn't say anything. Marianne asked, "Black Amber, are you in pain?"

"Linguist. Confusion (pain?). No more eyes."

I said, "They could fix the eyes, but there's more."

"Linguist, Red-Clay, Mica. Mica. Mica." Black Amber's fingers twisted against ours. I released the hand I'd been holding and she felt my face, pulling at my nostrils slightly as though they should be longer.

"Tom, I want to talk to you alone."

"When Black Amber goes back to sleep," I said. Marianne pushed Black Amber's other hand at me, sighed, and sat down on the human couch.

"Should have swum," Black Amber said, with almost a mean tone to it. "Killers."

Marianne said, "Do you mean us?"

"Bird. Bird who covered you. You."

I said, "Don't get her excited."

Marianne said, "Black Amber, I need to talk to Red Clay in private. Would you mind if we left you for a half hour?"

Black Amber said, "No spare moments."

"Tom, she's turning you into some kind of old-maidish martyr."

"Go take spare moments/deprive socially."

Before I could say, *That's the most coherent thing she's said this week*, Marianne said, "She needs social friction to keep her more alert."

Black Amber's lips rounded. "Castrate the bird/solve problems."

Marianne said in English, "Come on, Tom. Talk to me."

"You can speak in that language in front of her."

Marianne looked nervously at Black Amber, then said, "Okay, Tom, what I did with Karriaagzh was fucked, but why are you still giving me such grief about it?"

"Am I? I simply thought you might want to reconsider the relationship now that you . . ." I realized as I talked that I didn't want to suggest that she might prefer another human mate. Or other human mates, using that California casual cunt of hers. I tried to talk as properly and formally as I could. ". . . you might . . ."

"Might what, Tom?"

"You're Californian, radical. Look at Anne."

"And you're being a prig, Tom. I felt sorry for Karriaagzh, and I was curious, but it didn't do either of us any good. He forgot he couldn't put in brag claims and send you a challenge."

"Charming mating rituals he has."

"He wants to see you, Tom. Everyone thinks we should get back together."

"Do *you*? Would you want to marry me with permanent vows?"

"Tom."

"A real marriage?"

Black Amber said, "Argue noise, but smell sad, both."

Marianne slumped further into the couch and put her fingers against her temples, then cried. I felt stupid, like a jealous hick. "Tom, damn it, I'm trying to make sense of this. You've been so mean for the last four months, but you haven't kicked me out."

"You could betray me so easily now. With any human, any creature at all."

"Tom, stop speaking like you learned English as a second language."

I was startled. "So Karriaagzh wants to explain?"

"He just wants to see you. Take your shotgun if you want to."

Black Amber murmured, "Killer bird sound. Broke fear over millions of them." She sounded proud of herself. "Don't have to see ever again."

Marianne said, "Maybe the blindness is psycho-somatic?"

"Look at her eyes," I said. "They're filmed over."

"Will you go see Karriaagzh?"

"Yes, and I'll leave the twelve-gauge at home."

Marianne moved her body tentatively in a little breast jut, hip wiggle, not so much that I felt invited, enough to remind me.

Black Amber's nostril slits moved out and in. "Good," she said, then she wiggled herself deeper into the tube sofa and closed her eyes.

Marianne said, "Tom?"

"Yes."

"Anne thinks you and I have good synergy."

I didn't quite know how to take that. "Thanks."

She came up and kissed me, her tongue darting out a fraction of an inch. Then she twisted away from me and pushed the elevator button, back hunched, arms bent away from her body, knees slightly bent. The serious *Don't Touch* human posture. Before the elevator took her away, she said, "See Karriaagzh first."

I sat down at my terminal, sweating a bit, not sure whether I should be angry or fearful, and typed: TO KARRIAAGZH, EX-RECTOR. I UNDERSTAND YOU WANT TO TALK TO ME. RECTOR'S MAN RED CLAY (TOM GENTRY).

The computer was waiting for me. A pre-sent message flashed on my screen: TO RECTOR'S MAN RED CLAY. YES, COME TO THE RECTOR'S LODGE IN THE MORNING FOR BREAKFAST. WE WILL MAKE TIME FOR YOU. CADMIUM RECTOR, KARRIAAGZH EX-RECTOR.

Weirder yet, I thought. Chi'ursemisa came by with Drusah and asked, "Are you well?"

"Chi'ursemisa. Drusah?"

Drusah said from his scarred face, "We are well."

"I've been invited to have breakfast with Cadmium and Karriaagzh."

"We can feed Black Amber," Drusah said.

"You just put the formula in the pump and stick the nipple in her mouth, then press the button and hold the pump steady."

"I've watched," Chi'ursemisa said.

"Where's Daiur?"

"We sent him to his father's people," Drusah said.

I suddenly felt embarrassed, although I couldn't spot anything overtly sexual in their postures. Drusah's vocal cords thrummed roughly, as though he'd been tortured out of his pure Sharwani laugh, too.

Chi'ursemisa said, "Glad you understand."

Drusah rubbed his scar and imitated one of my smiles, which fit oddly under his cheekbones, one pointed, one broken.

I wondered when they planned to move out. They did plan to move out, didn't they? They followed me out to the living room and we sat around Black Amber's sofa, not saying much. It seemed as though we all, including Black Amber, wanted company, but weren't sure whether we needed to be with aliens. Amber stirred in her tube and moaned.

"Is she in pain?" Chi'ursemisa said.

Drusah said, "Better in pain than dead, perhaps."

Black Amber turned her head, our computers humming as she echolocated Drusah and looked toward him with her blind eyes. Habit? "No pain," Black Amber said. "No sex seizing."

Drusah got up and came over. He knelt by the tube and rumpled Black Amber's head hair. "Do you like that?"

"Touch always."

"Why don't you come out of the tube?"

"Cold."

"Feel inside the sofa, Drusah," I said.

He reached in by Black Amber's shoulders and drew his hand out quickly. "Artificial touch," he said. "Artificial womb."

"She wants to die this way."

"Dead already, comfortable," Black Amber said.

"What does she mean by that?" Drusah said.

"By Gwyng standards, she is dead, socially, but she didn't want to be so quickly dead, really."

"So she crawled into a fake womb," Chi'ursemisa said.

"Do you drug her?" Drusah's head hair flared, then smoothed down. He sounded angry. "Does she have full dignity?"

"She has full dignity." I didn't completely lie. Black Amber's bones were softening, and the Barcons gave me a specific neurotransmitter blocker for Gwyng pain nerves.

Marianne and Anne came in then, and I said, "I'm going to have breakfast with Karriaagzh and Cadmium in the morning. Anne, this is Drusah with Chi'ursemisa."

"Great," Marianne said in English. Anne hadn't seen Drusah before and she stared at his scars.

He said, touching his ruined cheekbone, "The scars are all honorable."

Marianne said, also in English, "Where are they going to live?"

I said, also in home talk, "They haven't said yet."

Chi'ursemisa said, also in English, "Isn't here okay?"

Marianne almost said something, probably *no*, then closed her mouth and smiled at me.

"Talk (tickle ears)," Black Amber said.

Drusah reached out and tickled her ears with his fingers. Black Amber thrashed slightly, then koo'ed. I couldn't have done that myself; I'd known Amber when she was Sub-Rector. The Gwyngs were partially right; this senile thing wasn't completely the Black Amber I'd known.

Anne said, "Do you take care of your old ones well, Drusah?"

"We love them like children," Drusah said, a warm

enough sentiment until I remembered that he and
Chi'ursemisa sent Daiur back to Hurdai's people.

"I know how difficult it is to take care of the elderly,
Tom," Anne said.

"The tube couch cleans up after her," I said. "All
I've really got to do is give her a bath at night, dump
the waste pouches and wash the tube out."

Anne said, "You have such patience, Tom."

Chi'ursemisa nodded. Marianne smiled, but muscles
twitched in her cheek. Anne looked at her and said,
"Really, Marianne, he does."

Then they all left when I had to slide Black Amber
out of the cocoonlike sofa onto a plastic sheet. Her arm
bones bent slightly. She lay shriveled and grey on the
plastic while I sponged her off, wiping inside the pouch,
cleaning her like a sick puppy.

She brought me to this, I thought, uncertain as to
whether *this* at this point was good or bad. Then I rolled
her over, washed her back, then dried her off before
helping her wiggle back into the tube.

"Thanks," she said, rubbing my eyebrows with her
furry knuckles. "Not alone."

In the morning, I dressed in my green uniform and
asked Chi'ursemisa if she'd wash and feed Black Amber while I went to see Cadmium and Karriaagzh. Marianne came up to us and said, "I'll do it."

*Oh, do make yourself indispensable even if you screw
around,* I thought, but I said, "Certainly, Marianne."
Indirect, sneaky, she was so different from Yangchenla.
If Marianne couldn't believe I was patient it was because she was patience squared. I was going to give up,
fall back in love with her, and ignore whatever she did.
She patted my cheek with nails at right angles to the
skin.

Chi'ursemisa laughed, bo'ing, bo'ing. I picked up
my wallet and tucked it in my tunic pocket, then looked
back at Marianne as I pushed the elevator button. She

didn't look like she'd won a victory. Maybe I am being
a prick about this, stingy with my sexual affections, I
thought. The elevator arrived. Our Shiny Black couple
with their new baby stared out at us as though we were
a theatre tableau. I looked back at Chi'ursemisa and
Marianne, saw Chi'ursemisa lay her hand on Marianne's shoulder, then got on the elevator.

"You will have another house soon," the male said
as the doors closed. "Will the Sharwani couple stay?"

"I don't know." I didn't even know if we'd keep the
floor in this building, too, or if I'd completely move out
to a Rector's Person's farm.

We all got out at the ground floor and took the same
bus out of Lucid Moment District through the open
floors of birds, then I stopped watching and began
thinking about Karriaagzh, my wife, her sister, Rhyodolite, Angleton, and Lisanmarl. Maybe it was abnormal not to want to fuck aliens? Maybe some of us were
as hard-wired to sleep with strangers as others of us
seemed to be to eat as much sugar as we could? Molly
said we'd all die out because eventually we'd all find
our perfect aliens. I wasn't sexually tempted, much, by
non-humans, but intellectually, man, they strung me
out a million miles.

And I couldn't beat Karriaagzh up. Even if he was
light for his size, he still weighed over three hundred
pounds and could kick like a Clydesdale.

All my thoughts chained together: alien sex, intellec-
tual curiosity, beating up Karriaagzh/being beaten up
by Karriaagzh, Marianne's blouse wet with her milk.
Finally, the bus stopped in front of the Academy main
gate and I got out and walked toward the Rector's Lodge
on its hill.

A Gwyng female showed me up to one of the high
semi-circular rooms overlooking the Academy grounds.
The room was empty except for a steam table, a chair
for me, a swing chair for Cadmium, its counterweights
resting on the floor, and a suede-covered pad with a

black wood armrest for Karriaagzh. I went over to the steam table and lifted one of the metal lids. Blood cakes.

The door opened. I dropped the lid as if I'd been caught spying. Cadmium said, "Red-Clay, relax (if . . .)."

Karriaagzh was in color! Partly in color, I realized as he came in, the new feathers chestnut and black, the old places still matted and grey, no tunic over them now. "Karriaagzh?"

"Red Clay," he said, accentless. He slumped on his hocks and waited until Cadmium adjusted the counterweights and got the swing chair up to about six feet. Then Karriaagzh came over to the steam table, right beside me, and took a plate and spatula. He said, "I'd like to get the blood cakes." I moved over and watched him put three of them on a plate. He said, "There are eggs under that one," pointing to the first dish.

I served myself while Karriaagzh took the blood cakes to Cadmium. Then Karriaagzh went over to his mat, stretched, roused all his feathers, the old grey ones, the new chestnut and black ones, and sat down, his eyelids closing from the bottom. When he'd settled down against the suede, he sighed, all the air rushing through his hollow bones. Poor old Karriaagzh again. I felt both manipulated and impressed.

"What are you going to do next?" I asked him.

Cadmium said, "Red-Clay," like I'd been impolite.

Karriaagzh opened his eyes. The muscles controlling his nictitating membranes bunched, then relaxed. "I'm sorry. I was terribly lonely and your mate could speak my language." The haw muscles bunched again.

Cadmium brought the swing down, laid his plate on the floor, then hauled himself up toward the ceiling. "Accept it," he said to me. I looked to see if his thumbs were curling back from the anger glands. Slightly.

He was Rector now; I was the Rector's Man. Karriaagzh closed his eyes and waited. I looked back at

Cadmium and then said, "Karriaagzh, I accept your apology, but why did you tell everyone?"

"I forgot what species I was dealing with," Karriaagzh said. Having said what he'd brought me in to hear, he got up and dusted off his renovated feathers. "After Cadmium takes full control, I'm going back to my own people. Then, perhaps, liaison work."

Cadmium said, "What do you think about a man you met on your planet?" He looked at Karriaagzh.

"Codresque," Karriaagzh said. "Tomas Codresque."

"He's with the CIA." Karriaagzh translated *CIA* to Cadmium for me.

Cadmium nodded and said, "It's all right. You'll have nothing to hide, Red-Clay."

"Me? What does this have to do with me?"

Karriaagzh said, "He's been recommended as a person who can help you with protocol." The word for *protocol* in Karst One also meant social flexibility and grace, authority of attitudes. Basically, it was a loosely constructed word, semantically speaking. I didn't like it.

"What about Marianne?" I said.

"We suggest that you and she stay mated," Cadmium said. "Once we learn more about your institutions, we will hire humans to counsel you."

"Yes, Rector," I said.

Cadmium brought the swing seat down to the floor and said, "Red-Clay, Red-Clay, she means more to you than you realize." He embraced me sideways, forcing it.

Karriaagzh said in Karst Two, "Hostile to authority (difficulties/deceptions in the past)."

Cadmium said, "Red-Clay, Red-Clay, not . . . don't. Be a friend."

"You're my superior," I said.

"Stiff neck," he said. My neck was literally rigid.

Karriaagzh came up to me now, all eight feet of him,

up to within a yard of me, and raised his crest. He said in English, "Don't be a fool."

My stomach squeezed; his nictitating membranes flashed over his eyes, drew back into the eyecorners. He backed up from me and then turned and left the room.

As soon as he was gone, Cadmium said, "Red-Clay, the agency person, Coodlescoo; we hired him for you."

"Cadmium, or should I say Rector?" I felt exposed, misunderstood.

"Cadmium, please."

"Codresque is a spy."

"Yes, but you need a caretaker at your Rector's People's house. We need to be reassuring. He can learn Karst One without surgery (mistrusts brain work). And he is not from your social group."

I remembered Codresque saying, *No American knows how to deal with me.* I would love him if he saw no difference between Angleton and me. "All right, Cadmium."

"And send the Weaver home."

"Why?"

He didn't answer, but his wrinkles deepened and his eyes grew oilier. She reminds him of all the dead, I realized.

"I will visit you and the Linguist. You are not reconciled?"

"I don't know. She helps me with Black Amber."

Cadmium shuddered. I realized then how difficult these times had been for him, how he'd had to push himself beyond the usual Gwyng limits. He sighed and walked in his rolling way over to the steam table. "Living dead," he murmured, almost to himself, but if he'd not wanted me to understand he could have used a Gwyng language.

"She's comfortable," I said.

"Thank you, I suppose, but no more." He served himself more blood cakes, then said, "I'm bringing your shopkeeper and her friends in as adopted pouch kin (kind people/no ambitions)."

"Cadmium."

He looked up at me.

"How did you get this job?"

"A mild concession to the Gwyngs. After a strong Rector, a usable Rector." His lips twitched into a circle, then pulled tight around his muzzle again. Analytics and Tactics probably listened to us. I doubted he intended to be weak.

"When I first met you, I thought you were a prig."

"I try to balance all the moralities," he said. Gwyng moralities, Federation moralities, Karst moralities—what a load, I realized. He said, "Adopt forgiveness as a morality."

"With Marianne?"

"We all have imperfect senses."

"No one species, much less one individual, can know the entire Universe." I remembered Karriaagzh saying something like that to me years ago.

Cadmium didn't answer that. He said, "You and Marianne need to pick your landscape for your country place. I will talk to her next."

When I saw Codresque again, he reminded me vaguely of a fat Gwyng, slightly bowlegged, wrinkled face. He came to see me in my apartment while Marianne went to the Rector's Lodge. Cadmium assured me that Karriaagzh would be at the Institute of Medicine getting his feather follicles reworked.

"Rector's Man Gentry, I understand that you might have reservations against me, but I think the Rector wants you to be more sure of yourself among your own kind."

"I think you're CIA, but Cadmium says that I won't have anything to hide."

Codresque's wrinkles deepened; how Gwyngish. I wondered what Cadmium was saying right now to Marianne. And Codresque didn't say anything, didn't deny being CIA, just stood there slightly hunched over.

I said, "Cadmium wants me to take Marianne back. He wants me to hire you as a servant."

Codresque said in Karst One, "I can serve you well."

I said in English, "You didn't have the language operation?"

He answered in stilted, technical Karst One, "No, we wondered if juvenile cell redevelopment and neural restructuring might make the individual more trusting than would be advantageous."

Okay, he *was* a spy, but Cadmium wanted me to hire him as a servant.

"Sir?" he asked.

"Yes, Codresque." I began to feel how one might enjoy having a servant.

"Could the uniform be tailored more?"

"It has to cover the middle leg joint and the upper arms." I remembered then having seen some uniforms that fitted better, more like topcoats than the usual baggy things. "We could do something with it."

He smiled at me, happy I was beginning to get the hang of how to use him. In English, he said, "I know of a shop in Paris that isn't convention bound. If you don't have the time for fittings, I can take measurements and have uniforms made to measure."

No time to go to Paris. Cadmium wanted Marianne and me to reconcile quickly and then get to work. We had to select a house, then begin work with Sharwani and Wreng cadets who'd started squabbling. "Made to measure would be fine." I'd see if I could find out precisely what that meant.

"We could send one of your better-fitting present uniforms as the muslin," Codresque said. He looked me in the eyes and suddenly seemed as formidable as when he had me strip at the big house in the South.

Marianne came home, then, and I tried to remember

how the introductions were done. "Marianne, this is Tomas Codresque, who'll be helping us."

Codresque bowed slightly. Marianne said, "Cadmium told me about him." Codresque's face remained impassive. Marianne continued, "Cadmium said he wanted us to take a drive. He loaned me a car and showed me how to drive it. It's Black Amber's old car."

"I can drive it," I said.

"If you would show me how, I can tend the sick Gwyng," Codresque said.

I got behind the wheel, noticing the radio and the box of paper tissues attached to the dash. Marianne said, "I'm not sure I like Codresque, but we will need some help. And you've been using Black Amber to avoid dealing with me."

"I haven't dealt with you, have I?" We pulled out of the basement into the city traffic. I set up the automatic system and leaned back. We were headed to the South Gate, going out a way I hadn't been before.

"I didn't know Karst had roads outside the city," Marianne finally said as we approached the industrial zone.

"Well, I guess they do. We've got a map." This was uncomfortably reminding me of Yauntra, of Filla, the Yauntra girl spy. Who, I had to admit, I would have fucked if she hadn't been so terrified. Maybe Cadmium had thought about that?

The Barcon guards at the checkpoint were in the shed phase, dark skin glistening over their oddly angled jaws. The one who checked our passes said, "Good trip, Rector's People."

As we drove away, I said in English, "I've never been south here before."

"How do you know Karst City is in the north?" Marianne asked.

I shrugged and said in Karst One, "I'd always translated this direction as *south*."

"I think it's psychological."

"Come on, Marianne."

"On Earth, the *northern* hemisphere is politically more powerful, now. But why do you translate into Terran coordinates here?"

I had the unpleasant feeling that she was also trying to make a point about moral coordinates. "Sorry," I said.

We drove into some hills covered with trees with bark like poplar trees, even more so, and long curved leaves. The road stayed level on stilts over the low places.

Marianne said, "Eucalyptus."

"Really?"

"Not really. Parallel development."

The countryside was funny here, bouncy with little creeks, small hills, and plants growing along tree limbs as we went further and further toward the equator, but still relatively near the coast.

"So, Tom, do you want me to leave?"

Don't say it so bluntly, I thought. "We've been ordered to reconcile."

"Tom, how hard do I have to say I'm sorry? You want me to slit a wrist?"

I obliterate all you fuckers . . . this relationship . . . Hurdai's dead. I began crying. Marianne said, "You sound awful," and began crying herself. I pulled the car over to the side of the road when we came off the bridge. We just sat crying for a while.

I said, "Do you want to leave me?"

"I don't want you to bully me."

"I'm not trying to bully you. I'm afraid you'll leave me now. You can go home. Maybe I'm not—"

"Tom, can't you get over being a scapegoated child?"

I sat back in the seat, my heart pounding. "Marianne."

"Anne told me that guys who were faithful were rare."

I looked over at her without speaking. She looked

haggard, hairs out of the restraining bandana plastered to her face, eyes swollen. "Marianne, you said you were sorry, didn't you?"

She nodded and pulled out some paper tissues to wipe her eyes. I'd noticed earlier that the car'd been equipped with them and felt angry now that we were such obviously emotional creatures. "Karriaagzh is getting his color back."

"His sister was so shocked. We'd socially and physically deformed him."

"What's the most important, Marianne: our lives before Karst or our lives here?"

"Are you trying to bu—"

"Marianne, I'm really asking. Me, you, both of us."

"I feel like a phony sometimes."

"Me, too. Like jail was more real than Lucid Moment District."

"Really, it's not true. Tom, I don't want to flounder all my life."

I began to sing the old Yalie song Cadmium and Rhyodolite had sung to me when I'd come back from Yauntra:

> Gentlemen songsters out on a spree,
> Lost from here to eternity.
> Lord, have mercy on such as we, ba, ba, ba.

Marianne covered her face with her hands. I said, "I don't mean to bully you." She laughed slightly and said, "We have more in common than we realized."

I said, "Were you afraid I'd stay on Earth?"

"Yeah." She shivered.

"Maybe I'm glad Cadmium put pressure on us."

"I've seen human friends do as much," she said, wiping her face again.

"Does it feel like a first date in some ways?"

She said, "First date of two divorced people."

Be careful, I told myself. "Let's go find a beach."

We drove until we could see a semi-circle of sand between rocks, parked the car, and walked down through briars and scrambled down a rubble slope to get to the beach. Marianne said, "It reminds me of California here."

"But wetter."

"Yes. Actually, I can't think of any place on Earth that looks just like it."

"But does it get too hot in the summertime?"

"Tom, we're only a hundred and fifty miles south of Karst City. It can't get too hot."

It was warmer than Karst City usually is, though. I said, "Do you want to be here with me? It would keep away Jereks."

Marianne looked at me in an *are you serious?* way, then said, "Do we have to be on this continent?"

"I like being relatively close to the city and it doesn't remind me of anything I don't want to remember."

"The hills look choppy. It's probably a multiple fault zone."

"We can ask. When we get back to Karst, let's see if we could get a Rector's People's House here."

We spread a blanket and sat on it looking at each other. Sex? Too soon. She handed me a bottle of sunscreen, then after we'd smeared ourselves with that, she lay her head on my arm and went to sleep. A killer and an adulteress. I gently moved around until I was comfortable and tried to sleep myself.

It was dusk when we woke up, with the sun dipping down into the hills behind us. Marianne's head had put my arm to sleep. We got up and stretched, then I said, "We'd better start back."

"We've got a tent under the seat."

I was about to say, *Karl will worry about us*, when I realized that we had a radio. We could tell Codresque we'd be late. Karl had friends in the building he could stay with.

We called in. Codresque answered, "Rector's People Gentry."

"Codresque, Tom here. We're staying overnight."

"I was briefed that you might. Can Karl stay with Granite Grit and Feldspar?"

"They're back. Sure. Is Black Amber all right?"

"She's alive. The other aliens are sitting with her. Sir, don't worry."

I'd feel guilty if Black Amber died when I was away, but I needed to be away. "It's all right," I said to Marianne. She pulled the tent out from under the seat, then pulled out two air mattresses and a picnic basket.

I took the tent and the picnic basket and began setting it up on the driest sand. *Slowly, go slowly.* After the tent was up, we sat on the air mattresses outside it eating villag and tomato sandwiches. "Whose idea were these?" I asked.

"Karl's."

"How has he been taking all of this? He seems almost to be avoiding me."

"He doesn't understand."

Poor Karl, I thought. I killed his playmate's father and quarrel with his mother. "It was hard for me to be among people who saw me as a criminal. I'm sorry if I overreacted." So what if I felt I was betrayed; life here was more difficult than we let ourselves realize.

"We can get away if we need to and just be people now."

I said, "What's simply human?"

She stared out at the water a while and then said, "Anne said that if having a faithful wife meant more to you than I got from not being faithful, that I should do what was most important."

"She and her husband have an open marriage, don't they?"

"It's not as much fun as she thought it would be, but it's the way their marriage works."

"Marriage is more than the sex."

"Yes, Tom."

The sky got darker, cloudy. After sunset, the ocean gleamed in streaks where fish or dolphins cut through phosphorescent plankton. Marianne asked, "Did they stock any dangerous animals here?"

"Just sapients."

She took off her clothes and ran down to the water that cupped light around her body. I thought it would be too much if the clouds parted when she came out and starlight gleamed off her. She came out like a shadow and sat down naked beside me, nipples twisted, chill bumps on her arms.

"It's colder than it looks," she said, looking out at the water. Then she looked at me, her eyes still red, and I pulled my clothes off and pulled her close.

We seemed very skilled and awkward at the same time. Working through the awkwardness seemed crucial.

During Black Amber's last days, Drusah and Chi'ursemisa helped Marianne and me. At the very end, we drove Black Amber down to the site for our Rector's People's House on a point overlooking the ocean near the beach where Marianne and I had worked out the beginnings of our reconciliation.

I wasn't sure whether Black Amber still could understand speech, but Drusah and I carried her on a stretcher to the spot where Support crews in bulldozers were leveling my house site. We tilted the stretcher so that she was facing the site. "I'll be a Rector's Man, here," I told her.

She called out with her ultrasonic voice, turning her head, mapping the place with sound. "Good," she said. "I/Mica picked well."

"Are you pleased with me?"

"You with you?"

I wasn't sure she knew what sense she was making, but yes, I was beginning to be pleased with me. "Yes."

She painted me with her ultrasonic voice and then fixed her blind eyes on mine, more alert than she'd been in weeks. "Take me to the water and sit with me," she said. "Roll me into the waves."

We all carried her down through the thorns to the beach. Drusah said, "We should touch her constantly now."

She was dying. We rolled her out on the sand and Drusah got water from the ocean in a bucket and put some shells in it. He guided her hand into it and she koo'ed, tried to flick water at him but her fingers were too weak.

Then we all sat around her, legs and hands touching her body until she died. I went up the hill to the workers and said, "Black Amber is dead. To whom do we report it?"

A small Gwyng said, "Consider it reported. The corpse is for the water."

I went back and saw Marianne crying against Chi'ursemisa's shoulder. Drusah was still stroking Black Amber's coarse shoulder fur, his fingers swollen. I said, "We can bury her at sea."

Drusah said, "Cadmium said corpses discomfort Gwyngs."

We all four guided Black Amber's body through the water, wading as far as we could, then swimming until we felt a current tugging at us. We let her body tumble into it and struggled out ourselves.

When we got back to the beach, we looked at each other in our Karst-issue bathing trunks, Marianne with her white bra covering her breasts, we others bare-chested, hairy, Drusah scarred by his own people. Marianne said, "I realize now that she cared tremendously about the Federation, even though . . ."

I remembered Black Amber crying oily Gwyng tears from a fake human face, the plastic bandages wrapping her when the Barcons put her back in Gwyng shape. I said, "She wasn't a bad guy."

Chi'ursemisa said, "Before Karriaagzh brought me here, I wanted to be pro-Federation. But that's not as simple as I thought it would be."

Marianne said, "When I first saw Alex, I knew the Federation wasn't simple."

I looked up and saw Cadmium come trudging through the sand toward us. He asked, "Is Black Amber truly gone?"

Drusah said, "Completely."

He came up to us and sat down, leaning back against his arms. His webs seemed dry, the skin on them flaking. We looked at each other. "Do you mind that we took care of her?" I asked him.

"It wasn't utterly abnormal," he said. "I could want the same thing myself some day."

The services, I thought, that conspecifics can't manage. I said, "Thanks for what you did for me, for us."

AFTERWORD

A series that began with *Becoming Alien*, went on to *Being Alien*, now, quite a distance from my initial concepts, ends with *Human to Human*. I'd like to thank John Betacourt and Dainis Bisenieks for help with the first book; Carol Deppe for help with two first chapters; Greg Keizer and Dr. Boyd Davis for their comments on the second book; and Amy Thomson for hers on this one. I especially want to thank my father, John R. Brown, for his readings of first drafts and Carol Smith for her proofreading of all three books.

The Oxford Companion to Animal Behavior stimulated many ideas about how the sense organs work, how sapience might evolve, and how sapients might behave. Among other sources, I should also mention *Mammalian Radiations*, the Johns Hopkins Press three-volume work entitled *Mammals*, the several collections by Stephen Jay Gould, and works of fiction by Ursula K. Le Guin, C. J. Cherryh, and James Tiptree, Jr. Also, Dr. Gregory Benford called my attention to an article on work that is a precursor to that of Joseph Weiss.

I also made extrapolations from the vampire bats at the Bronx Zoo, a female redtail hawk named Sigmund at the Carolina Raptor Rehabilitation and Research Center, and an Amazon parrot named Rocky. Whipped blood, live mice, and fresh sunflower seeds to you captives of us humans.

And thanks to the verbal people.

THE BEST IN SCIENCE FICTION